Alex Cross's *Trial*

FEATURING ALEX CROSS

Alex Cross's Trial

Cross Country

Double Cross

Cross

Mary, Mary

London Bridges

The Big Bad Wolf

Four Blind Mice

Violets Are Blue

Roses Are Red

Pop Goes the Weasel

Cat & Mouse

Jack & Jill

Kiss the Girls

Along Came a Spider

A complete list of books by James Patterson is in the back of this book. For previews of forthcoming books by James Patterson and more information about the author, visit www.jamespatterson.com.

Alex Cross's *Trial*

James Patterson
AND
Richard DiLallo

Doubleday Large Print
Home Library Edition

LITTLE, BROWN AND COMPANY
NEW YORK BOSTON LONDON

This Large Print Edition, prepared especially for Doubleday Large Print Home Library, contains the complete, unabridged text of the original Publisher's Edition.

Little, Brown and Company
Hachette Book Group
237 Park Avenue, New York, NY 10017

Little, Brown and Company is a division of Hachette Book Group, Inc. The Little, Brown name and logo are trademarks of Hachette Book Group, Inc.

ISBN 978-1-61523-103-4

Printed in the United States of America

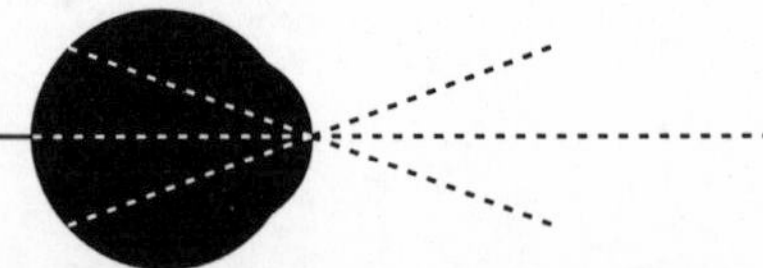

This Large Print Book carries the Seal of Approval of N.A.V.H.

For Susan, of course

A PREFACE TO *TRIAL*

By Alex Cross

A few months after I hunted a vicious killer named the Tiger halfway around the world, I began to think seriously about a book I had been wanting to write for years. I even had the title for it: *Trial*. The previous book I'd written was about the role of forensic psychology in the capture of the serial killer Gary Soneji. *Trial* would be very different, and in some ways even more terrifying.

Oral history is very much alive in the Cross family, and this is because of my grandmother, Regina Cross, who is known in our household and our neighborhood as Nana Mama. Nana's famous stories cover the five decades when she was a teacher in Washington—the difficulties she faced during those years of civil rights turmoil, but also countless tales passed on from times before she was alive.

One of these stories—and it is the one that stayed with me the most—involved an uncle of hers who was born and lived most of his life in the small town of Eudora, Mississippi. This man, Abraham Cross, was one of the finest baseball players of that era and once played for the Philadelphia Pythians. Abraham was grandfather to my cousin Moody, who was one of the most unforgettable and best-loved characters in our family history.

What I now feel compelled to write about took place in Mississippi during the time that Theodore Roosevelt was president, the early part of the twentieth century. I believe it is a story that helps illuminate why so many black people are angry, hurt, and lost in this country, even today. I also think it is important to keep this story alive for my family, and hopefully for yours.

The main character is a man my grandmother knew here in Washington, a smart and courageous lawyer named Ben Corbett. It is our good fortune that Corbett kept first-person journals of his incredible experiences, including a trial that took place in Eudora. A few years before he died, Mr. Corbett gave those journals to Moody. Eventually they wound up in my grandmother's hands. My suspicion is that what happened in Mississippi was too personal and painful for Corbett to turn into a book. But I have come to believe that there has never been a better time for this story to be told.

Part One

A GOOD MAN IS HARD TO FIND

Chapter 1

"Let her hang until she's dead!"

"Take her out and hang her now! I'll do it myself!"

Bam! Bam! Bam!

Judge Otis L. Warren wielded his gavel with such fury I thought he might smash a hole in the top of his bench.

"Quiet in the court!" the judge shouted. "Settle down, or by God I will hold every last one of you sons of bitches in contempt."

Bam! Bam! Bam!

It was no use. Warren's courtroom was overflowing with disgruntled white citizens who wanted nothing more than to see my client hang. Two of them on the left side began a chant that was soon taken up by others:

We don't care where. We don't care how.
We just wanna hang Gracie Johnson now!

The shouts from some among the white majority sent such a shiver of fear through the colored balcony that one woman fainted and had to be carried out.

Another bang of the gavel. Judge Warren stood and shouted, "Mr. Loomis, escort all those in the colored section out of my courtroom *and out of the building*."

I couldn't hold my tongue another second.

"Your Honor, I object! I don't see any of the colored folks being rowdy or disrespectful. The ones making the fuss are the white men in front."

Judge Warren glared over his glasses at me. His expression intimidated the room into silence.

"Mr. Corbett, it is my job to decide how

to keep order in my court. It is your job to counsel your client—and let me tell you, from where I sit, she needs all the help she can get."

I couldn't disagree.

What I once thought would be an easy victory in the case of *District of Columbia v. Johnson* was swiftly turning into a disaster for Gracie and her increasingly helpless attorney, Benjamin E. Corbett: that being myself.

Gracie Johnson was on trial for the murder of Lydia Davenport, a wealthy white woman who was active in Washington society at a level high enough to cause a nosebleed. Worse, Gracie was a black woman accused of killing her wealthy white employer.

The year was 1906. Before it was all over, I was afraid they were going to hang Gracie.

I had to be careful they didn't hang me while they were at it.

Chapter 2

"I will not tolerate another outburst," Judge Warren said to the spectators. He turned to look me in the eye. "And I suggest that you, Mr. Corbett, select your objections with greater care."

"Yes, Your Honor," I said, then immediately held my tongue in check with my teeth.

"Mr. Ames, you may resume questioning the defendant."

Carter Ames, the city attorney, was a little old man about five feet tall. He strode to the witness stand as if he were every inch of six-two.

"Now, Grace, let's go back to the afternoon in question, May twenty-third. In your testimony—before the unfortunate disruption occurred—isn't it true that you essentially admitted to murdering Mrs. Davenport?"

"Excuse me, sir, I said *no such thing,*" Gracie shot back.

"The court stenographer will please read the testimony given by Miss Johnson a few moments before the courtroom interruption."

"Got it right here, Carter," the stenographer said.

Wonderful. Ames and the court stenographer were on a first-name basis. No telling which parts of Gracie's testimony had been left out or "improved."

The stenographer flipped back the pages in his tablet and began to read in a droning voice.

"Miz Davenport was always a mean old lady. Never had a nice word for anybody. Ask me, she had it coming to her. The day before she got killed, she told me she was fixing to fire me because I was too stupid to know which side of the plate do the fish fork go on. She was a mean old witch, she was. I'm telling you, she had it coming."

I jumped up from my chair.

"Your Honor, obviously my client did not mean—"

"Sit down, Mr. Corbett."

I had one more thing to say—I just had to get it out.

"Your Honor, the prosecutor is deliberately twisting my client's words!"

Carter Ames turned to me with a smile. "Why, Mr. Corbett, I'm not twisting a thing. Your client has spoken for herself very clearly. I have no further questions, Your Honor."

"In that case, court will adjourn for a two-hour recess, so we can get ourselves a cold glass of tea and some dinner," the judge said. "I believe that Mrs. Warren said my personal favorite, chicken pot pie, is on the menu today."

Bam! Bam! Bam!

Chapter 3

The two-hour dinner break before Carter Ames and I gave our closing arguments seemed to last at least twice that long. I never had much appetite during a case, so I spent the interval pacing the block around the courthouse square, mopping my face and neck with a handkerchief.

Washington was in the grip of a torturous heat wave, and it was only June. The air was as thick and swampy as any summer afternoon back home in Mississippi. Carriage horses were collapsing. Society ladies called off their afternoon teas and spent their leisure time soaking in cool tubs.

Back home in Eudora I rarely had to wear the full lawyer suit with high stiff-starched collar and all the snaps and suspenders. Down south, folks knew how to survive the heat: move slowly, and wear light clothing.

It must have been ninety-five degrees when we finally returned to the courtroom. The newfangled electric fans barely stirred a breeze. Gracie's face streamed with perspiration.

The judge entered. "Are you ready, gentlemen?"

Carter Ames sauntered toward the jury box. He put on a big friendly smile and leaned in close to the jury foreman. Ames was justly famous for the high drama and fancy oratory of his closing arguments in murder cases.

"Gentlemen, I want you to join me on an important journey," he said, in his orotund voice. "I'll let you in on our destination before we commence—the Kingdom of Truth. Few who set out on the journey toward the Kingdom of Truth ever reach their destination. But today, gentlemen, I can promise you, that is where we shall arrive."

The smoke from Judge Warren's after-dinner cigar wafted blue through the air around the dandyish little city attorney. He slowly paced the length of the jury box, turned, and paced the other way.

"We are not going to make this journey by ourselves, gentlemen. Our companions on this journey are not of the fancy kind. They don't wear fine clothes and they don't ride first class. Our companions, gentlemen, are the facts of this case."

As metaphors go, it seemed fairly simpleminded to me, but the jurors were apparently lapping it up. I made a mental note to lay on an even thicker layer of corn pone than I had originally intended. It was the least I could do for Grace and her chances.

"What do the facts of this murder case tell us?" Ames asked. His voice dropped a few notes on the scale. "The first fact is this: Grace Johnson has all but *confessed* to the crime of murder, right here in front of you today. You heard her admit to a most powerful motive, the hateful emotions and vitriolic resentments she bore toward her employer."

It was all I could do to keep from jumping up and shouting "Objection!" Judge

Warren's earlier warning served to keep me in my seat.

"The second fact speaks even more loudly. Grace claims that Lydia Davenport shouted at her. Let me repeat that shocking claim, gentlemen. Lydia Davenport dared to shout at the woman who was a willing employee in her household. In other words, Mrs. Davenport deserved to die because she shouted at a *maid!*"

Ames was not just a skillful actor; when it came to the facts, he was also quite the juggler.

"Now let another fact speak to you, friends. The fact is, the court has appointed one of the capital's finest young attorneys to represent Grace Johnson. Now mind you, this is as it should be. Let the least among us have the best defense money can buy—your tax money, that is. But don't let the young gentleman fool you. Don't let his pretty words bamboozle you. *Let me tell you what he's going to try to do.*"

He waved his hand indifferently in my direction, as if I were a fly buzzing around his head.

"Mr. Corbett will try to cast doubt upon

these *obvious facts*. He will tell you that the Davenport house was bursting with employees who might have murdered Lydia Davenport."

Ames spun on his tiny heel and pointed a crooked finger at my client.

"But the *fact* is this: Only one person in that house admits out loud, in a clear voice, to having a motive for the murder. And *that person is seated right there! Grace Johnson!*"

He strode to the prosecution table and lifted a worn brown Bible. He opened it to a page he seemed to know by heart and began to read aloud.

"If you continue in my word, you are truly my disciples, and you will know the truth, and the truth will set you free."

He snapped the Bible closed with a flourish and held it high in the air.

"Gentlemen, we have arrived. Our journey is done. Welcome to the Kingdom of Truth. The only possible verdict is guilty."

Son of a bitch! Carter Ames had just destroyed my closing argument.

Chapter 4

The diminutive prosecutor threw a thin smile my way as he returned to his chair, his eyes dancing with the light of triumph. I felt a twinge in my stomach.

But now it was my turn to speak, and hopefully to save a woman's life.

I began with a simple declaration of the fact that no one had witnessed the murder, and then I discussed the other suspects: the Irish gardener, Mrs. Davenport's secretary, and her houseman—all of whom despised their employer and could have easily committed the murder. Of course, they were all white.

Then, since Carter Ames had stolen my thunder, I decided to finish up in another direction, a bold and risky one that brought tremors to my hands.

"Now, before you all go off to your jury room, I'm going to do something that's not often done. Mr. Ames claimed to have taken you to the Kingdom of Truth, but the *fact* is, he never even got close to his stated destination. He omitted the most important truth of all. He never mentioned the real reason Gracie Johnson is facing the possibility of losing her life.

"You know the reason. I don't even have to say it. But I'm going to say it anyway.

"*Gracie Johnson is colored*. That's why she's here. That's the only reason she's here. She was the only colored employee in attendance at the Davenport house that day.

"So there it is. She's a Negro. You gentlemen are white. Everyone expects that a white jury will always convict a black defendant. But I know that not to be true. I think—matter of fact, I truly believe—that you have more honor than that. You have the integrity to see through what the prosecutor is trying to do here, which is to railroad an innocent woman whose only crime was telling you honestly that her boss was a mean old woman.

"Do you see what we've found? We've turned up the most important *fact* of all. And that fact, the fact that Gracie's skin is black, should have no influence whatsoever on what you decide.

"That's what the law says, in every state in this Union. If there is a reasonable doubt in your mind as to whether or not Gracie Johnson is a murderer, *you . . . must . . . vote . . . to . . . acquit.*"

I started to go back to my chair, but then I turned and walked right up to Carter Ames's table.

"May I, Carter?"

I picked up his Bible, flipping through the pages until I appeared to find the verse I was seeking in the book of Proverbs. No one needed to know I was quoting from memory:

"When justice is done, it brings joy to the righteous."

I closed the Good Book.

Chapter 5

Carter Ames pushed his silver flask of bourbon toward my face. “Have a swig, Ben. You deserve it, son. Well done.”

What a sight for the funny pages we must have made—Ames barely five feet tall, me at six-four—standing side by side in the marble hallway outside the courtroom.

“No, thanks, Carter. I’d rather be sober when the verdict comes in.”

“I wouldn’t, if I was you.” His voice was a curdled mixture of phlegm and whiskey. As he lifted the flask to his mouth, I was surprised to see half-moons of sweat under his arms. In the courtroom he’d looked cool as a block of pond ice.

"Your summation was damn good," he observed. "I think you had 'em going for a while there. But then you went and threw in that colored stuff. Why'd you have to remind them? You think they didn't notice she's black as the ace of spades?"

"I thought I saw one or two who weren't buying your motive," I said. "Only takes one to hang 'em up."

"And twelve to hang *her,* don't I know it."

He took another swig from his flask and eased himself down to a bench. "Sit down, Ben. I want to talk to *you,* not your rear end."

I sat.

"Son, you're a fine young lawyer, Harvard trained and all, gonna make a finer lawyer one of these days," he said. "But you still need to learn that Washington is a southern town. We're every bit as southern as wherever you're from down in Podunk, Mississippi."

I grimaced and shook my head. "I just do what I think is right, Carter."

"I know you do. And that's what makes everybody think you're nothing but a goddamned bleeding-heart fool and nigger-lover."

Before I could defend—well, just about everything I believe in—a police officer poked his head out of the courtroom. "Jury's coming back."

Chapter 6

The cumbersome iron shackles around Gracie Johnson's ankles clanked noisily as I helped her to her feet at the defense table.

"Thank you, Mr. Corbett," she whispered.

Judge Warren gazed down on her as if he were God. "Mr. Foreman, has the jury reached a verdict in this case?" he asked.

"Yes, we have, Your Honor."

Like every lawyer since the Romans invented the Code of Justinian, I had tried to learn something from the jurors' faces as they filed into the courtroom—the haberdasher, the retired schoolteacher, the pale young man who was engaged to Congressman Chapman's daughter and had cracked a tentative smile during my summation.

Several of them were looking directly at Gracie, which was supposed to be a good sign for a defendant. I decided to take it that way and said a hopeful little prayer.

The judge intoned, "How find you in the matter of murder against Grace Johnson?"

The foreman rose in a deliberate manner, then in a strong, clear voice he said, "We the jury find the defendant guilty as charged."

The courtroom erupted with exclamations, some sobs, even an ugly smattering of applause.

Bam! Bam! Bam!

"I will have order in my court," said the judge. Damned if I didn't see a smile flash across Judge Warren's face before he managed to swallow it.

I slid my arms around Gracie. One of us was trembling, and I realized it was me. My eyes, not hers, were brimming with hot tears.

"It be all right, Mr. Corbett," she said quietly.

"It *isn't* all right, Gracie. It's a disgrace."

Two D.C. blueboys were heading our way, coming to take her back to jail. I motioned for them to give us a moment.

"Don't you worry, Mr. Corbett," Gracie said. "Jesus works in mysterious ways."

"God bless you, Gracie. We'll file an appeal."

"Thank you, Mr. Corbett. But now I got to tell you something."

"What's that?"

She leaned close to me, dropping her voice to a whisper. *"I done the crime."*

"What?"

"I done the crime."

"Gracie!"

"I got five chillun, Mr. Corbett. That old lady, she don't pay me hardly nothing. I needed money. So I meant to take the silver."

"And . . . what happened?"

"I was coming through the dining room with the silver chest in my hands. Miz Davenport walk in. She 'posed to be having a nap. Well, she screamed at me like she the devil. Then she come a-running at me."

Gracie was composed, very calm, almost in a trance as she spoke to me.

"I had the bone-handle carving knife in my hand. Not for her—I don't know, just in case of something. When she run at me, I turned. She run straight up on that knife, sir. I swear I never meant to do it."

The policemen apparently felt they'd been patient long enough. They came up alongside us and, taking hold of Gracie's arms, began to lead her away.

"But I tell you, Mr. Corbett..."

"What, Gracie?"

"I would do it again."

Chapter 7

As I walked all the way home from the courthouse on that hot June day, I still had no idea what life-changing things were in store for me and my family. Not a hint, not a clue.

Our house was quiet and dark that afternoon when I arrived. I walked through the front parlor. No sign of Meg, Amelia, or Alice.

In the kitchen a peach pie was cooling on a table. Through the window I saw our cook, Mazie, sitting on the back stoop, shelling butter beans into a white enamelware pan.

"Has Meg gone out, Mazie?" I called.

"Yes, suh, Mr. Ben. And she took the littl'uns with her. Don't know where. Miz

Corbett, she was in some bad mood when she went. Her face all red like, you know how she gets."

How she gets. My Meg, my sweet New England wife. So red in the face. *You know how she gets*. The gentlest girl at Radcliffe, the prettiest girl ever to come from Warwick, Rhode Island. Burning red in the face.

And she gets that way because of me, I couldn't help thinking. Because of my failure, because of my repeated failure. Because of the shame I bring on our house with my endless "charity cases" for the poor and disenfranchised.

I walked to the parlor and lifted my banjo from its shelf. I'd been trying to learn to play ragtime tunes since I first heard the new music that had come sweeping up from the South late in the old century. It was music as noisy and fast as one of the new motorcars that were unsettling horses all over the country.

I sat on the piano bench and tried to force my clumsy fingers to find the first offbeat notes of that skittering melody. The music seemed to be in such a hurry, but something about it took me back to a place and a time much slower, and maybe better, than any in Washington, D.C. The bumpy syncopation reminded me of the sound I used to hear coming from tiny Negro churches out in the country, in the woods outside Eudora, Mississippi, where I was born and raised.

As a boy I'd walked past those churches a thousand times. I'd heard the clapping and the fervent amens. Now that had all gotten blended in with a fast-march tempo and the syncopated melody of the old work songs. Mix it all together, speed it up, and somehow, from that corner of the South, down around where Louisiana, Mississippi, and Arkansas meet up, the music came out ragtime.

Whenever I heard that sound, whether issuing from a saloon on the wrong side of Capitol Hill or a shiny new phonograph in Dupont Circle, it sent me out of my Washington life and down the memory road to Mississippi.

And whenever I thought of Mississippi, I couldn't help seeing my mother's face.

Chapter 8

Eudora, the county seat, is located in an odd corner of southern Mississippi, sixty miles east of the Big Muddy and fifteen miles north of the Louisiana state line.

My father, the Honorable Everett J. Corbett, may have been the most important judge in town, but the only truly famous citizen in Eudora was my mother, Louellen Corbett. They called her "the Poetess of Dixie." She wrote sweet, simple, sentimental verses in such noted periodicals as *Woburn's Weekly Companion* and the *Beacon-Light* that captured the hearts of southern ladies. She wrote poems about everything dear to the southern heart—paddle wheelers on the Mississippi, moonlight on the magnolias, the lonely nobility of the aging Confederate widow.

But that one particular day in Eudora...

I am a boy of seven, an only child. I'm downtown with my mother on a summer afternoon.

Downtown consisted of the Purina feed and seed store, the First Bank, a few shops around the courthouse square, the Slide Inn Café, specializing in fresh seafood from the Gulf, and the Ben Franklin five-and-dime—about which my mother was fond of saying, "They sell everything you need and nothing you really want."

July was wide-open summer in south Mississippi, featuring a sun that rose early and stayed at the top of the sky all afternoon. The air near the Gulf is so humid at all times of year that you have to put your shoes near the stove at night to keep them from turning white with mildew.

I was wearing short pants, but Mama was "dressed for town"—a lacy flowing dress that swept the ground, a sky blue shawl with dark blue fringe, and her ever-present wide-brimmed straw hat. A boy always thinks of his mother as pretty, but on that afternoon, I remember, she seemed to be shining.

Our chore that day was to pick up eighteen yards of blue velvet Mama had ordered from Sam Jenkins' Mercantile for new dining room curtains.

"Mornin', Sam."

"Why, good morning, Miz Corbett," he said. "Don't you look nice today."

"Thank you."

For Mama, that was mighty few words to utter. I turned to look at her, but she seemed all right.

Sam Jenkins stood there peering at her too. "Is there something I can help you with, Miz Corbett?"

"Yeah," she said, "Sham. Oh. Excuse me."

Something *was* wrong. Why was my mother slurring her words?

"Did you come to pick up that fabric, Miz Corbett?" said Sam. Instead of answering, Mama squinted hard and rubbed the front of her head.

"Miz Corbett? You all right?"

Silence from my mother. Only a puzzled gaze.

Then that slurred, weak voice again.

"When doesh shoe . . . when . . ."

"Miz Corbett, have you been . . . have you been *drinking?"*

Mama shook her head slowly and kept rubbing her forehead. I felt the blood flush through my body.

"Don't be shilly. I sh . . . I . . . don't . . ."

I spoke very quietly. "Mama, what's wrong with you?"

"Ben, you better take your mama home now. Looks like she may have had a little touch o' the grape." He forced a laugh.

"My mama never drinks. She must be sick."

"I'm afraid she is, son. Whiskey sick."

Suddenly my mother's knees buckled. She drooped over to one side and then fell to the floor with a heavy thud.

Sam Jenkins turned to the back of his store. "Henry, come up here! I got a lady passed out drunk on the floor."

Chapter 9

From separate directions came two teenage boys. One was white, with red hair. The bigger one was black, as tall as he was skinny.

"Y'all help this boy take his mama out of here," Sam Jenkins said.

The white boy leaned down to Mama and tried to lift her. She was small, but he couldn't find the right angle to maneuver her into a standing position.

"Marcus, you gonna help me?"

"Mist' Sam, I think this lady sick," said the black kid.

"Nobody asked your opinion," said Mr. Jenkins. "Just get her out of the store!"

They lifted my mother up and carried

her out to the sidewalk, where they set her on a bench near the watering trough.

"Shit. She ain't sick," said the red-headed boy. "She's drunk as a monkey."

I was trying my best not to cry, but I couldn't stop the tears blurring my eyes. I was helpless and small, and something was terribly, terribly wrong with my mother. I believed that she might die right there.

The white boy disappeared back into the store, shaking his mop of red hair in disgust.

Then Marcus spoke very softly to me. "Want to hep me carry her down to the doctor?"

I remember nothing of how we got my mother to Dr. Hunter's house. I do remember hearing the doctor say, "Louellen isn't drunk. This is apoplexy. She's had a stroke, Ben. I'm so sorry."

I burst into tears.

Later on, when I understood what the doctor's words really meant, I wished Mama *had* been drunk. Everything in our lives was so different from then on. The next day she was in a wheelchair and looked twenty years older. Eventually she regained her ability to speak, but she left that chair only when she was lifted into the washtub or her bed.

She wrote a few poems about her condition—"A View from a Moving Chair" and "Words You May Not Understand" were the most famous ones—but she was always weak and often distracted.

To my surprise, she sometimes enjoyed talking about that day in Jenkins's store. She would laugh at the idea that she had been mistaken for a drunk, but she always repeated the lesson she had learned that day: "Just remember one thing, Ben. That was a *black* boy who helped us. He was the only one who helped."

I did as she instructed. I remembered it through grammar school, high school, college, and law school. I remembered it whenever colored people came to my office in Washington with worried faces and tears in their eyes, asking for my help.

But sometimes I couldn't help them. The way I couldn't help Grace Johnson.

I rested the neck of the banjo against my arm and began to pick out the notes of "Bethena," the saddest rag Joplin ever wrote. Every note in that jaunty, quick tune is minor, every shading of the melody is dark.

For all that, it made me feel better—a little homesick, maybe, but what's so wrong with that?

Chapter 10

I heard the click of the front door, then the happy, giggly sounds of Amelia and Alice hurrying inside.

This was followed by Meg's icy voice.

"Say a quick hello to your father, girls. Then wash up for supper."

Amelia poked her head through the parlor door, a happy little angel of seven in a red-and-white gingham sundress, shortly followed by Alice, another helping of strawberry shortcake in an identical outfit.

Those dresses were the only thing identical about the girls. Although they were twins, they barely looked like sisters.

Amelia was small, with fine, dark, beautiful features exactly like her mother's.

Alice was taller, blond and lanky, and had the misfortune of taking after her father, though I will say that our family looks had settled better on her face than on mine.

"Remind me again which one of you is which," I said with a stern expression.

"Daddy, *you know,*" said Amelia. Alice squealed in delight.

"No, I've completely forgotten. How am I supposed to be able to tell the difference when you look exactly alike?"

To Amelia, that was a scream.

Meg walked into the front hall. "Come along, girls. You heard what I said."

I pointed at Alice. "Oh, *now* I remember. You are... Amelia." And then, pointing at Amelia, "So that means you must be Alice."

"And *you* must be Mommy!" Amelia pointed at me, giggling at her own cleverness. Was there any sweeter sound in the world?

I knelt down and kissed her, then her sister, and gathered them both for a big daddy-hug.

"Where have you two been causing trouble today?"

In a ridiculously loud stage whisper Alice

said: "We're not allowed to say...but we were hiding in church."

Meg called again, with the business end of her voice: *"Girls!"*

"Mama says you're in trouble," Amelia reported. "She says you're in the doghouse."

"And we don't even have a dog!" Alice crowed with laughter.

"Girls!" That voice brooked no nonsense.

They ran from my arms.

Chapter 11

I will never forget the rest of that evening, not a moment of it. Not a detail has been lost on me.

"You and I are living in two different marriages, Ben. It's the truth, a sad truth. I'll admit it," said Meg.

I was flabbergasted by this announcement from my wife of nearly eleven years. We were sitting in the parlor on the uncomfortable horsehair sofa Meg's father had given us as a wedding gift. We had just finished an awkward supper.

"Two different marriages? That's a tough statement, Meg."

"I meant it to be, Ben. When I was at Radcliffe and you were at Harvard I used to look at you and think, Now, this is the man I could always be with. I honestly believed that. So I waited for you while you went to law school. All the time you were at Columbia, in New York, I was wasting away at my father's house. Then I waited some more, while you went to Cuba and fought in that war that none of us understood."

"Meg, I'm sorry. It was a war."

"But I'm still waiting!" She twirled around, her arms outstretched. And in that one gesture, in those few seconds, I realized the complete truth of what she was saying. Our house was not the one on Dupont Circle that Meg deserved, but a small frame bungalow on the wrong side of Capitol Hill. Cracks were visible in our plaster walls. The piano had broken keys. The roof leaked.

Through soft sobs Meg continued, "I'm not a selfish woman. I admire the cases you take, really I do. I want the poor people and the colored people to be helped. But I also want something for my girls and me. Is that so wrong?"

She wasn't wrong. Maybe I had let her down by worrying too much about my own conscience, not thinking enough about her expectations and the life she believed she was getting when she married me.

"I love you, Meg. You know I adore you." I reached and touched her face. Her dark hair fell across my fingers. We could have been back in Harvard Yard or walking in the moonlight along the Charles.

A sudden knock, and Mazie entered the room. " 'Scuse me, Mr. Ben. They's a man at the door. Says it's urgent."

"Who is it, Mazie?" said Meg.

"He say his name Nate, and . . ." She paused, reluctant to finish the sentence.

"Is he a colored man, Mazie?" I asked.

Meg said, "Of course he is, Ben. He's here to see you, isn't he?"

A pause.

"Please show the man in," I said.

Chapter 12

Right then and there, everything changed in our lives, certainly in mine. Meg looked at me with those big eyes of hers, as much in sorrow as in anger. I reached to touch her again, but she pulled away. She shook her head as if I were a child whose behavior had disappointed her. "You know this one by name?"

"I only know one man named Nate, and that's Nate Pryor. He was Tenth Cavalry. We rode together at San Juan Hill."

Nate appeared at the door just in time to hear Meg say, "The hell with you, Ben."

She walked past Nate and out of the room without so much as looking at him. Her passing set up the first decent breeze I'd felt all day.

"You can introduce us some other time," Nate said. His voice was deep, his enunciation precise. I shook his hand warmly and clapped his shoulder.

"I don't know what elixir you're drinking, Nate, but you look younger than you did the day Colonel Roosevelt drove us up old San Juan Hill."

"The only medicine I take is good old-fashioned hard work. The kind the Lord intended a man to make with his days. Maybe a little taste of 'shine once in a while, for a chaser."

I nodded, but then I looked into his eyes. "What brings you here, Nate? What's so urgent?"

"I'm here with a serious proposition. I wouldn't bother you, but it's something I believe only you can do."

Whatever the favor he was about to ask of me, I was fast losing the desire to hear about it. A sad tale, surely—hard times, ill health, someone's poor relative left penniless and in need of free legal assistance.

I tried to keep my voice gentle. "I've taken on about all the cases I can handle for a while."

"Oh, this is not a law *case*." He flashed a particularly charming smile. "Perhaps I should have mentioned that I came here today directly from the White House. This isn't *my* proposition. This is a request from the president."

I was astonished. "Roosevelt sent you here? To my home?"

"The man himself."

Chapter 13

The first time I ever laid eyes on Theodore Roosevelt—God, how he hated the nickname "Teddy"—I was surprised by how much he resembled the cartoons and caricatures with which the papers regularly mocked him. And now, on this fine summer day in the White House, I saw that the thick spectacles pinching his nose, the wide solid waist, and the prominent potbelly had only become more pronounced since he took up residence on Pennsylvania Avenue.

Roosevelt jumped up from his desk and charged across the room toward me before his assistant, Jackson Hensen, could finish his introduction.

"Captain Corbett, a pleasure to see you again. It's been too long."

"The pleasure is entirely mine, Colonel . . . uhm, Mr. President."

"No, no, no. I'll always prefer Colonel!"

The president waved me over to a green silk sofa near his desk. I sat, trying to contain my excitement at being in the Oval Office, a room that was airy and beautifully appointed but a good deal smaller than I would have imagined.

A door to the left of the president's desk glided open. In came a tall Negro valet bearing a tea tray, which he placed on a side table. "Shall I pour, sir?"

"Thank you, Harold, I'll do my own pouring."

The valet left the room. Roosevelt went to a cabinet behind his desk and took out a crystal decanter. "Except I'll be pouring *this*. What'll it be, Captain, whiskey or wine? I'm having claret myself. I never touch spirituous liquors."

That is how I wound up sitting beside TR on the green sofa, sipping fine Kentucky bourbon from a china teacup embossed with the presidential seal.

"I presume our old friend Nate Pryor

has given you some idea why I wanted to see you," he said.

I placed my cup on the saucer. "He actually didn't say much, to be honest. Only that it was to do with the South, some kind of mission. A problem with the colored people? Danger, perhaps."

"I've been doing a little checking on you, Ben. It just so happens that the place you were born and raised is the perfect place to send you. *Assuming* you agree to this assignment."

"Mississippi?"

"Specifically your hometown. Eudora, isn't it?"

"Sir? I'm not sure I understand. Something urgent in *Eudora?*"

He walked to his desk and returned with a blue leather portfolio stamped with the presidential seal in gold.

"You are aware that the crime of lynching has been increasing at an alarming rate in the South?" he said.

"I've read newspaper stories."

"It's not enough that some people have managed to reverse every forward step the Negro race has managed since the war. Now they've taken to mob rule.

They run about killing innocent people and stringing 'em up from the nearest tree."

The president placed the portfolio in my hand.

"These are papers I've been collecting on the situation: reports of the most horrible occurrences, some police records. Things it's hard for a Christian man to credit. Especially since the perpetrators of these crimes are men who claim to be Christians."

My first thought was that the president was exaggerating the problem. Northerners do that all the time. Of course I had heard of lynchings, but I hadn't known of any in Mississippi since I was a boy.

"They hang men, they hang women, for God's sake they even hang young children," Roosevelt said. "They do the most unspeakable things to their bodies, Ben."

I didn't say a word. How could I? He was talking about my hometown.

"I've tried discussing the matter with several southern senators. To a man, they claim it's the work of outsiders and a fringe element of white reprobates. But

I know damn well it's the Klan, and in some of these towns that includes just about every respectable white man."

"But Colonel," I said, "the Klan was outlawed forty years ago."

"Yes. And apparently it's stronger than ever now. That's why you're here, Captain."

Chapter 14

I was glad when Roosevelt reached for the decanter again. This talk of the sins of my fellow southerners had me upset, even a little angry.

"Colonel, I haven't spent much time down home since I finished law school," I said cautiously. "But I'd be surprised if there's a problem in Eudora. Folks there generally treat the Negroes well."

When he spoke, his voice was gentle. "Open your eyes, Ben. Since April there have been two men and a fifteen-year-old boy allegedly lynched within a few miles of your hometown. It's on the way to becoming a goddamn epidemic, and I—"

"Excuse me, sir. Sorry to interrupt. You said 'allegedly'?"

"Excellent! You're paying attention!" He thwacked my knee with the portfolio. "In this file you'll see letter after letter, report after report, from congressmen, judges, mayors, governors. Nearly every one tells me the lynching reports are greatly exaggerated. There *are* no lynchings in their towns or districts. The Negro is living in freedom and comfort, and the white southerner is his boon friend and ally."

I nodded. I didn't want to admit that had I been asked, that would have been very much like my own estimate of the situation.

"But that is *not* the story I'm hearing from certain men of conscience," he said. "I need to know the *truth*. I'm glad you don't automatically believe what I'm telling you, Ben. I want a man with an open mind, an honest and skeptical man like yourself who can see all sides of the question. I want you to go down there and investigate, and get to the bottom of this."

"But sir, what is it you want me to find out? Exactly what?"

"Answer these questions for me," he said.

"Are lynchings as common a fact of life as I think they are?

"Is the Ku Klux Klan alive and thriving down there, and if so, who is behind the outrageous resurgence?

"What in hell is the truth—the absolute truth? And what can a president do to stop these awful things from happening?"

He barked these questions at me in the same high, sharp voice I recalled from the parade ground in Havana. His face was flushed red, full of righteous anger and determination.

Then, softly, he asked, "Will you do it for me, and for this country, Ben?"

I did not hesitate. How could I? "Of course, I am at your service. I'll do what you ask."

"Bully! When can you go?"

"Well, sir, I do have a trial beginning next week in the circuit court," I said.

"Leave the judge's name with Mr.

Hensen. We'll take care of it. I want you in Mississippi as soon as possible."

He clapped his hand on my shoulder as he walked me to the door. From the breast pocket of his jacket he removed a folded scrap of paper, which he handed to me.

"This is the name of a man who will assist you down there. I believe he'll be able to open your eyes to the way your good people of Eudora have been treating their colored citizens."

"Yes, sir." I tucked it away.

"One more thing..."

"Sir?"

"I must have secrecy. A cover story has been arranged for you: you're in Mississippi to interview possible federal judges. If your real mission is exposed, I will deny that I had anything to do with your trip. And Ben, this could be dangerous for you. The Klan murders people—clearly."

In the outer office I gave the judge's name to Mr. Hensen, then walked down the steps of the North Portico to the curving driveway. To be honest, I hoped some friend or acquaintance might happen along and witness my emergence from that famous house, but no such luck.

I stepped out onto Pennsylvania Avenue and turned toward my office. I would have to work late getting everything in order. It seemed I might be gone for a while.

I had just passed the entrance to Willard's Hotel when I remembered the slip of paper the president had given me. I pulled it out and took a step back to read it in the haze of gaslight from the hotel lobby.

Written in the president's own bold, precise hand were four words:

ABRAHAM CROSS
EUDORA QUARTERS

I thought I knew everybody in Eudora, but I'd never heard of Abraham Cross. "The Quarters" was the Negro section of town. This was the man who was going to teach me about southerners and lynching?

The fact was, I had not been completely honest with Roosevelt. Had he asked me, I would have told him the truth. I already knew more than I cared to know about the horror of lynching.

I had seen one.

Chapter 15

The summer we both turned twelve, my best friend, Jacob Gill, and I made it a practice to slip out of our houses after supper and meet at the vacant lot behind the First Bank of Eudora. Once out of the sight of grown-ups, we proceeded to commit the cardinal and rather breath-taking sin of smoking cigarettes.

We'd blow perfect smoke rings into the hot night air and talk about everything, from the new shortstop just sent down from the Jackson Senators to play with the Hattiesburg Tar Heels, to the unmis-takable breasts budding on a lovely and mysterious eighth grader named Cora Sinclair.

More than anything, I think, we liked the

ritual of smoking—swiping the tobacco from Jacob's father's humidor, bribing Old Man Sanders at the general store to sell us a pack of Bugler papers without a word to our mothers, tapping out just the right amount of tobacco, licking the gummed edge of the paper, firing the match. We considered ourselves men, not boys, and there was nothing like a good after-dinner smoke to consecrate the feeling.

Then came a Monday night, early August. The last night we ever smoked together.

I will tell you how the nightmare began, at least how I remember it.

Jacob and I were a little light-headed from smoking three cigarettes in quick succession. We heard noises on Commerce Street and walked down the alley beside the bank to see what was stirring.

The first thing we saw was a group of men coming out of the basement of the First Methodist Church. I immediately recognized Leon Reynolds, the "dirty man" who did the sweeping and manure hauling in front of the stores around the courthouse square. He had a hard job, a big belly, and a sour-mash-whiskey attitude.

Across Commerce Street, on the sidewalk in front of Miss Ida Simmons's sewing and notions shop, we saw three colored teenagers standing and shooting the breeze. Lounging against the wall of Miss Ida's, they were facing the wrong way to see that there were white men bearing down on them.

I recognized the tallest boy as George Pearson, whose mother sometimes did washing and ironing for our neighbors the Harrises. Beside him was his brother Lanky. I didn't recognize the third boy.

If Jacob and I could hear their conversation this plainly, so could the men walking down the sidewalk toward them. George Pearson was doing most of the talking.

"Shoot, Lank, they couldn't do a damn thing 'round here without us," he said. "Let 'em try to get along without colored folks. Who'd curry their hosses and pitch their hay? Who'd they get to cut cane and pick cotton?"

Jacob looked at me. I looked back at

him. We knew black boys were not supposed to talk this way.

The white men walked right past us and stepped down into the street. I don't think they even registered our presence. When they heard what George was saying, they started walking faster, and then they ran. They were almost upon the three boys when one of the men boomed, "Hell, George, you one smart little nigger to figure all that out by yourself!"

Chapter 16

George Pearson turned, and I saw nothing but the whites of his eyes. It was stupid of him to be talking like that in the open on Commerce Street, but he quickly demonstrated that he was smart enough to run.

Jacob and I watched him leap the horse trough in one bound and take off sprinting through the skinny alley beside the church. Leon Reynolds and his pals gave chase, huffing and cursing and yelling "Stop, nigger!"

"We better go home, Ben," said Jacob. "I'm not kidding you."

"No," I said. "We're going after them. Come on. *I dare you*."

I knew Jacob would lay down his life

before taking off in the face of a dare. Sure enough, he followed me. We kept far enough back so as not to be seen. I had not been a very religious boy up till then, but I found myself praying for George Pearson to get away. *Please, God,* I thought, *make George run fast*.

The men chased him all the way to the end of Court Street, out past the icehouse. As they went along, a couple more men joined the chase. George seemed to be getting away! Then, from out of nowhere, a bucket came sailing out of the icehouse door, tangling his feet and tripping him up.

Within seconds the men were on George. Leon Reynolds punched him right in his face. The man next to him hocked up a big wad of spit and let it fly. Another man reached down, grabbed George by the testicles, and twisted his hand.

"Holy God," Jacob whispered in the bushes where we'd taken shelter. "They're gonna kill him, Ben. I swear to God."

The men yanked George up by one arm

and set him stumbling in front of them. They taunted and teased and pushed him toward the swampy woods behind the icehouse. One of them had a torch. Then another torch was lit.

"We gotta do something," I said to Jacob. "We *gotta*. I'm serious, boy."

"You crazy? What in hell can we do? They'll twist our balls off too."

"Run home and get your daddy," I said. "I'll try to keep up with 'em."

Jacob looked at me, plainly trying to gauge whether his departure now would mean he had failed to live up to my earlier dare. But finally he ran for help.

Leon Reynolds yanked George up hard by his ear. I found my hand clutching at the side of my own head in sympathy.

Two men lifted George as easily as if he were a cloth doll. Blood poured from his mouth, along with a load of bile and vomit.

One man held George at the waist while another pushed and pulled his head up and down to make him perform a jerky bow.

"There you go, nigger boy. Now you're

bowing and showing the respect you should."

Then, leaning in, with one firm tug, Leon Reynolds pulled George's ear clean off his head.

Chapter 17

I wanted to throw up.

I stood ankle deep in the muck of the swamp, batting at the cloud of mosquitoes that whined around my face and arms. I was hiding as best I could behind a tangle of brambly vines and swamp grass, all alone and completely petrified.

In no time at all, the men had fashioned a rope into a thick noose with a hangman's knot. It took even less time to sling the rope over the middle fork of a sizable sycamore tree.

The only sound in those woods was the awful grunting of the men, the steady metallic chant of the cicadas, and the loud beating of my heart.

"You know why you being punished, boy?" shouted one of the men.

There was no response from George Pearson. He must have fainted from the beatings or maybe the pain of losing his ear.

"We don't appreciate *boasting.* We don't appreciate it from no nigger boy."

"Now, come on, Willy, ain't it a little rough to throw a boy a rope party just for shootin' off his stupid-ass mouth?" said another.

"You got another suggestion, Earl?" Willy said. "What other tonic would you recommend?"

I looked around for Jacob. Surely he'd had time to get home and come back with his father.

The men carried George to the sandy ground underneath the sycamore. One of them held up his head while the others slid the rope around his neck.

I didn't know what I could do. I was just one boy. I wasn't strong enough to take on one of these men, much less all of them, but I had to do something. I couldn't just hide like a jackrabbit in the woods and watch them hang George Pearson.

So I finally moved out of the shadows. I guess the slosh of my feet in swamp water turned their heads. I stood revealed in the light of the moon and their torches.

"Would you looka here," said Willy.

"Who the hell is this?" said one of his friends.

"Ain't but a little old boy, come out to give us a hand."

I realized I was shivering now as if this were the coldest night of all time. "Let him go," I squeaked, instantly ashamed of the tremor in my voice.

"You follered us out here to hep this nigger?" said Willy. "You want us to string you up next to him, boy?"

"He did nothing wrong," I said. "He was just talking. I heard him."

"Willy, that's Judge Corbett's kid," said a tall, skinny man.

"That's right," I said, "he's my daddy. You're all gonna be in bad trouble when I tell what you did!"

They laughed as if I'd told the funniest joke they'd ever heard.

"Well, now, correct me if I'm wrong, young Master Corbett," said Willy, "but I believe the law in these parts says if a nigger goes to boasting, his friends and neighbors got every right to throw him a little rope party and teach him how to dance."

My throat was so dry I was surprised any sound came out. "But he didn't do anything wrong," I said again. For some reason I thought if I repeated myself, they would see the logic.

Willy put on a smile that held not a hint of amusement. "Boys, I believe we have got ourselves a pure-D, grade-A, number one junior nigger-lover."

The other men laughed out loud. Hot tears sprang up in my eyes, but I willed them not to fall. I would not cry in front of these awful bastards, these cowards.

I recognized a tall, skinny one as J. T. Mack, the overseer at the McFarland plantation. He slurred his words as if he were drunk. "If this boy is half smart as his daddy, he'll just turn his ass around and march on back home. And forget he ever come out here tonight."

In two steps Willy was on me, gripping my arm, then my throat. J. T. Mack moved in to grab my other arm.

"Hold on, son. You can't go home to daddy yet. We need a souvenir of your visit. Come on out of there, Scooter," said J.T.

Out of nowhere came a dapper young man in a green-and-white-plaid suit, his hair slicked back with brilliantine. He looked about sixteen years old. He carried a wooden box camera on a large tripod, which he set up in the clearing about ten feet from the motionless body of George Pearson.

Scooter stuck his head under the black cloak attached to the camera and then pushed back out. "I can't see nothing. It's too dark. Bring your light in close to his face," he said.

The two men with torches moved closer, illuminating the shining black skin of George Pearson's face. Scooter put his head back under the cloth.

With that, Leon pulled hard on the rope. George Pearson stood straight up and then he flew off the ground three or four feet. His eyes opened wide, bulging as if they might explode. His whole face seemed to swell. His body began trembling and jerking.

The horror of what I was seeing froze me in place. I felt something warm dripping down my leg and realized I had peed my pants.

No one was looking at me now or bothering to hold me. Slowly, slowly, I began to back away.

“Hope you got a good likeness, Scooter,” said J.T. “We’ll all be wanting a copy. Something to remember ol’ George by.”

Everybody hooted and laughed at that one. I turned and ran for my life.

Chapter 18

I suppose there might have been one good thing about the punishing southern-style heat wave that had settled over Washington: that night Meg had gone to bed wearing her lightest nightgown. As I opened the door to our room Meg was resting on our bed, pretending to read her leatherbound copy of the book of Psalms.

"Are you speaking to me?" I asked her.

"You weren't here to speak to until now," she answered without looking up.

I leaned down and kissed her and was relieved that she didn't turn away.

Meg was so lovely just then, and I wanted nothing more than to lie down beside her. But it wouldn't be fair, not with the knowledge running around in my head.

"Meg," I said softly, "I have something to tell you. I'm not sure how you're going to take it."

Her eyes hardened.

"I went to the White House tonight," I said.

Her eyes flashed. In one second the hardness melted into joy.

"The White House!" she cried. "Oh, I knew it! I *knew* Roosevelt would have to come around! You're one of the best young lawyers in town. How ridiculous of him to have waited this long to offer you a position!"

"It's not a position," I said. "The president asked me to . . . take on a mission for him. It could be for a month or two."

Meg sat straight up. The Psalms slid to the floor with a soft plop. "Oh, Ben, you're going to leave us again? Where?"

"Home," I said. "To Mississippi. To Eudora."

She exhaled sharply. "What could the president possibly want you to do in that godforsaken corner of nowhere?"

"I'm sorry, Meg," I said. "I can't tell you. I had to give Roosevelt my word."

Meg's rage exploded, and she cast about for a suitable weapon. Seizing the bottle of French eau de toilette I had given her for her birthday, she fired it against the wall with such force that it shattered. A dreamy scent of lavender filled the room.

"Meg, how could I say no? He's the president of the United States."

"And I'm your wife. I want you to understand something, Ben. When you go back to Mississippi, on your *mission,* you'd best be advised to purchase a one-way ticket. Because if you go, there's no point in coming back. I mean that, Ben. So help me, I'm serious. I can't wait for you any longer."

I heard a sound behind me. Meg and I turned to discover that we had an audience for this display: Alice and Amelia.

"Hello, girls," I said. "Mama and I are having a talk. An adult talk. Back to bed with both of you now."

Meg had already turned her face away from the door. I could see from the heaving of her shoulders that she was crying, and that made me feel awful.

I walked the girls back to their room, where I tucked them in, covering them gently with the light cotton sheets that sufficed on hot nights like this.

I kissed Amelia, then Alice. Then I had to kiss Alice again, and Amelia, in that order, to even things out.

As I rose to leave, Amelia threw her skinny arms around me and tugged me back down to her side.

"Don't go, Papa," she said in a voice so sweet it nearly broke my heart. "If you go, we'll never see you again."

The moment Amelia said it, I had the terrible thought that my little girl just might be right.

Part Two

HOMECOMING

Chapter 19

I was soon enough reminded of the dangers of the mission I'd undertaken for the president of the United States. Two days into my journey south, I was in Memphis, about to board the Mississippi & Tennessee train to Carthage, where I would switch to the Jackson & Northern for the trip to Jackson. I had just discovered some truly disturbing reading material.

I had been waiting when the Memphis Public Library opened its doors at nine a.m. A kindly lady librarian had succumbed to one of my shameless winks. She agreed to violate several regulations at once to lend me a number of back issues of the local newspapers, which I agreed to return by mail.

I had carefully chosen the most recent issues that carried sensational stories of lynchings on their front pages. Many of those appeared in the *Memphis News-Scimitar* and the *Memphis Commercial Appeal*.

I was instantly confused by one headline that declared, "Colored Youth *Hung* by Rope AND *Shot* by Rope." The article explained that after the fifteen-year-old boy was strung up by his neck—he'd been accused of setting fire to a warehouse—the mob shot so many bullets at his dangling corpse that one bullet actually severed the rope. The boy's body crashed to the ground, a fall that would surely have killed him had he not already been dead.

Another article blaring from the *News-Scimitar* concerned the lynching of a Negro who was the father of two young boys. The man was taken forcibly from the Shelby County Jail and lynched within a few yards of the entrance. The unusual thing here? A member of the sheriff's department had gone to the man's home and brought his sons to view their daddy's lynching.

The "coverage" in these pieces read more like the review of a new vaudeville show or a lady pianist at a classical music concert. To wit:

> The Everett lynching was far more gruesome than the Kelly lynching of but two weeks previous. Due to the unusual explosion of Thaddeus Everett's neck and carotid arteries, this hanging was both more extraordinary and interesting than the afore-mentioned Kelly death.

And from the *Memphis Sunday Times,* a "critique" of a different lynching:

> Olivia Kent Oxxam, the only woman privileged to be present at "Pa" Harris's lynching in the River Knolls region, declared it to be "One of the most riveting events of my lifetime. I was grateful to be there."

These articles made the lynchings seem so engrossing that they must surely surpass the new Vitagraph "flicker" picture shows for their entertainment value.

I folded the papers carefully and stashed them in my valise. Then I decided that the heat inside the train carriage was worse than the soot and grime that would flow in from the stacks after I opened the window. I made my move, but the damn window wouldn't budge.

I was pushing upward with all my strength when the gentleman in the opposite seat said, "Even a strong young man like yourself won't be able to open that window—without pulling down on the side latch first."

Chapter 20

I laughed at myself, then pulled on the latch. The window slid down easily. "I guess strength doesn't help," I said, "if you don't have some brains to go along with it."

My fellow traveler was middle-aged, paunchy, seemingly well-to-do, with a florid complexion and a gold watch fob of unmistakable value. He put out his hand.

"Henley McNeill," he said. "Grain trader. I'm from Jackson."

"I'm Benjamin Corbett. Attorney at law. From Washington."

"Miss'ippi?" he said.

"No, sir. Washington, D.C."

"Well, you are one very tall attorney,

Mr. Corbett. I would bet those Pullman berths play havoc with the sleep of a man your size."

I smiled. "I've spent my whole life in beds that are too short and bumping into ceilings that are too low."

He laughed and put away the book he'd been reading.

"Are you a journalist, too?" Henley McNeill asked.

"No."

"Well, I only ask on account of I saw you reading all those newspapers."

I decided to see where the truth might take me. "I was doing a little research . . . on the history of lynching."

He blinked, but otherwise betrayed no reaction. "Lynching," he said. "In that case, newspapers might not be your best source of information."

"How do you figure?"

"Well, sir, in my view, the newspapers don't always tell the truth.

"Let me give you a point of observation," McNeill continued. "Now, this is just the opinion of one man. But I'm a man who's spent his whole life right here in Mississippi. And my daddy fought for the Confederacy alongside Braxton Bragg at Stones River."

Henley McNeill seemed like a sensible fellow. This was the very type of man Roosevelt had in mind when he sent me down here to speak with the locals.

"The white man doesn't hate the colored man," he said. "The white man is just *afraid* of the colored man."

"Afraid?"

"Not afraid in the way you think. He's not afraid the colored man's going to rape his wife or his daughter. Although, let's be honest, if you turned a colored man loose on white women with no laws against it, there's no telling what might happen."

He leaned forward in his seat, speaking intensely. "What genuinely scares the white man is that the colored is going to suck up all the jobs from the whites. You just got out of Memphis, you saw how it is. It's the same in all the big cities—Nashville, New Orleans, Atlanta. You got thousands and thousands of Negroes running around looking for jobs. And every one of 'em willing to work cheaper than the white man, be they a field hand, a factory hand, or what have you."

I told McNeill that I understood what he was saying. In fact, it was not the first time I'd heard that theory.

"Yes, sir," he went on. "The black man has got to figure out a way to get along peaceable with the white man, without taking his job away from him."

He paused a moment, then leaned in to tap the side of my valise with an insistent finger. A smile spread over his face.

"And if the black man don't come to understand this," he said, "why, I reckon we'll just have to wipe him out."

Chapter 21

Home again.

Home to the town where I learned to read, write, and do my multiplication tables. Home to the town where my mama fell ill, stayed ill for many years, and died, and where my father was long known as "the only honest judge in Pike County."

My town, a little over three thousand souls, where I once set the Mississippi state record for the hundred-yard dash, shortly before I broke my leg in a fall from a barn roof. Where Thomas McGoey, the mail carrier, rang our doorbell and personally presented me with the letter announcing I'd been accepted at Harvard.

The last time I'd been home to Eudora was for my mother's funeral, six years ago. I remember being startled at the time by how much the town had changed. Most astonishing to me then were the two gas-powered motorcars parked beside the hitching posts.

Many other things had changed since that last mournful journey to my birthplace. But on this day, while I waited for Eudora Station's one ancient porter to summon the energy to unload my trunk, I found myself amazed to see how much this lazy little town resembled the one I knew when I was a boy.

The early-summer heat remained as overwhelming as I remembered, the whitish sun seeming to press down on everything under its gaze. The First Bank, Sanders' General Store, the Purina feed and seed, the Slide Inn Café—everything was just the same.

Eudora Town Hall still featured an oversized Confederate stars-and-bars hanging in the second-floor window above the portico. The same faded red-and-white-striped barber's pole stood outside the shop with the sign that said

"Hair Cuts, Shaves, & Tooth Extractions"—although no one had gone to Ezra Newcomb for a bad tooth since the first real dentist moved to town when I was eleven.

One difference I noticed immediately was that many of the doorways—at the depot, at the little vaudeville theater, at the Slide Inn—now bore signs marking certain entrances as "White" or "Colored." When I was a boy, everyone knew which places were for whites and which for Negroes.

At last the porter approached with my trunk and valises, accompanied by a gangly colored teenager. The porter asked, "Will we be taking these to your father's house, Mr. Corbett?"

I frowned. "How'd you know my name?"

"Well, suh, the stationmaster tol' me to hurry up and go help Judge Corbett's boy with his trunk, so I purt' much figured it out from there."

I gave the old man a dime and offered another dime to the boy if he would carry my luggage on to my destination. He threw that heavy trunk up on his shoulders as if it contained nothing but air and picked up my pair of valises with one large hand.

"I'll be staying at Maybelle Wilson's," I said. "I'm here on business."

We crossed to the First Bank and turned left onto Commerce Street. It was right then that I had the feeling that I had entered into one of Mr. H. G. Wells's fabled time-transport machines. "My God," I said under my breath. *"How can this be?"*

Chapter 22

There before me was my first sweetheart, Elizabeth Begley, instantly recognizable with her blond curls, her delicate face, a sweet young girl in a pretty pink-checked sundress.

I realized with a start this was neither a dream nor a memory. This really was Elizabeth Begley. *And she truly was eleven years old!*

Then I saw the very real and very grown-up Elizabeth Begley step out of Ida Simmons's notions shop and call out to the little girl standing before me.

"Emma? You wait right there for me."

I called out Elizabeth's name. She turned, and her face lit up instantly.

"Why, good Lord! Ben Corbett! The

heat must have gone to my eyes. This cannot be you!"

"It's Ben, all right. Your eyesight is just fine."

As was everything else about her. Elizabeth looked as beautiful as when I used to sneak glances at her all through our school years together. If anything, she'd gotten even prettier as a woman.

"Well, Ben, what brings you back to our little nothing of a town?" she asked.

I told myself to close my mouth, which had fallen open in astonishment, partly at the chance meeting, but also at the sight of this lovely woman.

"Oh, just some work for the government. Interviewing candidates for the federal bench, potential judges. And I suppose I needed a breath of good old Mississippi fresh air."

"Honey, everybody in town is just gonna be beside themselves with excitement to see you," Elizabeth said and beamed. "The famous Ben Corbett, the one we all thought had gone off forever to be a Yankee lawyer, has finally come for a visit! I know your father must be thrilled."

"I hope he will be," I said. "It's a surprise. The job I'm on came up suddenly."

I doubted that many people in town—especially my father—would be all that happy to see me. But that wasn't the kind of information to share with Elizabeth. Instead I remarked that Emma was as pretty as Elizabeth had been as a girl, which happened to be true, and made both of them smile.

"I see you've still got honey on your tongue, Ben," she said, with a hint of a blush. And then a wink, to show her sense of humor was intact.

"I'm just speaking the truth," I said, smiling. It really was good to see her.

"Ben, I would love to stand here and visit with you and get more compliments, but Emma is going to be late for her dance class," she said. "I do want to talk to you. Where is Mrs. Corbett? Did you abandon her at the station?"

"She stayed home," I said. "The children are involved in their lessons."

"I see," Elizabeth said, with an inflection that suggested she didn't quite comprehend that version of events. "It's been too long, Ben," she went on. "I hope we'll see each other again?"

"Of course we will. Eudora is a small town."

"And that's why we love it."

She took her daughter's hand and headed off toward the shade of the oak trees surrounding the town square. I turned around and stood watching Elizabeth and Emma as they walked away.

Chapter 23

Here's something I truly believe: a man should be able to walk through the front door of his childhood home without knocking. I was thinking this as I clutched the ring of the brass knocker on my father's front door. I may have spent the first eighteen years of my life here, but it was never *my* house. It was always *his* house. And he never let me forget it.

It was six years ago, at my mother's funeral, that I had last laid eyes on my father.

It hadn't gone well. I had just buried the most understanding parent a man could possibly have. When the service was over, I was left with a stern, distant, conservative father who had no use for a lawyer son who leaned the other way. After the funeral luncheon, after all the deviled eggs and potato salad and baked ham had been consumed, after the Baccarat punchbowl had been washed, dried, and put away, my father had an extra glass of whiskey and began to pontificate on the subject of my "Washington shenanigans."

"And if you don't mind, what might those terrible shenanigans be?" I asked. "How have I disappointed you?"

"Believe it or not, son, y'all don't have a lock on every form of human knowledge in that Yankee town you now call home," he said. "The news does travel down to Mississippi eventually. And everybody I know says you're the most *progressive* young lawyer in Washington." I had never heard that word pronounced with a more audible sneer.

I didn't answer. All the way down on the train, I had vowed to myself not to react to his temperamental outbursts.

"Your mother enjoyed that about you," he went on. "Your Yankee free-thinking ways. But she's gone now, God rest her soul. And I can tell you this, Benjamin.

You're a fool! You're up to your knees in the sand, and the tide's approaching. You can keep trying to shovel as hard as you can, but that will not stop the tide from coming in."

"Thank you for the colorful metaphor," I said. Then I went upstairs, packed my valise, and went back to Washington.

After that I heard from him only once a year, around Christmas, when a plain white envelope would arrive containing a twenty-dollar bill and the same handwritten note every year:

"Happy Christmas to yourself, Meg, and my granddaughters. Cordially, Judge E. Corbett."

Cordially.

Chapter 24

Now here I was, standing at his door again. And as much as it galled me to knock on that door, I could not come home to Eudora without seeing my father. I was sure he already knew that I was back.

Dabney answered the door. He had been my father's houseman since before I was born.

"Good Lord! Mister Ben! Shoot, I never expected to open this door and find you on the other side of it. The judge is gonna be absolutely de-*light*-ed to see you."

"Dabney, it's good to know you're still the smoothest liar in Pike County."

He smiled brightly and gave me a wink. Then I followed him to the dining room, breathing in the old familiar smell of floor wax and accumulated loneliness.

My father sat alone at the long mahogany table, eating a bowl of soup from a fine china bowl. He glanced up, but his face did not change when he saw me—eyes icy blue, his lips thin and unsmiling.

"Why, Benjamin. How nice of you to grace us with your presence. Did somebody die?"

My father's gift for sarcasm had not diminished. Immediately I found myself wishing I hadn't come running over to his house my first day in town.

"How are you feeling?" I asked.

"Sound body, sound mind. As far as I can tell. Why? Have you heard otherwise?"

"Not at all. I'm glad to hear you're well."

"What wonderful Yankee manners. I trust you are healthy yourself?"

I nodded. The silence between us was almost painful.

"So, Ben, you still busy up there freeing the slaves?"

"I believe it was President Lincoln who did that."

"Ah, that's right," he said, a wisp of a smile coming to his face. "Sometimes I forget my history. Care for some turtle soup?"

Soup? On a ninety-degree night in Mississippi?

"No, thank you."

"No turtle soup? Yet another in a succession of foolish choices on your part, Benjamin."

My father did not ask me to take a seat at his table.

He did not ask what brought me to Eudora after six years, and I wondered if it was possible that he knew.

He did not inquire after Meg, or ask why my wife had permitted me to travel all this way by myself. He did not ask about Alice or Amelia.

I thought of Mama, how much she would have loved having two little granddaughters in this house. It was always too quiet in here. I remembered one of her favorite expressions: "The silence in here is so loud, I can hear my own heart rattling around in my ribs."

Judge Corbett looked me up and down. "Where is your baggage?" he asked.

"I'm not staying here," I said. "I've taken a room down at Maybelle Wilson's. Actually, I'm here on business for the government. I have to check out some candidates for the federal courts."

I could have sworn this news made him wince, but he recovered quickly enough.

"Fine," he said. "Be about your business. Maybelle's should suit you perfectly. Is there something else?"

I saw no reason to prolong this agony. "Oh, no. Nothing. It was pleasant to see you again."

He waved for Dabney to ladle more soup into his bowl. He dabbed at his lips with a starched linen napkin. Then he deigned to speak.

"We should arrange another visit sometime," my father said. "Perhaps in another six years."

Chapter 25

"You need something for your belly, Mr. Corbett?" Maybelle called in a loud voice from the front parlor of her rooming house.

I had found the Slide Inn Café all closed up for the night, but still I declined Maybelle's invitation. "No, thank you, ma'am. I'm all taken care of."

"Just as well. Ain't nothin' in there but some old pone."

Maybelle's had never been known for luxury. In fact, the only thing the place was ever known for was a string of slightly disreputable boarders through the years. Now, I supposed, I was one of them.

The original Maybelle had died years ago, about the time the house was last given a fresh coat of paint. But Eudora tradition dictated that any woman who ran the place was referred to as "Maybelle."

Occasionally a shoe salesman or cotton broker spent a night or two at Maybelle's. Once or twice a year my father commandeered the place to sequester jurors during a trial. And there were, inevitably, rumors about women of uncertain morality using the rooms for "business."

A monk would have felt at home in my room: a narrow iron bed, a small oaken desk with a perilous wobble, and an equally wobbly cane-backed chair. On the bureau were an enameled-steel bowl and pitcher. And under the bed, a chamber pot for those times you didn't want to make the trip to the outhouse.

In the corner of the room was one small window, which somehow managed to admit all the hot air from outside during the day and to hold it inside all night.

I stripped down to my Roxford skivvies and positioned the chair directly in front of that window. I suspected there was no breeze to be had in town that night. Luckily, my room was provided with the latest advance in cooling technology:

a squared-off cardboard fan with the inscription “Hargitay’s Mortuary Parlor, The Light of Memphis.”

A lonely man sitting with his bare feet propped up on a windowsill, waving a funeral fan at his face.

Welcome home, Ben.

Chapter 26

It was too damn hot for sleeping. I figured I might as well do some detective work in my room.

I had put aside two newspapers from the collection of "lynching reviews" I'd brought from Memphis. Now was as good a time as any for reading.

These particular articles were of special interest. From the pages of the *Jackson Courier,* they told the stories of lynchings that had taken place right here in Eudora, and within the past three years.

I unfolded the first paper:

> Word of an horrific death by strangulation reached our office this morning. By the time this reporter

visited the alleged scene, no trace of said hanging was evident, save for a bloodied rope tossed aside in a pile of swamp grass.

The unanswered questions were obvious. Who told "this reporter" that the death was "horrific"? Why was he so careful to use the word "alleged"?

I picked up the other newspaper.

We learned of the death by lynching of Norbert Washington today. A witness at the lynching site in that area of Eudora called "the Quarters" said that Washington, a tobacco tanner at a plantation in nearby Chatawa, had been heard making rude and suggestive comments to a white lady in the Chatawa Free Library.

Upon investigation it was discovered that the town of Chatawa did not have a library, free or otherwise. That information notwithstanding, the eyewitness stated, "The hanging was most exciting, gruesome and, I must add, satisfying in its vengefulness for the niggerman's impertinence."

I was glad that I kept reading, even though I wanted to look away. The final sentences were, for me, the most startling:

> When interviewed, Chief of Police Phineas Eversman said that he was unaware of any lynching that previous evening in Eudora. A visitor in Chief Eversman's office, the respected Eudora Justice Everett Corbett, agreed. "I too know nothing about a lynching in Eudora," Judge Corbett said.

I let the newspapers fall to the floor. No wonder Roosevelt needed someone to sort out this tangle of contradictions, half-truths, and outright lies.

Loneliness also gives a man time for thinking. It broke my heart to be so far away from my family—and to have left on this trip without a single kind word between Meg and me. From my valise I drew a small pewter picture frame, hinged in the middle. I opened the frame and stared at the joined photographs.

On the left was Meg, her smile so warm, so bright and unforced, that I found myself smiling back at her.

On the right were Alice and Amelia, posed on the sofa in our parlor. Both of them wore stiff expressions, but I knew the girls were seconds away from exploding into laughter.

I studied the images for a few minutes, thinking only good thoughts. I wished there were some way I could blink my eyes and bring the pictures to life so that all three of them could be here with me.

Chapter 27

Early the next morning, I discovered that the current Maybelle, a pleasant and blustery woman, was not much of a cook. I sat at the dining room table, poking at breakfast: a biscuit as tough as old harness leather, grits that were more lumps than grits, and a piece of salt pork that was 100 percent gristle.

"Miss Maybelle, who belongs to that bicycle I saw leaning against the shed out back?" I finally asked. "I need to see a few people around town."

"I keep that for the boy runs errands for me after school," she said. "You welcome to borry it, if you like."

Five minutes later I was rolling up my pant legs to protect them from bicycle chain grease. Two minutes after that I was sailing down Commerce Street. I felt like a nine-year-old boy again, keeping my balance with my knees while extending my arms sideways in a respectable display of balancing skills.

I was nine again, but everything I saw was filtered through the eyes of a thirty-year-old man.

I rode the bicycle two circuits around the tiny park in front of the Methodist church, took a left at the minister's house and another left at the scuppernong arbor. At the end of the vine-covered trellis stood a simple white wooden structure that was unsupervised by anyone's eyes and universally known among the young people of Eudora as the Catch-a-Kiss Gazebo.

It was here that I came with Elizabeth the summer I was fifteen. It was here, on that same wooden bench, that I leaned in to kiss Elizabeth and was startled down to my toes by an open-mouthed kiss in return, full of passion and tongue and spit. At the same moment I felt her hand running smoothly up the side of my thigh. I felt the pressure of her nails. My own hand moved from her waist to her small, rounded bosom.

Then Elizabeth pulled away and shook her head, spilling blond curls onto her shoulders. "Oh, *Ben,* I want to kiss you and kiss you. And more. I want to do everything, Ben. But I can't. You know we can't."

I had never heard a girl talk like that. Most boys my age were hopeless when it came to discussing such matters—at least, in Eudora they were.

There were tears in Elizabeth's eyes. "It's all right," I said, but then I grinned. "But we could kiss some more. No harm in that." So Elizabeth and I kissed, and sometimes we touched each other, but it never went any farther than that, and eventually I went away to Harvard, where I met Meg.

Now I rode that bicycle fast down the lane, leaning into the curve, rounding the corner at the preacher's house, faster and faster, remembering Elizabeth Begley and the first taste of sex that had ever happened to me anywhere but in my own head.

Chapter 28

I pedaled that bicycle all the way from my growing-up years to the present day. And I began to see people I knew, shopkeepers, old neighbors, and I waved and called out "Hi." A couple of times I stopped and talked with somebody from my school days, and that was fine.

I rode over to Commerce Street, past the Slide Inn Café, past the icehouse where a bucket came flying out of the darkness just in time to trip up poor George Pearson and send him to his death by hanging.

The exhilaration of my first ride through town was fading under the glare of a morning sun that was beating down hard. I was out of training for Mississippi summers. My thirst was demanding attention, and I remembered a pump at the end of the cotton-loading dock at the gin, just down from the depot.

I pedaled down Myrtle Street to the end of the platform that ran from the cotton gin beside the tracks of the Jackson & Northern line. I leaned my machine against the retaining wall and turned to the pump.

As I worked the handle and reveled in the water—half drinking, half splashing my face—I heard a loud voice behind me, an *angry* voice.

"What the hell makes you nigger boys think you can come high-walkin' into our town looking for a job? All our jobs belong to white men."

At the other end of the platform were two large and burly men I recognized as the Purneau brothers, Jocko and Leander, an unpleasant pair of backwoods louts who had been running the cotton gin for Old Man Furnish as long as I could remember. The two of them towered over three scrawny black boys who looked to be fifteen years old, maybe even younger.

"Well, suh, we just thinking with the crop coming you might be needin' some mo' help round the gin," said one of the boys.

"That's the trouble with you niggers, is when you set in to tryin' to think," said Leander Purneau. He spoke in a friendly, jokey voice, which put me, and the boy, off guard. But then he popped him a solid punch on the side of his face and sent the boy down onto his knees.

The other boys skittered away like bugs from a kicked-over log. Suddenly I really was back in the past, and the boy on the ground was in serious trouble, like poor George Pearson had been.

There was one difference now—I was not a timid little boy. I was a grown man. As I wiped my wet hands on my shirt, I considered what I was about to do.

If I caused a commotion, made a scene, called attention to myself, I might endanger my mission even before it started.

But if I did nothing?

Fortunately, the boy on the ground rolled over and jumped up. He sprinted off down the platform, holding his jaw, but at least he was getting away.

And at that very moment, I felt something cold and hard jammed against the side of my neck.

It felt an awful lot like the barrel of a gun.

A deep voice behind me: "Just put your hands in the air. Nice and slow, *high,* that's the way to do it."

Chapter 29

"Now, I want you to turn around real slow, partner. Don't make any fast moves."

I did exactly as I was told. *Real slow.*

And found myself looking straight into the face of Jacob Gill. Jacob and I had been inseparable from as far back as I could remember, until the day I left Eudora for college.

"You son of a bitch!" I shouted at him.

Jacob was laughing so hard he actually held his stomach and doubled over. His laughter made him do a little jig of delight.

"You nearly gave me a goddamn heart attack," I said. "You're a jackass."

"I know," Jacob said, howling some more.

Then we hugged, seizing each other by the shoulders, stepping back to get a good look.

"How'd you even know it was me?" I asked.

"We don't have too many yellow-haired fellows ten feet tall hanging around," said Jacob. Then he added, "I saw you decide not to mix it up with Jocko and Leander. That was smart thinking on your part."

"I guess so," I said. I remembered the time Jacob left me in the swamp to watch what happened to George Pearson. I wished I could tell him why I'd held back this time.

"Hey, it's near dinnertime," Jacob said and lightly punched my shoulder. "Let's go get some catfish."

"That sounds good. Where we going?"

"Don't tell me you've turned into such a big-city boy you forgot Friday is catfish day at the Slide Inn?"

Chapter 30

I pushed the bicycle between us down Myrtle Street, toward the town square. Jacob stopped twice along the way to take a nip of whiskey from a pint he kept in his worn leather toolbox, and I said hello to a couple more people I recognized, or who remembered me.

The Slide Inn was alive with the hum of conversation, the smell of frying fish, the smoke from the cigars of the old fellows who always occupied the front table, solving the world's problems on a daily basis.

"Why aren't you staying at your daddy's?" Jacob asked as soon as we sat down at a corner table.

"You know my father," I said. "It seemed

like Maybelle's was the smart place to be. My father and I just don't get along."

"All right, then. But there is one question I been dying to ask: *What in hell are you doing back in Eudora?*"

"Nothing much," I said. "I've got a little business to tend to."

"Lawyer business?"

"Just a simple job for the Justice Department. I have to interview a few lawyers in the county, that's all it is. In the meantime—it's catfish!" I said.

Pretty soon Miss Fanny came from behind the counter bearing plates of crispy fried fish, sizzling-hot hush puppies, and ice-cold sweet-pickle coleslaw. The first bite was delicious, and every bite after. I asked Miss Fanny what time the place opened for breakfast, and made up my mind never to suffer through another of Maybelle's breakfasts.

"Hell, I look old, but you still look like a high-school boy, Ben," said Jacob. "Like you could run ten miles and never even break a sweat."

"Oh, I did plenty of sweating just riding that bike a dozen blocks," I said. "It'll take me a while to get used to this heat again. How you been keeping yourself, Jacob?"

"Well, let me see . . . you probably heard I turned down the offer to be ambassador to England . . . and that was right after I passed on the chance to be president of the university up in Tuscaloosa. Well, sir, it was shortly after that I made up my mind that the profession I was most suited for was as a carpenter's assistant."

"That's good," I said. "Honest work."

"Yeah, me and Wylie Davis are the men you want to see if you need a new frame for your window screens, you know, or a new roof for your johnny house."

Then there was silence, a good and acceptable kind of silence—nothing nervous or uncomfortable about it. The kind of quiet that is tolerable only between old friends.

It was Jacob who finally broke it.

"They were good days, Ben. Weren't they?"

"They were *great* days."

"We were friends! Right through it all."

"The best," I said. "We were like brothers."

We clinked our iced-tea glasses. Then Jacob spoke.

"But there is one thing I need to make very clear to you, Ben."

"What's that?" I tried to keep the note of concern out of my voice.

"You said we were like brothers?"

"Yeah? That's what I said."

"I just need to remind you of something."

"Well, go ahead, Jacob," I said.

"I was *always* the pretty one."

Chapter 31

Enough!

Enough idle thoughts about my long-ago romance with Elizabeth Begley.

Enough turning over in my mind the painful lack of affection between my father and me, the disgust in his face when he saw me for the first time in six years.

Enough reliving an old friendship like Jacob's and mine.

Theodore Roosevelt hadn't sent me to Eudora to take a rickety bicycle ride down memory lane. I had a job to do, and it might even help change history.

I paid the bill for our lunch, and Jacob left two bits for Miss Fanny. Then he headed off up Commerce Street to help

Wylie frame a new roof for the front porch of the town hall.

An old black man stepped off the sidewalk as Jacob passed, not to avoid a collision, but simply making the customary show of respect. Black men of all ages had been stepping down off sidewalks to get out of my way since I was five years old.

I rode the bicycle back to Maybelle's, changed my shirt, and set off on foot for the Eudora Quarters. On my way out, I made sure to tell Maybelle I had some interviews to attend to.

I considered trying to hire a horse and buggy, and couldn't think of anywhere in town to do such a thing. My father had three perfectly good horses in his barn, of course, but I was determined to do what I came to do without him.

ABRAHAM CROSS, EUDORA QUARTERS said the slip of paper the president had given me.

It was time for me to meet this Mr. Cross.

Chapter 32

I knew the streets of the Quarters almost as well as I knew the rest of Eudora. I knew the history of how it came to be. After the war, the slaves from all the plantations and farms in the vicinity of Eudora had been freed. Most of them had either left their previous lodgings or been turned out by masters who no longer wanted to provide housing for people they didn't own.

So the freed slaves built their homes where no one else wanted to live, in a swampy, muddy, mosquito-ridden low place half a mile north of the center of Eudora.

They gathered fallen logs from the woods and lumber from derelict barns to build their little houses. They laid boards across the swampy, pestilential ground to keep their children's feet out of the mud. They stuffed rags and old newspapers in the chinks in the walls to keep out the wind in winter.

They ate squirrel and possum, poke sallet and dandelion greens. They ate weeds from the field, horse corn, the leftover parts of a pig, and whatever else they could get their hands on.

Walking along there now, as the neighborhood changed from poor white to poorer black, I saw a colored man sitting on the porch of a shack painted a gay shade of blue. He nodded at me.

I returned his nod. "Pardon me, do you know a man by the name of Cross? Abraham Cross?"

He never blinked. His eyes didn't move from mine, but I had the feeling he was deciding whether or not I was worthy of the information I sought.

"Yes, suh," he finally said. "If you just keep walkin', you will come on a house with a strong smell of onions. That will be Abraham's house."

The sight of a white man walking on

this street was not a welcome one for most of the people I came across. They kept their eyes down as they passed, which seemed to be customary now in Eudora but had not been the case when I was a boy.

Within minutes I caught the sharp tang of onions on the air. I saw thick patches of the familiar blue-green stalks in the yard of a small red house.

Suddenly, from the space between two houses, one little boy came running, followed by two more, and two more in pursuit.

"He gonna snatch you and eat you," the lead boy shouted.

Then I saw what was chasing them—a wild pig, huge and hairy and grunting, bearing down on the boys with a pair of very bad-looking tusks.

"That ain't the most beautiful animal in the world," said a colored man standing on the porch of the red house.

I answered, "That is a face not even a mother could love."

I looked closer. The man was taller than me, by at least three inches, and older, by at least fifty years.

"But she sure is beautiful when she's angry," he said.

We both laughed.

Then he said, "Begging your pardon, sir, but I get the idea you might be looking for someone."

"Well, as a matter of fact, I *am* looking for a man. His name is Abraham Cross."

"Yes, sir. You lookin' at him."

I must have appeared surprised.

"You was expectin' some young fella, weren't you, Mr. Corbett?"

"No, I—I really had no idea who to expect..."

"Well, sir, I confess I was expectin' a young fella myself. So I guess at least one of us was right."

Chapter 33

Maybe it was because he looked like a picture of silver-haired wisdom. I just don't know. But the truth is, I liked Abraham Cross from the moment I met him.

When he shook my hand, he grasped my shoulder with his other hand, so that I felt well and truly gripped.

"From this moment, Mr. Corbett—"

"Call me Ben," I said.

"From this moment, Mr. Corbett," he said pointedly, "I am happy to be of service to you as a guide and advisor. With luck, we may also become friends."

I told him that I felt luck would be on our side.

He offered me a seat on his porch, which had a view of everyone passing along the boards from one end of the Quarters to the other. Abraham greeted everyone—man, woman, child—with a friendly wave and a personal word of greeting. I think if that hairy old boar had come back, Abraham would have waved and said howdy.

Abraham Cross had the way of a man at ease with himself. He wore dark woolen trousers, a neatly ironed white shirt, and a navy blue bowtie. I don't know if he'd dressed up because he was expecting me or if he dressed this way every day.

On his head was a faded blue baseball cap with the initial *P* faded to near invisibility. I asked him what the *P* stood for.

"Pythians," he said. "Does that mean anything to you?"

"Weren't they athletes in ancient Delphi?" I said.

"Well, sir, I may be old but I ain't as old as the Greeks in old Delphi," he said, laughing.

Then he explained.

His greatest love in his young life, he told me, was baseball. After the War between the States he headed north, where a few Negro teams played.

"Notice I said they 'played.' I didn't say they 'flourished.' Anyways, I made the team in Philadelphia. We was porters and butlers, iron men, lawn mower men during the week. On the weekends we played baseball."

At Abraham's nod, I followed him off his porch and toward the little "downtown" of the Quarters.

We were passing the colored general store, Hemple's, where you could see the canned goods inside through gaps between the boards. By the front door stood a neat pyramid of beautiful peaches.

Abraham reached into his pocket for a couple of pennies, which he took inside to the old man at the cash box. He came back out and selected a nice fat peach from the side of the stack.

"Were you any good?" I asked the old man.

He smiled. He looked past me to a broom standing just inside the door. He asked me to hand it to him.

"You want to know if I was any good?"

He held the broom short, like a baseball bat. Then he tossed that beautiful peach into the air.

He swung.

He connected. Tasting a fine spatter of peach juice on my face, I watched it sail up and up, into the hot afternoon sky.

"Don't bother to go lookin' for that peach," he said.

"I believe it is gone," I agreed.

"In a minute or two it's gonna be in Loo-siana," he said with a grin. "They always said tall, skinny boys like you and me can't play baseball. They say we too far from the ground. I'll tell you something, I proved they don't know everything."

He wiped the broom handle on his shirt and put the broom back inside.

We walked a few minutes in silence. Then Abraham stopped, his face suddenly serious.

"I could talk baseball and swing at soft peaches all day," he said. "But you and I have some other business."

"Yes, we do," I said.

"This is serious business, Mr. Corbett. Sad business. My people are worse off now than they were the day Mr. Lincoln signed the Emancipation."

Chapter 34

"We don't have to go far to find a lynching tree," Abraham said. "But I know how tired you young fellas get from walking in the heat of the day. I reckon we'd best take the hosses."

The two "hosses" Abraham led out from a rickety blacksmith shop were mules—in fact, they were mules that had hauled one too many plows down one too many cotton rows. But those skinny animals proved their worth by depositing us, less than twenty minutes later, at a secluded swampy area that was unmistakably the site of a lynching.

Unmistakably.

A cool grotto tucked back in the woods away from the road. Big branches interlaced overhead to form a ceiling. The dirt was packed hard as a stone floor from the feet of all the people who had stood there watching the terrible spectacle.

Abraham pointed to an oak at the center of the clearing. "And there's your main attraction."

Even without his guidance, I would have recognized it as a lynching tree. There was a thick, strong branch barely a dozen feet from the ground. The low dip in the middle of the branch was rubbed free of its bark by the friction of ropes.

I walked under the tree. The hard ground was stained with dark blotches. My stomach churned at the thought of what had happened in this unholy place.

"Somebody left us a greeting," Abraham said. "That would be the Klan."

He was pointing behind me, to the trunk of a sycamore tree. About five feet up, someone had used an odd-looking white nail to attach a plank with crude lettering on it:

BEWARE ALL COONS!
BEWARE ALL COON LOVERS!

"I've never seen a nail that color," I said.

"You never seen a nail made out of human bone?" said Abraham.

I shuddered, reaching up to haul the plank down.

"Don't waste your strength, Mr. Corbett," he said. "You pull that one down today, there'll be a new sign up there next week."

His face changed. "We got *company,*" he said.

Chapter 35

The double-barreled shotgun pointed our way was almost as big as the girl holding it. It was so long and heavy I was more afraid she would drop it and discharge it accidentally than that she might shoot us on purpose.

Abraham said, “What you fixin’ to do with that gun? That ain’t no possum you aimin’ at.”

I was distracted by the fact that she was very serious *and* very pretty. She wore a simple cotton jumper, stark white against the smooth brown of her skin. A perfect face, with delicate features that betrayed the fierceness of her attitude. Deep brown eyes flashed a steady warning: *keep away from me*.

"What y'all doing messin' around the lynching tree?" she said.

"You know this girl, Abraham?"

"I surely do. This is Moody. Say hello to Mr. Corbett."

Moody didn't say a word to me. She kept her barrel trained on my heart. If she was going to stare at me this way, I couldn't help looking back at her.

"Well, if you know her," I said, "maybe you should tell her not to go around pointing firearms at people."

"Moody, you heard the man," said Abraham. "Put it down. Now, granddaughter."

"Oh, Papaw," she said, "what you bring this white man out here for?"

Abraham reached out and pushed the gun barrel away. Moody pulled back from him as if he were trying to take away her doll.

"She's your granddaughter?"

"That's right."

It struck me that the girl had seemed as willing to shoot her grandfather as to shoot me. She walked boldly up to me, around me, looking me over as if I represented some species of animal she had never observed before and already didn't like.

"Mr. Corbett is here from Washington," said Abraham.

"You working for him?" said Moody. "Why would you?"

"We working together," said Abraham.

"Well, if you ain't working for him, how come he calls you Abraham, and you call him Mr. Corbett?"

"Because he prefers it that way." Abraham knew that wasn't so, but he fixed me in place with a look that stifled the protest in my throat. "Mr. Corbett is here by the instructions of the president of the—"

"*Abraham,*" I said. "We're not supposed to talk about any of this."

He nodded, dipped his head. "You are right, Mr. Corbett," he said.

Moody gave me a disgusted look and said, "You should have let me shoot him while I had the chance."

Chapter 36

When I was growing up, gumbo was not something most white people would eat, unless they were Catholic and lived down on the coast. Gumbo was food for black people, or Creole people. Like chitlins and hog ears, it was the kind of thing mostly eaten out of necessity. Or so most people thought. My mother's cook, Aurelia, used to whip up a big pot of sausage-and-crawfish gumbo and leave it to feed us through Friday, her day off.

So when Abraham suggested we stop in at a little gray shanty of a saloon with a crooked sign on the door, GUMBO JOE'S, I was a happy man. Also along for the meal was Moody and her brother Hiram, a handsome boy of nineteen with aspirations to be a lawyer.

I was surprised at the idea of a Negro restaurant in Eudora, but when I stepped inside the place, I saw it was 95 percent saloon, with a little cooker perched beside the open window in back. On the flame sat a bubbling pot.

An old black man came out from behind the rickety bar. I couldn't help flinching at the sight of him: he had no chin, and his right arm was severed just below the elbow.

Without our asking, he brought three small glasses and a bottle of beer. "Y'all want gumbo?"

"We do," said Abraham.

So much for a menu.

Abraham poured beer into all three glasses, and I took one. It wasn't cold, but it tasted real good.

"What happened to that man?" I said softly.

"The war," said Abraham. He explained that the old man had been a cook for Pemberton's army at Vicksburg. The Yankee mortar shell that crashed through the mess tent was no respecter of color or rank.

"He lost half his face fighting for the side that was trying to keep him a slave," I said.

"Wasn't fighting, he was cooking," said Abraham. "A lot of us did. The pay was good. Better than we got staying home. Those was good times, if you didn't get killed."

The War between the States had been officially over for forty-three years but had never actually ended in the South. The Confederate battle flag still flew higher than Old Glory, at least at our courthouse. There were Rebel flags hanging on the fronts of stores and from the flagpoles of churches. Ever since I was a boy I had recognized the old faded butternut cap as the sign of a Confederate veteran.

There had always been men with wooden legs or wooden crutches. I knew that an empty sleeve pinned up inside a suit jacket meant an arm had been left on a battlefield in Georgia or Tennessee. Maybelle's handyman, otherwise a handsome old gent, had a left eye sewn shut with orange twine. The skin around that eye burned to a god-awful dry red that would have scared me if I'd been a child.

"That old man behind the bar?" said Abraham. "Before the war, he was trying to become a professional fiddler."

I shook my head. "And now he has no chin to lean his fiddle on," I said.

Abraham's face broke open in a big smile. So did Moody's and her brother's. "Aw now, Mr. Corbett, I was fooling on you. Old Jeffrey wasn't no fiddler. He was slingin' beer back before the war, and he been slingin' beer ever since."

Moody saw the look on my face and busted out with a guffaw. "Papaw, *Mr.* Corbett ain't too swift, is he?"

Chapter 37

The chinless old man returned, bearing in his good hand a tray with three steaming bowls of dark gumbo.

"Look like we maybe gonna have some music too," Hiram said, and his face lit up in a smile.

Two or three men had drifted in, still shiny-sweaty from the field. They ordered beers and shot nervous looks in our direction. The more I thought about it, the more I realized how out of place I was in here. It was the Negroes' place; who was I to come in and sit down as if I belonged?

At least they had the courtesy to let me sit there, which would certainly not be the case if one of them tried to order a beer in a white barroom.

I was delighted to see a grizzled middle-aged fellow taking out a banjo, tuning it up while his buddy drummed his hands on an overturned gutbucket. The thin, listless woman between them waited for the banjo player to plink a little chord, and then without any introduction or ritual, she set in to wailing.

Lawd, I been blue
Since my man done left this town…

The little hairs on my neck prickled.

"You heard the blues before, Mr. Corbett?" asked Hiram.

"I have—one time," I said. "On Beale Street in Memphis."

Sho done been blue
Since my man done left this town…

"You like the way she sings?" Moody said.

"I do," I said. "I like it a lot."

Moody shrugged, like she didn't much care which way I answered her question.

"I'm a devotee of ragtime music," I told her.

"You a what?" said Moody. "A deevo—what did you say?"

"Admirer," I said. "I'm an admirer of ragtime."

"No, that word you used—what was it again?"

Moody had a bold way of speaking. I must admit I wasn't accustomed to being addressed by a colored girl without the customary "yes, sir" and "no, sir."

"Devotee," I said. "One who is devoted to something. I think it's from the French."

"That's a pretty word," she said, "wherever it come from."

He beat me, then he leave me
And now he ain't been coming round.

When that lament ended, the banjo man put down his instrument and brought out a battered guitar.

Once again I was swept up in the mournful repetition, the slangy bent notes from the singer echoed by the guitar, the way it all fell together into a slow, rhythmic chant of pure feeling. This music was made from leftover parts of old field songs and hymns and slave music, but to me it sounded like something entirely new, and something quite wonderful.

Chapter 38

My belly was stuffed full of gumbo and rice. My tongue still burned from the red pepper. I remarked to Abraham on the staying power of the cayenne.

"Here, take a chaw on this," said Abraham. From his satchel he brought forth a length of brown sugarcane. I smiled. That's what our cook Aurelia used to prescribe for a sore throat or any other minor childhood complaint: a suck on a piece of sweet cane.

"You got enough for family?" said Moody.

"I got plenty, but it don't look right for a gal to chew cane," Abraham said.

She put on such a pout that Abraham

laughed and brought out a piece for her and another for Hiram.

"My granddaughter is incorrigible," said Abraham. "I hope you can forgive her."

"I don't need him forgiving me," she said.

Her grandfather's face darkened. "Moody? Watch your mouth."

She dropped her eyes. "Yes, sir."

"See now, Mr. Corbett, she got so comfortable settin' here next to you that she's done forgot how she s'posed to act. If you was any other kind of white man, she could be in big trouble right now, sassing you that way. Same thing goes for Hiram. *Even more so*." I had the feeling he said this more for Moody's and Hiram's benefit than for mine. Moody kept her eyes riveted fiercely on the floor beside our table.

"See, when you're colored, you always about this close—" he held up his fingers, indicating a tiny space—"to sayin' the wrong word. Or lookin' the wrong way. And that means you this far from gettin' beat up, or kicked, or punched, or cursed. Or gettin' strung up and killed by the KKK."

I took a long sip from my beer.

"Everything a colored man does can be a crime these days," he said.

"I don't quite understand," I said.

Moody's eyes came up. "Let me tell him, Papaw."

He hesitated, but then he said, "All right."

"They's a young fellow called Whitney," she said, gazing intently at me. "He spent a day hoeing out the flowerbeds around ol' Miz Howard's house, then when she was done he told her how much it was. She didn't want to pay. Said he hadn't worked that many hours. Then she calls up the sheriff and says Whitney done said something dirty to her. Well, she got him arrested, but that wasn't enough for 'em. They come drug him out of the jail and hung him up. Killed him. All because he asked for his pay." Her eyes blazed.

"That's the *truth,*" said Hiram.

"Sammy Dawkins brung his empty Co-Cola bottle back to Sanders' store to get his penny back. Ol' Mr. Sanders tells him niggers don't get the penny back, just white folks. Sammy argues with him and next thing you know he's in jail. *For wanting his penny!*"

"Keep your voice down," Abraham said.

"There was a couple boys sitting on the sidewalk downtown. They was talkin' to each other quiet like, telling about this strike of colored men up in Illinois. Well, sir, somebody overheard what they said, and next thing you know a bunch of men jump on these boys. One of 'em, they knocked out all his teeth."

"We get punished for 'boasting,' and for 'strutting,' and for talking too loud, and for casting the evil eye. We get arrested for 'walking too fast,' or 'walking too slow,' or taking too long to say *yassuh.*"

Moody was furious now. Her voice carried to tables nearby. Some of the people stopped their own conversations to listen.

"Colored man looks at a white woman, they kill him just for thinkin' the thoughts he ain't even thought," she said. "If he even looks at a white woman, it must mean he wants to rape her or kill her.

When they're the ones doing most of the raping and killing around here!"

"Now, calm down," Abraham said.

"Don't tell me to calm down! I know what it's like. It happens to me too, Papaw."

"I know, child."

"You don't know what happened yesterday. I was bringin' the basket of ironing back to Miz Cooper, you know she got that boy Dillard, he's not right in the head. Well, he out there pulling weeds in the kitchen garden. He looked at me. All I said was, "Howdy, Dillard," and he says somethin' real rude, like, 'Maybe you want to go with me, Moody' or somethin' like that. I just ignored him, Papaw. I just kept walking. But he come up behind me and grab me, like, you know, touching my titties."

"Hush," said Abraham sternly.

"It's what happened, Papaw," she said. "Then he says 'Aw come on, Moody, you a nigger girl, and ever'body knows that is all a nigger girl wants.'"

And with that, she couldn't keep the tears in. She folded her arms on the table and buried her head. Hiram stroked her neck.

I spoke softly: "We're going to do something, Moody. That's why I'm here with your grandfather."

There was silence. Then Moody looked up at me and she was angry.

"*Go home, Mr. Corbett*. That's what you could do. Just pack up your bag, and go home."

Chapter 39

"I guess you prayed for mail, Mr. Corbett," Maybelle said as I walked past the kitchen of the rooming house the next morning. "And the Lord answered."

She held out a plate with a pair of blackened biscuits and another plate with three envelopes. My heart lifted. But my happiness faded when I glanced through the letters and found that none of them had come from Washington.

I smiled down at the biscuits, thanked Maybelle, and put them aside for disposal later.

On my way over to the Slide Inn, I thumbed through the mail. First I opened a flyer inviting me to a "social and covered dish supper" at the Unitarian church in Walker's Bridge, one town west of Eudora. In the right-hand margin was a handwritten addition: *"Ben—Hope to see you at the supper. Elizabeth."*

The next envelope also held an invitation. This one was a good deal fancier than the first, engraved on heavy paper, wrapped in a piece of protective tissue.

Mr. and Mrs. L. J. Stringer
request the pleasure of your company
at supper
on Saturday, July fourteenth,
nineteen hundred and six
at eight o'clock in the evening

Number One Summit Square
Eudora, Mississippi
R.S.V.P.

What was this world coming to? A fancy-dress invite from L. J. Stringer, of all people!

It was hard to believe that the sweet, kindly boy with whom I'd spent a good portion of my childhood was now in such a lofty position that he could send out invitations engraved on thick vellum.

And that on his way to manhood, L.J. had invented a machine that shot twine around cotton bales in one-eighth the time it took four men to do the job.

The Stringer Automatic Baler. Without it, Cotton would no longer be King.

I eased into a rear table at the Slide Inn Café. I ordered coffee and a big breakfast of grits and eggs, patty sausage and biscuits. I thought about L. J. Stringer for a moment or two, but my heart was heavy at the absence of a single letter from home.

Why hadn't Meg written? I didn't really need to ask myself that. I knew the answer. But even if she was too angry—why hadn't she allowed the girls to write?

I decided to detour by the post office just to make sure no letters had been accidentally sent to Judge Everett Corbett's home.

Meantime I took a slurp of the Slide Inn's good chicory coffee and tore open the last of my three letters, the one without a return address.

At first I thought the envelope was

empty. I had to feel around inside it before I found the card.

It was a postcard, like any other postcard. In place of a picture of the Grand Canyon or Weeki Wachee Springs, the card bore a photograph of a young black man dangling from a rope. His face had been horribly disfigured. The whip marks on his bare chest were so vivid I felt like I could touch them.

On the other side of the card was a handwritten message:

THIS IS THE WAY WE COOK
COONS DOWN HERE.
THIS IS THE WAY WE WILL
COOK YOU.
WE KNOW WHY YOU ARE HERE.
GO HOME, NIGGER-LOVER.

Chapter 40

I didn't go home, of course; I couldn't — my mission was only just getting started. So I actually talked to some candidates for federal judgeships. And I continued my secretive investigation for Roosevelt. I even squeezed in a few hours at L. J. Stringer's party and remembered what a good friend he was.

A few weeks later, I felt I needed a haircut, and I knew where to go: Ezra Newcomb's.

During my visit, I congratulated Ezra, Eudora's only barber, on the sharpness of his blade. This resulted in my receiving a nine-point instructional course on the most important techniques involved in properly sharpening a straight razor.

(The truth was, I had brought my own dull razor along, hoping to have Ezra sharpen it.)

"You got to start her off real slow, then you swipe down the strop real fast," he was saying.

This was exactly the lesson I had gotten from Ezra the last time he cut my hair, when I was a boy of eighteen.

"Just don't understand it," Ezra said. "A boy goes all the way up to Harvard and they don't teach him how to sharpen a razor."

"I must have been out sick the day they gave that class."

Ezra laughed and swept the bib off me with a dramatic flourish. He returned my sharpened razor to me. I handed him a quarter and told him to keep the change. He whistled at my generous big-city tipping habits.

Then I stood outside the barbershop in the bright September sun, admiring the dangerous gleam on the edge of the blade.

"Why, Ben, you're looking at that razor the way most men look at a pretty girl!"

I turned around to see Elizabeth Begley standing right there beside me. We were practically elbow to elbow.

"I was admiring Ezra's handiwork. In all my years of trying, I have never been able to put half as good an edge on a razor."

"Oh, Ben, I don't believe there's anything you can't do," she said, "if you decide to go after it."

Now what was this craziness? Was my old girlfriend flirting with me? Was I flirting right back?

I flicked the razor shut and slipped it into my pocket.

"Come walk me to Jenkins's store," she said. "I bought new boots for Emma and she's already been through the laces. That's not right."

We walked the sidewalk of Commerce Street, which was fairly deserted at this hour.

"A little bird told me you were the *guest of honor* at the Stringers' dress party the other night," she said.

"I wouldn't say guest of honor," I said. "But I guess some people are a little curious what I'm doing back here."

"You must tell them all you've come

to visit *me,*" Elizabeth said with a smile. "That will get their tongues wagging."

She laughed, and so did I.

"Speaking of people who love to talk behind other people's backs..." She nodded in the direction of Lenora Godwin, who was walking toward us on the sidewalk across the street, apparently lost in thought.

"Lenora was at the party," I said. "She's still as well dressed as ever."

"Did she look ravishing?" There was a slightly caustic edge to the question.

"She may still be the 'Best Dressed,'" I said, "but I was wondering why the 'Most Popular Girl' at Eudora High wasn't there."

"It's simple, Ben. She and her husband were not invited to attend."

I was surprised to hear this. I knew that Eudora "society," such as it was, was a small, intimate group. Surely Elizabeth would be included.

"I think you know my husband is Richard Nottingham, the state senator," Elizabeth said. "Richard is known to be the political kingmaker."

"I did know that," I said.

"Well, then, put it together. L. J. Stringer never sits down to dinner with anyone more important than himself. Some people say that Richard will be the next governor," she said.

"And what do you think, Elizabeth?"

"He certainly wants to be governor. But I... I don't want to leave Eudora."

We had reached Jenkins's store now. "Thank you for walking with me, Ben. And for our talk. Now I have boot laces to buy."

To my disappointment, she didn't invite me in with her. But Elizabeth leaned in and lightly kissed my cheek, then disappeared into the store—the same one where my mother had collapsed when I was just a boy.

Chapter 41

My mother used to say, "When you're truly in love, you see the face you love in your coffee cup, in the washstand mirror, in the shine on your shoes." I remembered those words as I sat at my regular table at the Slide Inn, sipping a cup of strong and delicious chicory coffee.

Miss Fanny brought my breakfast of fried eggs, creamy salty grits, a slice of cured ham, and buttermilk biscuits, but I only had eyes for my coffee cup, and Mama's words haunted me. I couldn't stop thinking about Elizabeth. *Yes, Mama. I see her face in the surface of my coffee.*

Elizabeth.

If I were not feeling so lonely and

abandoned by my wife, would I be having these feelings? Probably not. But I was feeling lonely and abandoned, and worse—aroused.

Elizabeth.

My reverie was broken by Fanny's exclamation as she looked past me and out the window.

"That boy is like to drive me crazy, late as he is. Look at him, running up here like his shirttail's on fire!"

A gangly colored boy of about sixteen was headed for the café in a big, sweaty, arm-pumping hurry—such a hurry, in fact, that he almost dashed in the front door without thinking.

Then he saw Fanny and me staring at him. He remembered his place, ducked his head, and went around back.

Miss Fanny went to meet him. Through the window to the kitchen I saw the two of them in serious conversation, the boy gesticulating wildly.

I waited until Miss Fanny came back out front, then lifted my finger for more coffee. She brought the tin pot over to me.

"What's the trouble?" I said.

"Big trouble," she said quietly. "Seems

like there was another hangin' party last night."

I kept my voice low. "You mean . . . a lynching?"

"Two of 'em," she said.

Chapter 42

I took another sip of coffee and noticed that my hand was shaking some. Then I folded my napkin and headed back through the kitchen as if I intended to visit the privy. On the way I detoured to the side of the room where the boy stood over a sinkful of dirty dishes.

"What happened, son?" I said. "Please, tell me everything."

At first the boy just stared at me without speaking a word.

Fanny came up behind us. "It's okay, Leroy. This here's Mr. Corbett. He's all right to talk to."

At last the boy spoke. "You know who is Annie?" he said. "The one cook for Miz

Dickinson? She got a girl, Flossie, little older than me?"

I didn't know who he was talking about, but I nodded so he would continue.

"Well, it was that Mr. Young," he said, "Mr. Jasper Young."

I knew Jasper Young, who owned the hardware and feed stores. He was a quiet, grandfatherly man who exercised some influence behind the scenes in Eudora.

"What does Jasper Young have to do with it?"

"I can't say." The boy stared down at his dishes.

"Why not?"

He shot a look at Miss Fanny. "Lady present."

"Aw, now, come on, Leroy. Not one thing in this world you can't say in front of me!"

He wiggled and resisted, but at last he turned his eyes away from Fanny and fixed them on me.

"Mr. Young want some lovin' from Flossie. She didn't want to go along with it. So he . . . he *force* the love out of her."

What an incredible way to put it.

He force the love out of her.

The rest of the boy's story came quickly.

Flossie had told her mother of the rape. Annie told her husband. Within minutes, her husband and son, crazed with rage, broke into Jasper Young's home. They smashed china and overturned a table. Then they beat Jasper Young with their fists.

A neighbor summoned a neighbor who summoned another neighbor. Within an hour, no more than that, Annie's husband and her son were hanging from ropes in the swamp behind the Quarter.

"Where are they, exactly?" I asked the boy.

"Out by Frog Creek."

That was not the place I'd visited with Abraham, but I knew where it was.

I practically ran all the way back to Maybelle's. I didn't ask if I could borrow the bicycle, I just climbed on and rode out the old McComb Road, toward the swamp.

Toward Frog Creek.

Chapter 43

I came upon a vision of horror, all too real. Two men, one young, one older, naked and bloody, dangling from ropes. Already the smell of rotting flesh was rising in the morning heat. Flies were on the bodies.

On the ground beneath the stiff, hanging bodies, amid the cigar butts and discarded whiskey bottles, sat a woman and child. The woman was about thirty-five years old. The boy was no more than four. He was touching the woman's face, touching the tears on her cheeks.

The woman saw me and her face furrowed over in rage. "You go on, now," she shouted. "They already dead. You cain't do no more to hurt 'em."

I walked closer and she drew the boy to her, as if to protect him from me.

"I'm not going to hurt anybody," I said. "I'm a friend."

She shook her head fiercely. *No*.

I wanted to comfort her terrible sobbing, but I stayed back. "Are you Annie?"

She nodded.

Now that I was close to the dangling bodies, I saw the welts left by whips, the bloody wounds covering almost every part of their bodies. The older man's arm hung down from his shoulder by a few bloody tendons. As the younger man slowly twisted, I saw that his testicles had been severed from his body.

My voice finally came out choked. "Oh, I am so sorry."

I noticed a pink, rubbery thing in her hand, something she kept stroking with her finger as she wept.

She saw me looking. "You want to know what it is? It's my Nathan's tongue. They done cut his tongue out of his head. Stop him from sassin' them."

I looked up. Blood was thickly caked around the older man's mouth.

"Oh, Jesus!"

"Ain't no Jesus," she said. "There ain't no Jesus for me."

She wept so terribly I could not hold myself back. I knelt by her in the clearing.

For a moment all was quiet, but for her sobbing.

Then a noise. A rustling in the underbrush, a crackling of twigs. I saw birds fly up in alarm.

Someone was there.

No doubt about it.

Someone was watching us.

And then out came several people, some men but also women, black people from the Quarters come to cut down the father and son who had been murdered.

Part Three

SOUTHERN FUNERAL FAVORITES

Chapter 44

Could anyone possibly pedal a bicycle as slowly as I did going back to Eudora?

I looked all around me. Although my little town still looked much as it had when I was a boy, now it was stained and tattered almost beyond recognition.

Now the whole place was poisoned by torture and murder. The proof was still swinging from that oak tree out by the banks of Frog Creek. I thought about going to the police, but what good would it do? And besides, it would raise the question of why I had gone out to the scene of the lynchings.

"You all soakin' wet," Maybelle said as I trudged up onto her porch. "Set here with me and have a lemonade."

I put myself in a porch rocker and prepared to be disappointed, but the lemonade was cold, sweet, delicious.

"Oh, I almost forgot," Maybelle said. "You had a visitor while you were gone. Senator Nottingham's wife."

"Elizabeth? Did she leave any message?"

"No, she said she would stop by again. But that reminds me, I know how much stock you put in getting the mail, and you did get some today. I put it in the front hall."

On the hall table was a square, cream-colored envelope with my name written in Meg's delicate hand.

I took the stairs two at a time. Inside my room, I removed my jacket and settled into the chair at the window for a good read.

Dear Ben,

I know I ought to be ashamed for not having written sooner. The girls have done very little else but remind me. They have pestered me about you night and day. But I've been busy doing almost all the housekeeping, because Mazie had to go up to Trenton on account of her sister has been "ill."

Do not worry about me. Other than sore muscles from wringing out the wash and from scrubbing the floors in the house, I am in good physical shape.

These opening lines filled me with joy. My wife was still my wife. My fears were unjustified. The letter sounded so much like her—the teasing complaints, the emphatic descriptions, even the hint that she regarded Mazie's sister's problem as nothing more than a love of the grape.

Later on, when I reflected on this moment, I wished I had stopped reading at that point.

Ben, I might as well get to the point. I have suffered and wept many nights over this. Finally I have reached my decision. There is no reason for me to delay the pain for both of us, and pain there will surely be when I tell you what is in my heart.

I think it would be best for all

involved if I move back in with my father.

I read that last sentence again…and again…

I doubt this will truly come as a surprise to you. You know that we have not been in love, as husband and wife must be, for some time now.

My hand was shaking now. The paper began to rattle and my eyes burned.

I rested my head back against my chair. "*I'm* still in love, Meg," I said out loud.

I have prayed much about this matter, and have spoken to my father about the situation.

I should have known. Meg had consulted the one god in her life, the almighty Colonel Wilfred A. Haverbrook, U.S. Army, Ret. No doubt the colonel had agreed with her that her husband was a miserable failure.

I know that my decision may strike you as a terrible mistake on my part. Yet I believe it is the only correct solution to our dilemma. We must be honest with each other and ourselves.

I think it best if you do not come home at this time. I will be in touch with you by post or wire, as I begin the steps necessary to bring about a most painful but inevitable result.

Cordially, your wife
Meg

I have often heard the expression "It hit him like a punch in the stomach," but I had never felt it myself. Suddenly I knew exactly what it meant. The letter struck me a blow that caused a physical ache so sharp I had to bend over. Then I sat up. Perhaps I'd missed a word, or an entire sentence, and reversed the meaning of the thing.

I grabbed the letter and read it again. I read it out loud.

Eventually I turned it over and found another message scrawled on the back in pencil, a child's handwriting.

Daddy, me and Alice miss you terrible, just terrible. Pleas come home soon as you can. I love you, your dauhgter, Amelia.

And that is when I felt my heart break.

Chapter 45

I poured cold water from the pitcher into the basin, then washed my face with the coarse brown soap, scrubbing so hard I threatened to take the skin off.

Next I took a sheet of writing paper from my valise, along with a pen Meg had given me for the first anniversary of our marriage: a beautiful Waterman pen.

I pulled the wobbly chair up to the wobbly table and uncapped the pen. Immediately I felt all my lawyerly eloquence disappear.

Dear Meg,

As your husband, and your friend, I must tell you that you have some things wrong. I do love you. You are simply wrong to say that I don't. A separation like this is a rash thing to do, especially considering that we have never even discussed these problems face to face.

I don't care about your father's opinion of our marriage. But I do care that our parting will break the hearts of everyone involved—Alice, Amelia, my own heart, even yours.

Before you take any further action, please, my darling Meg, we must discuss this—together, as husband and wife, as mother and father of our two little daughters, as Meg and Ben who always planned to spend our lives together.

Suddenly I came out of my writing trance...

"Mr. Corbett! Mr. Corbett!"

It was Maybelle, hollering from the foot of the stairs.

I quickly wrote,

Your loving and faithful husband,
Ben

"Mr. Corbett!"

I put down the pen and walked out to the landing.

"What is it, Maybelle?" I called.

"Mrs. Nottingham is here to see you. She's here on the porch. She's waiting on you, Mr. Corbett. Hurry."

Chapter 46

There Elizabeth was, standing on Maybelle's wide wraparound porch. She had put on another bonnet and seemed even more attractive than she'd been this morning.

She reached out for my hand. "I came to apologize, Ben."

I took her hand. "What do you mean? Apologize for what?"

I said this for the benefit of Maybelle, whom I could see lingering in the parlor, trying not to be observed.

"Let's go look at Miss Maybelle's rose garden," I proposed. "It's in full bloom this time of year."

I made a motion with my eyes that disclosed my real meaning to Elizabeth.

She nodded and followed me around the porch toward the backyard.

Maybelle's roses were actually in sad shape, a few blossoms drooping among a profusion of weeds.

"I'm sorry for this morning," Elizabeth said. "The way I ran off."

"You didn't run, you walked. I watched your every step," I said and smiled.

"You can still be funny, Ben."

"Sit on the bench," I said. "I won't bite you."

Smoothing her dress, she sat on the stained marble bench amid the raggedy roses.

Sitting close to her, I was fascinated by her every gesture, word, movement. I noticed the way Elizabeth touched her mouth with the knuckle of her second finger, giving herself a little kiss before coming out with an opinion. And the slow southern musical rhythm of her speech. *Lord, what was getting into me? Probably just loneliness. Or was it being rejected by my wife?*

"You were surprised I came to see you again so soon?" she said.

"I'm always glad to see you, Elizabeth,"

I said. Then added, "Yes, I'm surprised you're here."

"I do have an ulterior motive," she said. "We're having a luncheon after church on Sunday. Will you come?"

"We?"

"Richard and I."

"Sure, I'll come," I replied.

I caught the faint scent of rose water, and I noted the curve of her nose, and remembered being very young and in love with that little nose.

"Wonderful," she was saying. "Come about one, Ben. We'll have some nice people in. I'll try not to have any of those you were subjected to at L.J.'s."

She stood. "I can't be late picking up Emma from her lesson. She's quite the little pianist, and I guess I'm quite the doting mother."

I stood, and we smiled. This time, there was no kiss on the cheek.

But I watched Elizabeth walk away again, every step, until she finally disappeared behind the rooming house porch.

Chapter 47

Washington, D.C.

That same afternoon, Senator John Tyler Morgan, Democrat of Alabama, stood in the lobby of the Willard Hotel, yelling at the general manager.

"I have never been refused service in my life! That insufferable man in the elevator had the nerve to tell me he was holding the car for an *important personage*. He told me to get off that car and wait for another car!"

Senator Morgan was so angry that specks of saliva were speckling the lapels of the general manager's morning coat.

"Senator, I am so sorry for the inconvenience—"

"Not an *inconvenience!* It's a goddamned *insult!* Who the hell was he holding the elevator for, the goddamned president of the United States?"

As he roared this question, the great glass doors of the lobby flew open at the hands of two uniformed guards. In walked Theodore Roosevelt.

He took one look at John Tyler Morgan in midrampage and the poor little cowering manager. Then Roosevelt thundered, "Unless my eyes deceive me, the man at the center of that ruckus is none other than the senior senator from the great state of Alabama. Good morning, John!"

The famous Civil War general and southern statesman was stunned into silence. No one had called him John in many years.

"Morning, Mr. President," he finally managed to say.

"Come ride the elevator with me, John!"

A few minutes later, having deposited the red-faced Morgan on his floor, Roosevelt had a good laugh at his expense. "And the newspapers call *me* a gasbag? Senator Morgan, my friends, is the royal

Chapter 48

The inner door opened and a pair of adjutants appeared, escorting a distinguished-looking black man with a Vandyke beard and a wide woman of a darker, more African appearance, with a wise face and a spectacular sweep of hair that plainly was not entirely her own.

Mr. Roosevelt bowed to the man and kissed the lady's gloved hand. He could never be seen doing such a thing in public, but here in private he was all too happy to pay honor to W. E. B. Du Bois, the great Negro writer and crusader, and to Ida B. Wells-Barnett, the passionate antilynching campaigner, such a modern and audacious woman that she dared to and supreme emperor of gasbags! Did you see how quickly I deflated him simply by using his Christian name?"

Appreciative laughter from his aides trailed the president to his suite. Roosevelt grew serious the moment he passed through the door.

"Good morning, Mr. President. We're all ready for your meeting," said Jackson Hensen, his capable assistant.

"Well, get them in here. No need to dawdle."

"Yes, sir. They're on their way up in the service elevator."

Roosevelt chuckled. "How did they take to that?"

"I understand the gentleman was... displeased," Hensen said.

append her husband's name to her own when she married.

"My sincere apologies for the indignity of bringing you up in the . . . back elevator," the president said.

Du Bois bowed slightly. "It is not the first time I have ridden in the servants' car, Mr. President," he said. "I am fairly sure it will not be the last."

Mrs. Wells-Barnett perched her sizable self on the upholstered chair beside the fireplace.

"Now, Mr. Du Bois," said the president, "I have received quite a lot of correspondence from you about these matters. I want you to know that my administration is doing everything within our power to see that these local authorities start observing the laws as—"

Roosevelt was surprised when Ida Wells-Barnett interrupted.

"That's fine, Mr. President," she said. "We already know all that. You don't have to coddle us or pour on all that old gravy. We know what you're up against. We're up against the same. White men get away with killing black men every day."

Roosevelt's eyes flashed behind his

spectacles. "Well, Madam, I think I may be able to do something finally," he said. "That's why I agreed to this meeting."

Du Bois said, "Yes, sir, but—"

"If you will try to refrain from interrupting your president," Roosevelt demanded, "I will further explain that I am taking steps right now to learn the true situation in the Deep South. Once I have all the facts, I assure you I intend to act."

"I appreciate that," Du Bois said.

"We're not asking for public displays any more than you are," said Wells-Barnett, warming to the discussion. "As you recall, sir, when you invited Booker Washington to dine at the White House, it caused a political headache for you and accomplished absolutely nothing for the cause of colored people."

"Booker T. Washington is the whitest black man I know," grumbled Du Bois.

Roosevelt sat ramrod straight in a large leather armchair. Jackson Hensen loomed over a tiny French desk in the corner, taking down in shorthand everything that was said.

"Mr. Roosevelt, let me put this as simply as possible," said Wells-Barnett.

"What we have at the present time is an epidemic of lynching in the South. The problem is getting worse, not better."

Jackson Hensen decided to speak up.

It was an unfortunate decision.

"I understand what you are saying, Mrs. Wells, Professor Du Bois," he said carefully. "But at the same time you are telling us these terrible stories of lynching, we have it on excellent authority that there is also an epidemic of white women being raped and molested by Negroes all over the South. I've seen the numbers. The crime of rape is at least as prevalent as the crime of lynching, is it not?"

"That simply isn't true, young man." Du Bois's voice was an ominous rumble. "I don't know where you're getting that insidious, completely inaccurate information."

Wells-Barnett interrupted. "Just this morning, Senator Morgan was telling people in the lobby of this hotel that he intends to repeal the antilynching laws now in effect."

Jackson Hensen made a skeptical sound. "With all respect, Mrs. Wells-

Barnett, I seriously doubt Morgan can muster the votes to do such a thing."

Then Du Bois: "I disagree, young man. I disagree—vehemently!"

"That's enough!" said the president. He got to his feet and paced the floor behind his desk. "I've heard enough of this squabbling. I *am* determined to get to the bottom of the problem. And I will!"

The president's flash of anger silenced everyone. They all stared at him dumbly: the combative Du Bois, the passionate Wells-Barnett, the young and arrogant Hensen.

Now Roosevelt spoke, quietly and with purpose. "At this very moment I have sent a personal envoy to the Deep South on a dangerous mission, to investigate this entire question of lynching. He is a man I trust," Roosevelt continued. "A native of those parts. I have connected him with certain others who can show him the situation from all sides. I haven't told you his name because I'd rather this situation remain confidential until he's done his job. And then I will do whatever I deem necessary to *remedy* the tragic situation in the South."

Ida Wells-Barnett rose from the sofa. "Thank you, Mr. President. I gladly tell anyone who asks that you are the best friend the Negro has had in this office since Mr. Lincoln."

Roosevelt shook her hand enthusiastically.

Du Bois was forced by Mrs. Wells-Barnett's action to rise from the sofa and offer his own hand. "Thank you, Mr. President," he said.

"Yes. Thank you, sir." The president shook his hand. "Let's hope we can make progress on this."

"I've been hoping for progress all my life," Du Bois said.

Roosevelt kept the fixed smile on his face until the two were out of the room. Then he frowned and uttered an epithet.

"Sir?" said Hensen.

"You heard what I said."

"Is there something I should do about this?"

"Get a message to Abraham Cross. Tell him I want a report from him and Ben Corbett immediately—if not sooner."

Chapter 49

I went down to Young's Hardware—the only such store in town—and bought myself a bicycle. Then I wheeled my purchase out into the hot sun. The machine was a beautiful silvery blue, with pneumatic tires to smooth out the bumps and ruts of Eudora's dirt streets.

I took my maiden voyage on my new machine out to the Quarters, to see Abraham Cross.

On this day Abraham and I did not head for the swamp. We rode his mules along the Jackson & Northern tracks, then turned east on the Union Church Road. This was fine open ground, vast flat fields that had been putting out prodigious quantities of cotton for generations.

Every mile or so we encountered a clump of trees surrounding a fine old plantation house. These plantations had been the center of Eudora's wealth, the reason for its existence, since the first slaves were brought in to clear the trees from these fields.

"You don't mean they lynched somebody right out here in the open?" I said.

"You stick with me," Abraham said, "and I'll show you things that'll make your fine blond hair fall out."

At that moment we were riding past River Oak, the McKenna family plantation. In the field to our left about thirty Negro workers were bent over under the hot sun, dragging the cloth sacks that billowed out behind them as they moved down the row, picking cotton.

We passed out of the morning heat into the shade, the portion of the road that curved close to the McKennas' stately home. On the front lawn two adorable white children in a little pink-painted cart were driving a pony in circles. On the wide front veranda I could see the children's mother observing their play and a small army of black servants hovering there.

This was a vision of the old South and the new South, all wrapped into one. There, gleaming in the drive, was a handsome new motorcar, brass fittings shining in the sun. And there, rushing across the yard in pursuit of a hen, was an ink-black woman with a red dotted kerchief wrapped around her head.

Abraham was careful to ride his mule a few feet behind mine, to demonstrate his inferior position in the company of a white man. I turned in the saddle. “Where to?”

“Just keep riding straight on ahead to that road beyond the trees,” he said.

“You don’t think that lady’s going to wonder what we’re up to?”

“She don’t even see us,” said Abraham. “She just happy to sit up on her porch and be rich.”

We passed once more out of the shade and turned our mules down the long line of trees flanking the McKennas’ pecan orchard.

Soon we arrived at another clump of trees shading an intersection with another dirt lane. The western side of this crossing formed a natural amphitheater, with a gigantic old black gum tree as its center.

Beneath this tree someone had built a little platform, like a stage. In a rough semicircle several warped wooden benches were arranged, their whitewash long faded. Obviously they had been hauled out of some derelict church and placed here for spectators.

"What is this, a camp revival?" I said.

Abraham pointed up at a sturdy low branch of the gum tree. The branch extended directly over the little wooden stage—or rather, the stage had been built directly under the branch. Three ropes were carefully knotted and hanging from the branch, three loops waiting for heads to be slipped in, waiting for someone to hang.

"Good God!" I said as I realized what I was seeing.

"For the audience," Abraham said as he gestured around at the benches. "They come to watch the lynching. And they need a place to sit. Nothing worse than having to stand while you waiting to watch 'em hang a nigger."

That was the first time I'd heard Abraham use that word, and his eyes burned fiercely.

I almost couldn't believe it. Across that fence was the McKennas' impeccable lawn, acres and acres of flawless mown grass. I could see beds of bright orange daylilies sculpted into the landscape from here to the big house.

To one side of the stage, I noticed a low table with a small bench behind it. Maybe that was for shotguns and rifles, to keep them out of the dirt.

"What's that table for, Abraham?"

He answered with a weak smile. "That's where they sell refreshments."

Chapter 50

If I thought that obscene place was the worst abomination I was going to see—a serene amphitheater constructed for the pleasure of human beings torturing other human beings—I was wrong.

Our journey was just beginning.

We turned south, along back roads, until we were riding beside the fields of the Sauville plantation. I asked if they too had a theater for lynching.

"I don't believe so," said Abraham. "Why bother building your own when there's such a nice one already established in your neighborhood?"

We rode past the showy Greek Revival pile of the Sauville home, past miles of fields with colored folks in them, picking cotton.

After riding for most of an hour, we came to a long, low cotton barn with a tall silo for storing grain at one end. The place was neatly kept and obviously much in use; the doors at one end stood open, revealing deep rectangular bays stuffed to the ceiling with the first bales of the new crop.

The most successful farmers used barns like this for storing their cotton from year to year, selling only as they needed cash or the price reached a profitable level.

"You telling me they've lynched somebody here?"

"I'm afraid so. This was where Hiram Frazier got hanged. And a couple more since."

"How on earth could you hang somebody in a barn this low? Looks like his feet would drag on the ground."

He pointed to the end of the barn by the silo. "The folks watch from in here. But they hang 'em inside the silo. Don't even need a tree."

I shook my head. I thought of Jacob

Gill and the pint he kept in his leather toolbox. I wished for a taste of that whiskey right now.

Abraham led the mules to a slow, muddy stream, where they drank. The old man knelt down, cupped some water in his hand, and drank too.

"It don't look like much, but it taste all right," he said.

I was thirsty but decided I could wait.

We climbed up on the mules. Abraham's animal groaned as he brought his full weight down on its back.

"I declare, I don't know who's in worse shape," Abraham said, "this poor old mule or me."

I smiled at him.

"There's one more place I need to show you, Ben," he said. "Then I reckon we'll be ready to write an official report for Mr. President."

As his mule started off, I saw Abraham wince in pain and try to hide it. He saw that I had noticed and forced a smile.

"Don't worry about me, Mr. Corbett," he said. "I'm old, but I ain't even close to dyin' yet."

But as he turned away and the smile

dropped from his face like a mask, I realized that Abraham was a very old man, and probably a sick man as well. His face had the hidden desperation of someone hanging on for dear life.

Or maybe just to make this report to the president.

Chapter 51

I suppose Abraham was wise to save the worst for last. We rode the mules through a peach orchard south of the Chipley plantation, making a roundabout circle in the general direction of town. The air was heavy with the smell of rotting fruit. For some reason no one was picking these peaches.

At the end of the orchard we emerged into a peaceful wooded glen. At the far side stood two huge old trees. From the fruit dotting the floor of the glen, I made out that these were black cherry trees; we had a nice specimen growing in back of the house the whole time I was growing up.

From the tree on the right hung a black

man. At least, I think it was a man. It was mostly unrecognizable. Flies buzzed around it. It had been there a while.

I didn't want to go closer, but I found myself moving there as if my legs were doing all the thinking for my body. I could see that the man had been young. He was caked with blood, spit, snot, mud, and shit. His head was distended, swollen from the pressure of hanging. His lips were swollen too, like balloons about to pop.

I began to gag and I turned away. I fell to one knee and heaved.

"Go ahead, Ben," Abraham said. "It's good to be sick, to be able to get rid of it like that. I wish I could. I guess I'm just gettin' too used to seein' it. It's a bad thing to get used to."

I took out my handkerchief and wiped the edges of my mouth. The wave of nausea was still sweeping over me.

"That's Jimmy Patton up there," he said.

"What happened to him?"

"He worked over at the gin for Mr. Purneau," Abraham said. "Last Saturday he got drunk like he always does after he gets his pay. He was walkin' home and somehow he got hold of a gun. Don't know if he brung it with him, I never knowed Jimmy to carry a gun. Anyway he popped it off right there a couple of times on Commerce Street, down at the end there by the depot. He didn't hit anybody, but a couple of men saw him. They brought him here."

"We can't leave him up there," I said.

"Well sir, we have to," said Abraham.

"Why is that?"

"Because they told the people came to cut Jimmy down they wanted him left here as a warning for the others."

"You afraid to cut him down, Abraham? This man needs to be buried."

"We got no way to carry him."

"Across the mule's back," I said. "I can walk it, or I can ride with you."

"I'm an old man, Mr. Corbett. I can't climb that tree."

"Well, I can, but I don't have a knife," I said.

Abraham produced an excellent bowie knife with a bone handle.

It was only when I was directly under Jimmy Patton's body that I saw someone had severed his fingers and toes. Where his digits should have been there were bloody stumps.

I made quick work of climbing the cherry tree.

"Yes, sir," Abraham said. "Sometime they cut off pieces. To take for souvenirs. And sometimes they sell 'em, you know. At the general store. At the barber shop. Ten cent for a nigger toe. Twenty-five cent for a nigger thumb."

I waved my hand at the ugly explosion of blood on the front of Jimmy Patton's trousers.

"That's right," said Abraham. "Sometimes they don't stop at fingers and toes."

I felt light-headed and nauseated again. "Just—just stop talking for a minute, would you, Abraham?"

I sawed at the rope with a knife for what seemed like an hour. Jimmy Patton finally fell to the ground with a sickening thud.

Somehow I managed to climb down that tree. Somehow I got the Indian blanket out from under Abraham's saddle and wrapped it around the dead man.

With Abraham's help I got Jimmy onto the mule. His body was so stiff from rigor mortis that I had to balance him just so, like a pine log.

"We better get out of here," Abraham said. "Somebody watching us for sure."

"Where? I don't see anybody."

"I don't see 'em," he said, "but I know they watching us, just the same."

We made it back through the peach orchard, onto the road, all the way back to town without meeting a soul. I walked the mule by its rope, hoping it would help to be out front. But there was nowhere to walk without breathing in the smell of Jimmy Patton's decomposing flesh, the coppery smell of his blood.

"I'm ready to write that report, Abraham," I said.

"Yes, sir," he said. "I imagine you are."

Chapter 52

Suddenly it was Sunday, and I was back in a world I recognized. I didn't admit to myself why I felt so lighthearted. I splashed my face with lilac water and clipped a fresh collar to my shirt, but it wasn't until I was standing at the bright yellow door of Elizabeth Begley's white mansion that I admitted what had made me so happy yet apprehensive: *the prospect of seeing her again.*

The door swung open even before I could knock. At a house so grand, I naturally expected to be greeted by a servant, but instead I found the door opened by its owner, Elizabeth's husband, a short, bald man with an amiable smile. "You must be the famous Benjamin Corbett of Washington, attorney at law," he said.

"I am," I said. "And you must be the much more famous Richard Nottingham, senator and man of influence."

He smiled. "You've got that just about right," he said, grabbing my hand. That hand had not been shaken so vigorously since Roosevelt operated it at the White House. Maybe it was a habit of politicians to inflict pain on new acquaintances, as an aid to memory.

"Lizzie talks so much about you I feel like we already know each other."

Lizzie. The familiarity of the nickname made me wince inwardly.

"I've been looking forward to meeting you," I said. "She speaks fondly of you."

"Oh, now, he's making that up," said Elizabeth, coming up behind her husband. "Don't lie, Ben. Richard knows I haven't spoken fondly of him in years!" She threw her husband a big stage wink. "At least, not in public."

Nottingham laughed. "Isn't she a delight?"

I agreed that she was, in a most unspecific murmur. Then I followed them into a small drawing room off the rear of the center hall.

"Ben, Richard and I are so happy you came. There may be a few people here you don't know—"

This looked a lot like the gathering at L. J. Stringer's mansion: the same aging stuffed shirts, the same overstuffed dresses, a faint smell of mothballs.

Elizabeth led me to a stout couple on the fringed velvet loveseat. "This is Senator Oscar Winkler and his dear wife, Livia."

I noticed that state senators dropped the "state," turning themselves into real senators. Senator Winkler clasped my hand. "Nice to see you again, Ben."

I was surprised he remembered me. Many years ago, as political editor for the *Eudora High School Bugler*, I had interviewed Senator Winkler for a column entitled "Eudora Looks Forward." He had been warm to me and wise in his comments. One thing he said I had never forgotten. He said it, then asked me not to print it: "The southern man who figures out a way to bridge this terrible divide between the black and the white will enjoy all the blessings our Lord can bestow."

I shook the senator's hand and kissed his wife's. As I was straightening up I heard Elizabeth say, "And I do believe you already know this fellow."

I turned. To my astonishment, I found myself smiling and extending my hand to one Judge Everett Corbett.

He shook it quite formally and made a little bow. "Ben, always a pleasure," he said. "I hope your business down here is going well."

Richard Nottingham clapped his hands. "Lizzie, I heard just a bit too much preaching this morning, and presently I'm about to starve to death." Everything the man said had that odd quality of being humorously intended but not actually funny. "Could we *please* have our dinner?"

Chapter 53

I was pleased about two things immediately. One, Elizabeth seated me next to herself at the table; two, turtle soup was *not* on the Nottinghams' menu.

I'd eaten a skimpy breakfast, expecting the usual six- or seven-course southern exercise in dinnertime excess. Instead I found the food a touch on the dainty side: deviled eggs, shrimp rémoulade, cucumber sandwiches, various cheeses, and a big silver dish of pickles.

My father was also dishing it up: the personification of silver-haired charm, as he could be at those times when he let himself be roped into a social event.

"I really owe you and Elizabeth a debt of gratitude," he told Nottingham. "If it weren't for you, who knows if I'd even get to see my son again before he heads home!"

I recognized that as a clear signal. Now that we'd seen each other and been observed acting cordially toward each other, my job was done. I was welcome to go back to Washington anytime.

"Oh, I'm not going home yet, Father," I said over the back of the settee. I held up my glass of claret. "I'm grateful too, Richard. My father and I don't get to see each other enough. It's so rare to see him in such a cheerful and expansive mood."

My father gave out a little laugh. "Ben is quite a character," he said. "He's come down to tell us all where we went wrong. He thinks the South ought to be able to change overnight."

Richard Nottingham was glancing from my father to me, as if wondering whether this dispute was going to lead to blows among all this expensive china and crystal.

"I'm just hoping for a South that returns to the rule of law," I said. "I just want a place where the Ku Klux Klan is not hanging black men from every available tree."

I knew that I was treading dangerously here, but I couldn't help myself.

"Now you're being plain ignorant," my father said. "You don't seem to remember that the Klan was outlawed about forty years ago."

"I remember it very well," said Livia Winkler. "My daddy said it was the end of civilization."

Senator Winkler cleared his throat. "Now, Judge, you know as well as I do that outlawing something does not guarantee that it ceases to exist," he said. "As a matter of fact, that's one of the best ways to ensure its continuing existence—to forbid it!"

They glared at each other. It struck me that they'd had this argument before, when I was nowhere around. It also reminded me that there were many good men and women in the South, even here in Eudora.

I was about to say something in support of Winkler when a servant girl walked in bearing a large round cake, frosted white, on a silver platter.

Nottingham brightened. "Why, Lizzie, is that a hummingbird cake?"

"Of course it is. I had them make it just for you. Richard's going off to Jackson next week. We'll miss his birthday, but we can all celebrate tonight."

Something happened then that sent an electrical jolt through my body. It was all I could do to keep from bolting upright in my seat.

As she said these words to her husband, I felt Elizabeth's hand gently pat the inside of my thigh.

"Ben," she said, "you must try the cake."

Chapter 54

"No, sir."

"No, not today, Mr. Corbett."

"No, sir, nothing today."

Maybelle always had the same answer to the question I asked her at least once every day. First I would check the table in the front hall, then I'd convince myself that a letter had come and Maybelle was keeping it from me because she knew how anxiously I waited.

I would go ask her, and she would say, "No, sir."

It had been more than a week since I'd written to Meg. I'd imagined that my love had fairly leapt off the page when she read it and that she would write back immediately.

That letter had not yet arrived.

Meanwhile I was keeping someone else waiting: President Roosevelt expected a report on what I had found out about lynching in and around Eudora. I had spent the past two evenings on a long letter to the president that gave precise locations, right down to the species of the hanging trees. I included the names of victims and the approximate times and dates of their murders.

Then I showed the letter to Abraham. He read it and said, "If it was me, I'd make it like a telegram. Short and sweet. 'Dear Mr. President, it's worse than you heard. Send the Army. Stop.' "

Abraham was right. I remembered years ago at Las Guasimas when Roosevelt spoke to me for the first time. He glared down from his horse. "Do we have provisions for an overnight, Captain?"

"Sir, I ordered the men to double their rations and to fill their canteens—"

"Stop!" Roosevelt commanded. "That was a yes-or-no question."

"Yes, sir," I said.

And now it took Abraham to remind

me of Roosevelt's fondness for a concise report.

"Send it to him in a wire," he said.

"That's a good idea. But I can't send it from Eudora."

The telegraph operator in town was Harry Kelleher, who was also the station-master. The moment I left the depot after sending my wire to the White House, Kelleher would personally see that the contents were passed on to every man, woman, and child in Eudora.

"Where can I go, Abraham?"

"Where's the closest place where everybody doesn't know who you are?"

I thought about that. "McComb," I said.

McComb was the nearest sizable town, a farm center and railroad hub ten miles north. When I was growing up, McComb was nothing but a crossroads, but when the Jackson & Northern railroad extended its line and located a terminus there, it outgrew Eudora. McComb was only an hour's carriage ride away, and it boasted Sampson's, a fine restaurant specializing in New Orleans–style food: Creole jambalaya, grits and grillades, steak Diane.

Most of all, it had something that was sure to lift my spirits. I had seen the handbill only the day before, hanging on the front wall of the *Eudora Courier* office.

TOMORROW! ONE NIGHT ONLY!
THE INIMITABLE AUTHOR, SATIRIST, &
RACONTEUR
MR. SAMUEL LANGHORNE CLEMENS,
WHO MAY DECIDE TO APPEAR ALONGSIDE
MR. MARK TWAIN
DOORS OPEN AT 7 O'CLOCK
THE TROUBLE TO BEGIN AT 8 O'CLOCK
MCCOMB CITY LYRIC THEATRE

My favorite author in the world was just a carriage ride away.

And then another thought struck me. I didn't have a carriage, but I knew someone who did.

Chapter 55

When I pushed my carefully composed telegram across the desk to the man behind the barred window at the McComb depot, his eyes bugged. "I ain't never sent a wire to the White House before," he said in a loud voice.

A few people waiting for the next train turned their heads to give me an appraising glance.

I smiled at the man. "Neither have I," I said gently. "Could you please keep it down?"

"I sent one to the president of Ole Miss one time," he bellowed, "but that ain't the same thing. You mean for this to go to the real president, in the White House, up in Washington?"

"That's the one," I said.

I would have to tell Abraham that his idea of coming to McComb for anonymity had failed. I wondered whether there was anyplace in the state of Mississippi from which you could dispatch a wire to 1600 Pennsylvania Avenue without causing a fuss.

"Yes, sir," the man was saying, "one time I sent one to Governor Vardaman, and there was this other time a fellow wanted to send one—"

"I'm glad you and I could make history together," I said. "Could you send it right away?"

"Soon as the station agent comes back from his break," he said.

I forced myself to remember that I was down South, where everything operated on Mississippi time, a slower pace than in other places. After the man's break would be soon enough.

I hurried out to Elizabeth's carriage, where she sat surveying the panorama of McComb.

Half the town had burned to the ground just a few years before, but a sturdy new town had already been put up to replace it. At one end of the business district stood a fine new depot and the famous McComb Ice Plant, which iced down thousands of train cars full of southern fruits and vegetables for the trip north.

All the way at the other end of downtown, on Broadway Street, stood the only other building that really interested me—the Lyric Theatre, where Twain would perform tonight.

First we repaired to Sampson's, where I ordered crab gumbo and Elizabeth ordered—what else?—turtle soup. We chatted and relived old times throughout the Pompano en Papillote and the Snapper Almondine, the bread pudding and the egg custard. It was the finest meal, and dining companion, I'd had since returning to the South.

With a rare sense of satisfaction, Elizabeth and I strolled down the new sidewalks of Front Street to the theater. Men in waistcoats and women in fancy crinolines were milling about the entrance, and I couldn't wait to go in.

"You look like a child on Christmas morning," Elizabeth said and laughed merrily.

I lifted my hat to the man I'd engaged to water our horse and keep an eye on the carriage. "It's better than that," I said. "Christmas comes once a year. But Mark Twain comes once in a lifetime."

Chapter 56

Let me put this simply. Mark Twain remains to this day the funniest, most intelligent and entertaining person I ever saw on any stage or read in any book.

By then he was an old man, over seventy, but he wore his famous white suit, smoked his famous cigar, and constantly ran his long fingers through his famously unruly hair. His voice was as raspy as an old barn door. He sounded at all times as if he were about ten seconds away from erupting in a violent rage.

"Nothing needs reforming," he said by way of beginning, "so much as other people's habits."

The audience roared in recognition of a universal truth.

"Best forget about the animals. Man is the only one with the true religion..."

The audience waited. Sure enough, the rest of the sentence arrived with perfect timing.

"Yep... several of them."

He was amusing, biting, sarcastic, ferocious, and bitter in his repudiation of nearly everything and everyone. Elizabeth laughed as hard as I did—harder sometimes. I kept sneaking glances at her: shoulders shaking, handkerchief pressed to her mouth. I was happy she was having such a good time.

I was no author, no satirist, no raconteur, but I did know that the humor of this man Clemens was different. Besides being funny, every word he spoke was the absolute truth. The bigger the lies he pretended to tell, the more truthful the stories became.

When he talked about his struggles with trying to give up whiskey and his beloved cigars, we all laughed because we had struggles of our own, and he helped us see that they were ridiculous.

When he read from his book *Huckleberry Finn,* a passage in which Huck is bemoaning the fancy clothes the Widow Douglas has forced him to wear, we laughed because someone had once forced us into Sunday clothes too.

Occasionally Twain landed with both feet in an area that made this audience a little restless, as when he said:

"We had slavery when I was a boy. There was nothing wrong with slavery. The local pulpit told us God approved of it. If there were passages in the Bible that disapproved of slavery, they were not read aloud by the pastors."

Twain paused. He looked deadly serious. I saw men shifting in their seats.

"I wonder how they could be so dishonest..."

Another long pause. And then: "Result of practice, I guess."

The laughter came, and I saw Elizabeth dab at her eyes.

After more than an hour of effervescent brilliance, it became clear that Twain was exhausted, clinging to the podium. A man pushed an armchair in from the wings, and Twain asked our permission to sit down.

He sat down and lit a cigar, which drew another round of applause.

He was finishing up. When he spoke this time, I felt he was speaking directly to me.

"There's a question I'm interested in," he said. "You-all might have an opinion on this. Why does a crowd of people stand by, smitten to the heart and miserable, and by ostentatious outward signs pretend to enjoy a lynching?"

The room fell so quiet you could hear the nervous cough of one man at the back.

"Why does the crowd lift no hand or voice in protest?" Twain said. "Only because it would be unpopular to do it, I think. Each man is afraid of his neighbor's disapproval—a thing which, to the general run of the race, is more dreaded than wounds and death."

Still the audience sat rapt, unmoving.

"When there is to be a lynching, the people hitch up and come miles to see it, bringing their wives and children," he said. "Really to see it? No—they come only because they are afraid to stay at home, lest it be noticed and offensively commented upon.

"No mob has any sand in the presence of a man known to be splendidly brave. When I was a boy, I saw a brave gentleman deride and insult a mob, and drive it away.

"This would lead one to think that perhaps the remedy for lynchings is to station a brave man in each affected community. But where shall these brave men be found? That is indeed a difficulty. There are not three hundred of them on the earth."

That's exactly what Mark Twain said that night. I looked around and saw almost everyone in that audience nodding their heads, as if they all agreed.

Chapter 57

Apparently Elizabeth's carriage horse had never encountered an automobile before, at least not after sundown, and not in such profusion.

With all the sputtering and clanging and light-flashing and honking in the streets around the Lyric Theatre, the frightened old horse bucked and snapped at the air. It took some fancy rein work to get us safely back on the road to Eudora.

The trip home made the trouble worth-while. The stir of a breeze in the sultry night. A fat full moon that seemed stained yellow around its edges.

"I saw *Charley's Aunt* in that theater," Elizabeth said. "I saw Maude Adams in Jackson when she came through as

Peter Pan. And they were both wonderful. But they didn't touch my heart the way Mr. Twain did. Or make me laugh until there were tears."

"It's a very special evening," I said. "Couldn't have been any better."

I waited. She didn't answer.

"It is," she finally said. "It's very special to me too."

These last words caught in her throat. I glanced at her: even in the faint moonlight, I could see the shine of tears in her eyes.

"What's the matter?" I asked.

"Oh, you know what it is, Ben," she said. "I should be riding home with Richard. I should be sharing memories of Mark Twain with him. I should be in love . . . with Richard."

I knew what I wanted to do then. I wanted to tell Elizabeth my own troubles, Meg's and mine, tell her how lonely I felt, how devastated when Meg proposed *(by letter, no less!)* that we put an end to our marriage.

Instead, I drove along in silence. The breeze disappeared, and the moon went behind a cloud.

"Why did you ask me to go with you tonight?" she said.

"I thought you would enjoy it," I said. "And I guess I've been . . . lonely."

"Oh, Ben," she said. "Oh, Ben." Then she took my hand in hers, and held it for a long moment.

We were riding past the town limits sign now. It was late; Commerce Street was deserted. The clip-clop of the horse's hooves echoed off the storefronts.

I finally pulled to a stop in front of the Nottingham home. I clicked open my watch. "Ten minutes till midnight," I said. "Very respectable."

"Respectable," she said with a little smile. "That is one thing you are. It's a good thing, Ben."

I walked her to the yellow door flanked by a pair of flickering gaslights.

"Thank you for a beautiful evening," she said. She pressed her lips to mine, her body soft against mine. The embrace lasted only a few seconds, but for those seconds, I was lost.

"Ben, do you want to come inside?" Elizabeth said in a whisper.

"I do," I whispered back. "I most certainly do. But I can't."

Then Elizabeth disappeared inside her house, and I went back to Maybelle's. I had never felt more alone in my life.

Chapter 58

I was still waiting for an answer from the White House. Maybe my telegram had been *too* concise? Too curt or disrespectful to send to the president? Maybe Roosevelt had forgotten about me?

I walked downtown to get out of the rooming house, to do something other than wait. Pretty much every human being within ten miles came to town on Saturday. For a few hours in the morning, the sidewalks of Eudora buzzed with the activity of a much larger town.

I was standing in front of the Purina feed and seed, discussing the weather with Mr. Baker, when I saw an old lady and her grown daughter hurrying along the sidewalk toward us, as if getting away from something.

"I don't care what anyone says," the younger woman said as they passed, "they are human beings too. It isn't right! Those boys are acting like heathens!"

Mr. Baker and I tipped our hats, but the ladies failed to notice us.

I excused myself and walked up Maple Street, around the corner where they had appeared. What I saw made my heart drop.

Three white men, maybe my age, were holding the heads of two black boys under the surface of the horse trough in front of Jenkins' Mercantile.

They were *drowning* those boys. It scared me how long they were submerged after I came around the corner and saw them. Then, as if on cue, they were yanked up from the water. They spluttered out a desperate heaving breath, and then their heads were plunged into the water again.

Those boys were just kids—twelve or thirteen at the most.

When their heads came up out of the

water again, they cried and begged the men to please let them go.

"Whatsa matter, you thought them white ladies was gonna save you?"

Their heads went back under.

I remembered the closing words of Mr. Clemens's address: *"Where shall these brave men be found? There are not three hundred of them on the earth."*

I took three long strides forward. "What's going on here? Let 'em up. Do it now."

The white men whirled around. In their surprise, they jerked the heads of their victims clear of the water. The boy on the left used the moment to make his escape, but the largest man tightened his grip on the other boy's arm.

He was a mean-looking fat man with red hair, bulging muscles, and a tooth missing in front. "These niggers was sassing us," he said.

"Turn him loose," I said.

"Shit, no."

"He's about twelve years old," I said. "You men are grown. And three of you against two little boys?"

"Why don't you mind your own damn

bidness," said the second man, who had a greasy head of black hair and a face that even his mother could not have loved much. "These nigger boys was out of line. We don't allow that in this town."

"I'm from this town too," I said. "My father's a judge here. Let him go."

I guess I sounded just official enough for Big Red to relax his grip. The black boy took off like a shot.

"Look what we got here, men," said Red then. "A genuine nigger-lover."

Without warning he charged and struck me full force with the weight of his body. I went flying.

Chapter 59

I was slammed down on the hard dirt street, and before I could catch my breath Red jumped on top of me.

"Reckon I'll have to *teach* you how to mind your own business."

I was trying to figure a way out of this. I had once watched Bob Fitzsimmons demolish an opponent with a third-round knockout. That was one way to do it. But there was another way to win a fight.

I reached up and pressed my thumbs into the soft, unprotected flesh of the fat man's throat. I got my leverage, then slung him off me, right over my head. Red landed face-first in the dirt and scuffed up his lip. Blood was coming out of his nose too.

I jumped to my feet and his buddies charged at me. The first ran hard into a right uppercut. He dropped like a rock and was out cold in the street.

Now there were two dazed bullies down, but the third got behind me and jumped on my back. He started pounding his fists into my ribs.

I knew there was a thick wooden post supporting the gallery in front of Jenkins' Mercantile, so I leaned all my weight into the man, propelling us backward, smashing him right into it. His arms unraveled from my neck and he lay on the ground twitching. He'd hit that post pretty hard, maybe cracked a couple of ribs.

"Nigger-lover," he spat, but then he struggled up and started to run. So did the other two.

It was quiet again, the street empty.

Well, almost empty.

Chapter 60

Standing on the board sidewalk beside Jenkins's display window was the dapper local photographer, Scooter Willems. Today he looked extra-fashionable in a seersucker suit with a straw boater. As always, he had his camera and tripod with him. I wondered whether he had just photographed me in action.

"Where'd you learn to fight like that, Ben?"

"Boxing team at college," I said.

"No, I mean, where'd you learn to put your thumbs in a man's throat like that? Looks like you learned to fight in the street," Scooter said.

"I reckon I just have the instinct," I said.

"Mind if I take your photograph, Ben?"

I remembered the night I first saw him, photographing George Pearson. "I *do* mind, Scooter. My clothes are a mess."

"That's what would make it interesting," he said with a big smile.

"Maybe for you. Not for me. *Don't take my picture.*"

"I will honor your wishes, of course." Scooter folded the tripod and walked away.

I tucked my shirt into my torn trousers, and when I brushed my hand against my chin, it came back bloody.

Moody Cross stepped out of Sanders's store with a sack of rice on one hip and a bag of groceries on her arm. She walked toward me.

"You are beyond learning," she said.

I used my handkerchief to wipe off the blood. "And what is it I have failed to learn, Moody?"

"You can go around trying to fight every white man in Mississippi that hates colored people," she said, "but it won't do any good. There's a lot more of them than there is of you. You can't protect us. Nobody can do that. Not even God."

She turned to walk away, but then she looked back. "But thank you for trying," she said.

Chapter 61

In four weeks of living at Maybelle's, I'd come to realize that my room was so damp, so airless, so overheated night and day, that nothing ever really dried out.

My clothes, my hand towel, and my shave towel were always damp. My hair was moist at all times. As much as I toweled off, powdered with talc, and blotted with witch hazel, my shirts and underclothes always retained a film of moisture. This stifling closet at the top of Maybelle's stairs was a punishment, a torture, a prison.

And besides, there was so much to keep me awake at night.

I longed for a letter from home.

And maybe because I didn't hear, I wrestled with thoughts of Elizabeth. I could still feel our kiss in front of her house.

I wondered if Roosevelt had ever gotten my wire. Surely he would have sent some answer by now. What if that telegraph operator in McComb had taken exception to the facts as I was reporting them?

And here I was, quite a sight, if anyone happened in to see me. I lay crosswise on the iron bed, naked, atop sweat-moistened sheets. I had tied a wet rag around my head; every half hour or so, I refreshed it with cool water from the washbasin.

But no one could win the battle against a Mississippi summer. Your only hope was to lie low and move as little as possible.

"Mr. Corbett."

At first I thought the voice came from the landing, but no, it came from outside.

Beneath my window.

"Mr. Corbett."

A stage whisper drifting up from three stories below.

I swung my legs to the floor, wrapped the top sheet around myself, and walked over to the window. I couldn't make out anyone in the mottled shadows under Maybelle's big eudora tree.

I called softly, "Who's out there? What do you want?"

"They sent me to get you," the voice said.

"Who sent you?"

"Moody Cross," he said. "Can you come?"

I didn't think it was a trap, but it paid to be careful. "What for? What does Moody want?"

"You got to come, Mr. Corbett." The fear in the voice was unmistakable. "They been another lynchin'."

"Oh God—where?"

"Out by the Quarters."

"Who is it?"

"Hiram," the man said. "Hiram Cross. Moody's brother is dead."

Chapter 62

I felt a deep surge of pain in my chest, a contraction so sharp that for a moment I wondered if I was having a coronary. Almost instantly I was covered with clammy sweat.

I heard the voice from outside again.

"Somebody overheard Hiram say that one day white folk would work for the black," the man whispered hoarsely. "Now Hiram swinging dead from a tree."

I felt the room beginning to turn—no, that was just my head spinning. I felt a strange chill, and a powerful force rising within me.

"Stand back," I said loudly.

"What's that, Mr. Corbett?"

"I said stand back. Get out from under this window!"

I heard branches strain and creak as the man obeyed.

Then I leaned my head out the window and threw up my supper.

Chapter 63

Moody did not shed a tear at her brother's funeral. Her face was an impassive sculpture carved from the smoothest brown marble.

Abraham fought to stay strong, to stand and set a brave example for all the people watching him now. And although he managed to control his expression, he could do nothing about the tears spilling down his face.

Swing low, sweet chariot.
Coming for to carry me home.

It must have been the hottest place on earth, that little sanctuary with one door in back and one door in front and no windows at all. It was the Mt. Zion A.M.E. Full Gospel church, three miles out of town on the Muddy Springs Road, and it was jammed to overflowing with friends and relatives.

Early in the service, a woman fainted and crashed hard to the floor. Her family gathered around her to fan her and lift her up. A baby screamed bloody murder in the back. Half the people in the room were weeping out loud.

But Moody did not cry.

Nobody knows the trouble I've seen.
Nobody knows but Jesus.
Nobody knows the trouble I've seen.
Glory hallelujah!

"I knew Hiram from the day he was born!" cried the preacher. "I loved him like a father loves his son!"

"Yes, you did!" shouted an old lady in the front row.

"Tell it, brother!"

"Amen!"

"I carried the baby Hiram to the river," the preacher went on, "and I dipped him in the river of life. That's right, I held him under the water of Jesus until he was baptized, and he come up sputtering, and then he was lifted up in the Holy Spirit and the everlasting light of Jesus—"

"That's right, Rev!"

"—so that no matter what might happen to Hiram, no matter what fate might befall him as he walked the earth, he would always have the Lord Jesus Christ walking right there by his side!"

"Say it, brother!"

"Now, children," the preacher said with a sudden lowering of his tone, "we know what happened to our son and brother Hiram Cross! We know!"

"Hep us, Jesus!"

"The white man done come for Hiram, done took him and killed him," the preacher called.

"We should think of our Lord, and how brave he was on that last night when he set there waiting for the Roman soldiers to come. He knew what was gonna happen. He knew who was coming for him. But he did not despair."

Instantly I found myself wanting to disagree, wanting to cry out, to remind him of the despairing words of Jesus on the cross, *My father, my father, why hast thou forsaken me?*

"Hiram was just that brave," said the preacher. "He didn't bow down or beg them to spare his life. He went along without saying a word, without letting them ever get a look at his fear. We should all strive to be as courageous as our brother Hiram."

"That's right!"

"The white man killed Hiram!" he hollered again. "But my friends, we are not like the white man! We cannot allow ourselves to be like that. The Bible tells us what to do. Jesus tells us what to do. It's plain to see. We have to do as Jesus did, we have to turn the other cheek."

There were groans from the congregation. It seemed to me that most of them had been turning the other cheek their entire lives.

Abraham's head had drooped until his chin was nearly resting on his chest. Moody continued to gaze straight ahead at the plain wooden cross on the rear wall.

"As the Lord tells us in Proverbs, *'Do*

not say, "I'll pay you back for this wrong!" Wait for the Lord, and he will deliver you.' God does not want us taking matters into our own hands.

"That is our charge, brothers and sisters. That is what the Lord tells us, in the book of Matthew: *'Love your enemies and pray for those who persecute you, that you may be sons of your Father in heaven.' "*

"How long, Brother Clifford?" came a voice from the back. "How long we 'posed to wait? Till the end of all time? How long?"

"We wait until the Lord makes his will clear," the preacher said calmly. "We wait like the children of Isr'al waited, forty years out in that desert."

The insistent voice spoke again:

"But how long? How long do we go on forgiving? How many of us got to die before it's time?"

And that is when I saw one shining tear roll down Moody's face.

We shuffled along, following behind Hiram in his pine box, out the narrow front door. The choir took up an old hymn.

I sing because I'm happy.
I sing because I'm free.
For His eye is on the sparrow
And I know He watches me.
And I know He watches me.

Chapter 64

A blinding light came. Then another bright flash.

We were leaving the church, just making our way down the rickety steps.

Another stunning flash of light came.

At first I thought it was lightning, then I realized lightning doesn't come from a clear blue sky. I blinked, trying to regain my power of sight, and then saw what was causing it: Scooter Willems and his camera, with its flash-powder apparatus.

Beside him were three large men I did not recognize, white men with twisted smiles on their faces, guns at their sides.

Moody left the line of mourners and marched straight over to Willems, right up to him.

“Show some respect,” she said to him. “This is my brother’s funeral.”

“Sorry, Moody,” Scooter said, almost pleasantly. “I thought you might want a photograph for your memory book.”

“I don’t need no photograph to remember this,” she said. “I’ll remember it fine.”

The pallbearers were sturdy young men about the same age as Hiram. They slid Hiram’s coffin onto the back of a buckboard. I made my way over to where Moody was glaring at Scooter and his bodyguards.

Scooter turned to me. “Moody’s all het up because I wanted to take a memorial photograph of the funeral.”

“Too bad you didn’t take a memorial photograph of the lynching,” Moody said. She turned on her heel and fell in step with the other mourners behind the wagon.

“Leave her alone, Scooter,” I said.

Scooter frowned. “Like I said, I just wanted to commemorate the event.”

I turned to leave, but Scooter wasn’t quite finished talking.

“Hey, Ben, how’s about I take one of you against this ocean of colored folks.”

I spun around at him. "Put your damn camera away. Go back to Eudora, where you belong. Leave these folks alone."

I noticed two little black boys listening to our conversation. As I turned to leave, Scooter spoke to them.

"Hey, little boys, I'll give you each a nickel to let me take your picture." He held out his hand with two nickels in it.

I pulled nickels out of my own pocket and handed one each to the boys. "Y'all run on," I said.

They did.

And I went to join Hiram's funeral procession.

Chapter 65

Abraham handed me a huge slice of chess pie. It was a southern funeral favorite because it could be made quickly, using ingredients most people kept on hand—milk, eggs, sugar, butter.

Abraham's house was overflowing with dishes and platters and baskets of food, and mourners eating as much as they could.

A question swam into my mind. How did Scooter Willems know Moody? I distinctly recalled him calling her by name, as if they were old friends. Were they? And how could that be?

I excused myself and threaded my way through the crowded little parlor, through the overpopulated kitchen, out the back door. I saw Moody sitting in the yard on an old tree stump, glaring at the ground.

"Moody," I said.

She did not acknowledge me.

I reached out to touch her shoulder. "Moody."

She pushed my hand away. "Don't put your *white* hand on my *black* shoulder," she said.

I drew back and put my hands in my pockets.

"Do you know Scooter Willems?" I asked.

She lifted her head and looked at me. "Who?"

"'Scooter Willems. That photographer from outside the church."

"I never seen that man in my life. He ain't nothin' but a buzzard, pickin' the meat off of dead people's bones."

"If you've never seen him, how did he know your name?"

"I don't know."

Moody looked into my eyes. For the first time since we'd met, she didn't look the least bit feisty or defiant. She looked downtrodden. Defeated. The heartbreak of Hiram's death had drained all the anger from her.

I put my hand on her shoulder again. This time she reached up and patted my hand.

"I've been going to funerals since I was a baby," she said. "This one is different. Ain't no 'peaceable joy' around here."

"What do you mean?"

"We used to burying the old folks," she said. "You know—after they lived a whole life. After they married and had their own kids, maybe even their grandkids. But lately, all these funerals for the young ones. And Hiram...I mean, Hiram..."

Moody began to cry.

"He weren't nothing but a baby himself," she said.

I felt tears coming to my own eyes.

"Here." I thrust the pie under her nose. "Eat some of this. You need to eat."

It was useless advice, I knew, but it was what I remembered my father saying to people at funerals. *Eat, eat...* Now I understood why he'd said it: he just couldn't think of anything else to say.

Moody took the plate from my hand.

Chapter 66

Moody was right. No "peaceable joy" came into Abraham Cross's house that day.

The bottle of moonshine was gradually consumed. The ham was whittled away until nothing but a knuckly bone was left on the plate. The pies shrank, shrank some more, then disappeared entirely. The afternoon lingered and finally turned into nighttime, with ten thousand cicadas singing in the dark.

I shook hands with Abraham. Moody gave me a quick little hug. I made my way through the remaining mourners, out the front door.

Fifty yards from the house, in front of the fig tree where I had parked the bicycle, stood three large white men. I couldn't make out details of their faces in that shadowy street, but I knew where I'd seen them: these were the same men who'd been standing with Scooter that afternoon at the Mt. Zion church when he took his photographs.

One of them spoke. "You looking for some trouble, Corbett?"

I didn't answer.

Looking back on it, I guess one man must have been smoking a pipe. I saw him move and smack something hard against the trunk of the fig. Sparks flew in a shower to the ground.

"We asked you a question," said the man in the middle. "Serious question."

"Abraham! Moody!" I yelled.

I don't know if they heard me. If they did, I don't know whether they came out of the house. In less time than it took for me to get my arms up, the three men were on me.

Kicked in the head. In the face. I tasted blood. I fell face-down on the ground, hard. A knee went into my stomach, fists whaling at me all over. Someone stomping on the side of my rib cage. I could not get my breath. Something tore into my neck. It felt like fire.

"Looks like you found it—*trouble!*" a man grunted, and drew back to get a better angle for kicking me. He delivered a stunning blow to my knee. I heard a cracking crunch and felt a wild sear of pain and thought he had shattered my right kneecap.

That was the last thing I remembered for a while.

Chapter 67

The next thing I was aware of—voices.

"You gotta use a higher branch. He's tall."

Something was in my eyes. *Blood.* I was blind from all the blood.

"Use that next branch, that one yonder," said a second man. "That's what we used when we hung that big nigger from Tylertown."

"He wasn't tall as this one. I can't hardly see up this high."

"Hell he wadn't. I had to skinny up the tree to put the rope way over."

Every inch of my body was experiencing a different kind of pain: sharp pain, dull pain, pain that throbbed with a massive pounding, pain that burned with a white-hot roar.

I thought, *It's amazing how much pain you can feel and still not be dead.*

"This nigger-lover is tall," the second man said, "but that 'un from Tylertown, he had to be six-foot-six if he was a inch."

I groaned. I think they were lifting me—hands under my armpits, digging into my flesh, cutting into me, dragging me off to one side.

A thud—something hurting my back. Then I felt the damp ground under me.

A crack—something landed hard on my left knee. I guessed that knee was shattered too.

"This rope is all greasy. I can't get aholt of it."

"That's nigger grease."

I felt the coarse hemp rope coming down over my face, dragging over my nose, tightening against my neck.

And I thought: *Oh, God! They're hanging me!*

Then I flew up into the air, like an angel—an angel whose head was exploding with terrible pain.

I could not see anything. I thought my

eardrums had burst from the pressure in my skull.

But they hadn't tied the noose right. Maybe the one who thought I was too tall was inexperienced. The rope was cutting under my jaw, but it had not gone tight. I got my hand up, somehow worked my fingers between the rope and my neck. I dangled and kicked as if I could kick my way out of the noose. *They are hanging you, boy,* was the chant that went through my head, over and over, like a song, an executioner's song.

Crack! I felt a sting on my back. Was it a bullwhip? A buggy whip? A willow branch?

"He's done. Or he will be," the voice said. "We can go. Let's get out of here."

The air smelled of woodsmoke. Were they going to burn me? Was I going to go up in flames now?

That heat grew and grew. I struggled to see through the blood. *It sure is hot up here. Maybe I'm already in hell. Maybe the devil has come and got me.*

"We better get out of here, J.T.," said the voice.

"Not yet."

"Listen to me. They're still awake over in the Quarters. They're angry."

"Let 'em come out here," the other man said.

"They'll be looking for Corbett. He's just like one of them."

"Yeah, he is. Just like a nigger. Wonder how that is?"

I heard the crack of a branch. The voices began to fade. The heat that had burned me alive began to fade away. Then I was alone. There were iron hands around my neck, squeezing and squeezing. No air. No breath. No way to breathe.

Oh, God. My mouth was so dry.

And then I was gone from the world.

Chapter 68

A few moments of consciousness. Then I blacked out again.

Awake.

Asleep.

Awake.

The wakeful times were a nightmare of confusion.

Terrible pain. There was something snapping at my feet, something with fierce sharp claws. Raccoons? Possums? A rabid fox? I didn't know if I was still alive.

I was surely dead for a while, then the bugs woke me with their biting, sucking my blood, little no-see-ums biting my neck and arms, mosquitoes big as bats sucking the blood from my veins, and then rats jumped onto my legs and ran up and down my body, squeaking, snapping at my privates.

Then a flash of light, so bright I saw the spackle of blood outlined on my swollen eyelids.

Was I dead? Was I in a different world? In my delirium I heard something. Maybe the angels singing. Or was it a dog barking—

Another flash, so bright it nearly shook me.

The pain in my skull increased. I felt the blood pumping through a vein in my forehead. I imagined it bursting, the blood running in a stream down my leg.

I tried to make a fist. *My fingers are gone!*

Oh my God. Maybe not. I couldn't feel anything on that side.

I couldn't taste the air.

I could only feel my tongue swelling up in my mouth, choking me. And my fingers were gone.

In my overheated brain I saw Mama at her desk, in that flowing white gown she wore under her housecoat. The violet inkstand, the silver pen. Mama smiled at me. "I think you'll like this poem, Ben. It's about you, baby."

I sat on my little stool in the room off her bedroom that smelled like lavender and talcum powder. I saw myself sitting there as if I were a figure in a drawing—a precise, detailed sketch of Mama and me.

Then the pain came swelling up through my chest, through my neck, and up into my brain.

Another flash of light.

And once again, nothing.

Chapter 69

Morning comes to a man hanging from a rope as it comes to a man sleeping in his bed—the chatter of birds, a faint breeze, the bark of a dog.

Then comes the pain again.

So much blood had clotted on my eyelids and eyelashes that I couldn't open them.

I breathed in short sharp intakes of air. The fingers of my right hand wedged into the rope had kept open just enough of a passage for a trickle of air down my windpipe. It had kept me alive. Or maybe *somebody* had spared me. Maybe the one who said I was too tall? Maybe someone I knew?

The rest of my body was pure pain: so

intense, so complete, that the pain now seemed like my normal state.

"Look, Roy, ain't no colored man. That man white."

The voice of a child.

"Dang," said another voice. "Look like they done painted him red all over."

A dog barked.

"Worms!" the first boy yelled.

I could only imagine what kind of horrible creatures were crawling on my skin.

"Worms!"

I felt something licking my foot. Then it barked.

"Worms! Get away from him, he *dirty!*"

Ahhh. Worms was the dog.

It was so hot. I should surely be dead by now. I think the pain radiating from my knees was keeping me alive. It wasn't that I had a will to survive.

I thought of stories from the war, wounds so horrible or amputations so unbearable that men begged their comrades to shoot them, to put them away. If I could speak, I would ask these boys to fetch a gun and shoot me in the head.

I felt something sharp poking my stomach. I must have flinched or jumped a little, and gave out a groan. The boys shrieked in terror.

"Oh, Jesus, the man alive!"

"Run!"

I heard them running as fast as they could, running away from the monster. I heard Worms barking as he ran after them.

I wanted to tell them to please come back and cut me down. Oh, how I wanted to lie on the ground just once more before I died.

That was not to be. I couldn't just hang here like this, waiting to die. The best I could hope for was to hasten it along.

I began wriggling my dead hand, trying to get it out from between the rope and my neck.

Part Four

"MY NAME IS HENRY"

Chapter 70

"My name is Henry."

I could barely hear.

"Can you hear me? I said my name's Henry."

I could barely see.

I could, however, tell that the person speaking to me was a *woman*. An ancient, bent-over colored woman.

"*Henry*. My name is *Henry*," she said. "You in there, Mist' Corbett?"

Most of her teeth were missing, producing a kind of whistly lisp as she leaned closer and spoke to me.

"Come on now, eat this," she said. She held out a spoonful of something. I opened my mouth. She stuck it in. God, it was delicious: black-eyed peas cooked to death, mashed to a paste.

While moving the food around my sore, battered mouth, my tongue discovered the gaping hole on the left side where two teeth had been.

"Where am I?" I croaked.

"Abraham house," Henry said. She poised another spoonful in front of my mouth.

I will never forget the taste of those peas. They remain to this day the single most wonderful food I have ever encountered.

I heard a familiar voice: "Now would you look at Mr. Corbett, settin' up and eatin' baby food all by himself." Moody came around from the head of the narrow cot where I lay, at the center of their parlor, in exactly the spot where Hiram's coffin had been.

Perhaps I was still in the midst of my delirium, but I thought she looked happy that I was alive and awake.

"This is Aunt Henry who been looking after you," she said.

"Henry?" I asked.

"Don't you be calling me Henrietta," she said.

Moody sat on the little footstool beside my bed. "You been through a pretty rough time, Mr. Corbett," she said. "When they cut you down, we just knew you was dead. But Papaw felt a pulse on your arm. So he run and got Aunt Henry. She's the one with the healing touch."

"Don't make him talk now, child," Aunt Henry said. "He still wore out." Every time I opened my mouth she stuck in more of the black-eyed-pea mush that was bringing me back to life, a spoonful at a time.

"She been pouring soup in you with a funnel," Moody said. "She done washed you and powdered you, shaved your face. When your fever went up, she sent me to the icehouse for ice to put in your bed. When the cut places started to scab, she put salt water on 'em so they wouldn't scar."

"How long have I been here?"

"Eight days since they cut you down," she said.

I felt the dull pounding ache in both knees. I remembered how those men had kicked my feet out from under me, then gone after my knees with the toes of their boots.

"Did they break my knees?"

Aunt Henry frowned. "Near 'bout," she said. "But you got you some hard knees. All battered up and cut up. But ain't broke."

"That's good." I managed a weak smile.

"It *is* good," Aunt Henry said. "Soon as you finish this here peas, you gonna have one more little nap, and then we gonna see if we can get you walkin'."

Moody said, "You'd best get him up *running,* Aunt Henry."

I shifted onto my side. "What do you mean?"

"The ones that hanged you gonna find you," Moody said. "Then they gonna hang you again."

Chapter 71

Aunt Henry was right. My knees weren't broken. But they certainly were not happy when called upon to do their job.

Armed with wobbly wooden crutches and a short glass of whiskey, I went for a late-afternoon stroll between Moody and Abraham. My body ached in a hundred different places, all tied together by the pain in my knees. When I bent my leg to take a step, the knee shot a white-hot arrow of pain to my hip. My neck was still raw from the rope, and the mangled fingers of my right hand were twisted and so blackish blue they might yet go gangrenous and have to come off. The sweat rolled down my back, into the swollen whip welts, stinging like fire ants.

But I kept on, hobbling down the muddy board walkway. I knew I was damned lucky to have survived, with no broken bones. My pain was nothing. It would be gone in a few days, or weeks at the worst. I could deal with that.

But inside, I felt another, more disturbing pain. I had been beaten and left for dead. I had disappeared from the world, and hardly anyone had come looking for me. I mattered to virtually no one. Meg. Elizabeth. My father. My daughters. Jacob, my childhood best friend. The entire town of Eudora. I had mostly been forgotten. A few people from town *had* come, good, kind folks. L. J. Stringer had actually visited a few times. But my own father hadn't come once.

"Abraham," I said. "Could I ask a favor?"

"Ask it," he said.

"Can you stop by Maybelle's and see if she's got any letters for me?"

He shook his head. "I went by this morning. Nothing there." Then he added, "Nothing for you from the White House, either."

I kept on, but the pressure of the

crutches under my arms was getting to be too much to bear. Everything from my neck down was one big aching mass of bruises.

"Does Maybelle know what happened to me?" I asked.

"Mr. Corbett, everybody in Eudora knows what happened to you. I'll tell you something I believe. There's good and bad in Eudora Quarters, good and bad in the town of Eudora—probably in equal numbers. Problem is, there's cowards in both places. That's why the bullies can have their way, Mr. Corbett."

"Abraham," I said with a sigh. "For God's sake. We've been through a good bit together. Would you please call me Ben?"

He patted my shoulder. "All right, Ben."

"Thank you."

"You welcome." He smiled. "But now you got to call me Mr. Cross." Abraham laughed out loud at that.

As I picked my way past the door of Gumbo Joe's, two old ladies looked up and waved at me. "I pray for you, sir," one of them said to me.

"Thank you, ma'am."

We went on a few more yards. “The colored folks appreciate what you was trying to do, Mist—Ben,” he said. “We know your heart is not the same as some the rest.”

Moody spoke up. “Yeah, and the white folks know it too. That’s why they goin’ to kill him.”

Chapter 72

"You just plain don't need me no more." Aunt Henry said it straight out as she dabbed at the wounds on my back with one of her secret potions.

"Fact is, Mist' Corbett, you hardly even got any scabs left on you," she said. "These is all healed up real good."

I twisted around on my chair to pull on my shirt, wincing from the pain.

"Now don't you be foolin' with me," Aunt Henry said. "You walkin' good with no crutch."

I knew she was right. Aside from the occasional shock of pain in my neck, or in my knees, I was feeling almost human again. I had no further need for Aunt

Henry's fussing and babying, which I had come to enjoy.

And it was time for me to go back to Eudora.

Frankly, I felt a bit reluctant to leave. There was something good about life as it happened in this modest little house. Certainly, the opportunity to see Moody every day was something I had enjoyed. But as much as that, I had enjoyed getting to know Abraham. With everything going against him—the death of his grandson, the increasing fear in the colored community, the lifetime of bigotry he had endured—Abraham was a man at peace with himself.

Just the night before, on a warm rainy evening when the mosquitoes were at their droning worst, we sat on a bench underneath the overhang of the porch.

We were working our way through a basket of hot corn muffins Moody had just brought out of the oven. I smiled up at her. She ignored me and turned back inside.

"Sometimes a man can sense something," Abraham said. "Something small that can blossom up into trouble."

"You mean, because we haven't heard from Roosevelt?" I asked. "I don't understand that at all. I almost got hanged for him."

"This got nothing to do with the president," he said, gazing off into the darkness. "I'm talking about another kind of business. Right here in my house."

I swallowed the rest of the muffin and wiped my mouth, inelegantly, on the back of my hand. I knew exactly what he was talking about. I had been hoping he wouldn't notice.

"Nothing has happened, Abraham," I said softly. "Nothing is going to happen."

He didn't look at me.

"I love that girl just about as much as I ever loved anybody," he said. "Including her mama. And including even my dear departed wife. As for you—well, I done took you into my house, hadn't I? That ought to show you, I hold you in high regard. You a fine man, Ben, but this just can't be. *It can't be*. Moody . . . and you? That is impossible."

"I understand that, Abraham. I don't think you ought to worry. Maybe you hadn't noticed, but Moody hasn't spoken a kind word to me since the day we met."

He put his hand on my shoulder.

"And maybe you hadn't noticed," he said, "but that's exactly how you can tell when a woman is in love with you."

Chapter 73

From the day after my hanging, someone was always awake and on guard at Abraham Cross's house. During the day and the evening, Abraham and Moody took turns keeping watch from the front-porch rocker. Since I was the cause of all this, I took the dead man's shift, from midnight till dawn.

Some nights I heard Abraham stirring, and then he would come out to sit with me for an hour or two.

One night, along about four a.m., I thought I heard his soft tread on the floorboards.

I looked up. It was Moody standing there.

"Mind a little company?" she said.

"I don't mind," I said.

She sat down on the bench beside the rocker. A foot or two away from me—a safe distance.

We sat in our usual silence for a while. Finally I broke it. "I've been busting to ask you a question, Moody."

"Wouldn't want you to bust," she said. "What is it?"

"Is that the only dress you own?"

She burst out laughing, one of the few times I'd made her laugh.

It was the same white jumper she'd worn the day I met her and every day since. Somehow it stayed spotless, although she never seemed to take it off.

"Well, if you really want to know, I got three of these dresses," she said. "All three just alike. Of all the questions you could have asked me, that's the one you picked?" she said. "You are one peculiar man, Mr. Corbett."

"I sure wish you would call me Ben. Even your grandfather calls me Ben now."

"In case you hadn't noticed, I don't do

everything he does," she said. "I'll just keep on calling you Mr. Corbett."

At first I thought it was moonlight casting that delicate rim of light around her face, lighting up her dark eyes. Then I realized that it was dawn breaking, the first streak of gray in the sky.

"I'll be moving back to Maybelle's tomorrow," I said. "It's time."

Moody didn't reply.

"It'll be better for Abraham once I'm out of here," I said. "And for you."

No answer.

I said, "The only reason those bastards come around is because I'm here."

Nothing. She stared out at the street.

"Thanks to y'all, I'm much better now. I'm feeling fine. I've got some decisions to make."

Her silence and stubbornness just went on and on, and I gave up trying to pierce it. I sat back and watched the gray light filling in all the blank dark spaces.

I think we sat another ten whole minutes without a word. The sun came up and cast its first shadows of the day.

At last Moody said, “You know I ain’t never gonna sleep with you.”

I considered that for a moment.

“I know,” I said. “Is it because I’m white?”

“No,” she said. “Because I’m black.”

Chapter 74

"I am just as sorry as I can be, Mr. Corbett, but we simply have no rooms available at this time," Maybelle said to me. "We are full up."

The dilapidated rooming house seemed strangely deserted for a place that was completely occupied.

"But Abraham came by and paid you while I was incapacitated," I said.

"Your money is in that envelope on top of your baggage," she said, pointing at my trunk and valises in a dusty corner of the center hall. "You can count it, it's all there."

"You accepted my money," I said, "but now that I need the room, you're throwing me out? That makes no sense."

Up till now, Maybelle had maintained her best polite southern-lady voice. Now the tone changed. Her voice dropped three notes.

"Look, I ain't gonna stand here and argue with the likes of you," she said. "I don't know how I could make it any clearer. *We got no rooms available for you*. So if you don't mind, I will thank you to go on and leave the house now."

"I can't carry this trunk by myself," I said.

"Why don't you get one of your nigger friends to help you," she snapped. "That's what I would do."

"I'll take the valises and send someone back for the trunk," I said.

I stuffed the envelope in my pocket, picked up a bag in each hand, and walked out into the blazing noonday sun of Eudora. Now what?

Sweet tea. That's what I needed, a frosty glass of tea. And time to think things through. I went to the Slide Inn Café and sat at my usual table. I sat there for almost twenty minutes. I could not seem to get the attention of a waitress. Miss Fanny wouldn't even meet my eye.

Oh, they saw me. The waitresses cast glances at me and whispered among themselves. The other customers—plump ladies in go-to-town dresses, rawboned farmers, little girls clinging to their mamas' skirts—they saw me too. When I dared to look back at them, they turned away. And I remembered what Abraham had said: *There's cowards in both places. That's why the bullies can have their way.*

Finally, Miss Fanny approached with a glass of tea, dripping condensation down its sides.

She spoke in a quiet voice. "I'm sorry, Mr. Corbett. We don't all feel the same way about you. Personally, I got nothing against you. I like you. But I ain't the owner. So you'd best just drink this tea and be on your way. You're not welcome here."

"All right, Miss Fanny," I said. "Thanks for telling me."

I drank the tea in a few gulps. I put a quarter on the table. I hoisted my valises and walked out into the street.

As I passed Miss Ida's notions shop, I saw Livia Winkler coming out.

"Miz Winkler," I said, touching the brim of my hat.

She suddenly looked flustered. Averting her eyes, she turned around and hurried back into the shop.

I crossed the street, to the watering trough in front of Jenkins' Mercantile. I scooped up a handful of water and splashed my face.

"That water is for horses, mules, and dogs," said a voice behind me. I turned.

It was the same fat redheaded man who with his two friends had jumped me at this very place, when they were holding those boys' heads underwater.

This time he held a branding iron in his hand.

I was too exhausted to fight. I was hot. I was still a bit weak and wobbly from everything I had been through. But Red didn't know that. I straightened up to full height.

"Use your brain," I said. "Turn around and walk away. Before I brand *you*."

We stared each other down. Finally he broke it off—shook his head in disgust, spat on the sidewalk near my shoes, and walked away. He looked back once. I was still there, watching him go.

Then I turned and headed in the direction of the one person in Eudora I believed would help me.

Chapter 75

"Well, damn, Ben! I could have used some warning, you know? I got about the biggest family and the littlest house in the whole town, and you want to move in here? Damn it all to hell, Ben!"

That was the warm greeting I got from Jacob Gill, my oldest friend in the world, my hope for a roof over my head that night.

"Sorry, Jacob," I said, "but I didn't know anywhere else to go."

He looked me over. I looked right back at him. Finally he crossed some line in his mind. He sighed, picked up one of my valises, carried it through the tiny parlor and into the tiny dining room.

"I reckon this is the guest room now,"

he said, and finally offered up a half smile. "I'll get some blankets; we can make a pallet on the floor—unless you want to sleep out in the smokehouse. Got nothing hanging in there, it might be more private for you."

"This will be fine," I said.

Jacob's house was a sad sight on the inside. The few pieces of furniture were battered old castoffs held together with baling wire and odd ends of rope. The cotton batting was coming out of the cushions on the settee. In the kitchen, a baby's cradle gave off an unpleasant aroma. A skinny cat nosed around the pantry, no doubt hoping to meet a mouse for lunch. Jacob said, "You want a drink?"

"Just some water would be good for me."

"The pump's on the back porch," he said. "I need me a finger or two myself."

He didn't bother to pour the whiskey into a glass. He pulled the cork and took a big slug right out of the bottle.

"Well, that's just fine, ain't it? Drinking straight from the bottle, and it ain't even lunchtime yet."

This observation belonged to Charlotte, Jacob's wife, who came in from the back porch with an infant in one arm and a pile of laundry in the other.

"Hello, Charlotte. Ben Corbett."

"Yeah, I know who you are." Her voice was cool. "I heard you were back in town."

"Ben's gonna be staying with us for a few days," said Jacob. "I told him he could sleep in the dining room."

"That's grand," Charlotte said. "That's just wonderful. That oughta make us the most popular family in Eudora."

Chapter 76

The second night I was at the Gill house, after a supper of leftover chicken parts and grits, Jacob suggested we go for "a walk, a smoke, and a nip."

First he poured whiskey from the big bottle into a half-pint bottle, which he stuck in his trouser pocket.

He walked and drank. I walked and looked anxiously down every dark alley.

"You sure are one hell of a nervous critter tonight," Jacob said.

"You'd be nervous too, if they beat you half to death and strung you up and left you for dead," I said. "Excuse me if I tend to be a bit cautious after almost being lynched."

A man came down the steps of the

First Methodist church, looking as if he had been waiting for us.

I recognized him: Byram Chaney, a teacher at the grammar school. Byram had to be well up in his seventies by now; I had thought of him as elderly years ago, when he was teaching me how to turn fractions into decimals.

"Evening, Jacob," he said. "Ben."

Jacob turned toward the streetlight to roll a cigarette. "I hope Byram didn't startle you, Ben," he said.

"Glad you could join us this evening, Ben," Byram said. "I think getting a firsthand look at things will be worthwhile for you. Jacob spoke up for you."

Suddenly I realized that Byram Chaney had, in fact, been waiting for us. I turned to Jacob to find out why.

"I haven't told him yet," Jacob said to Byram.

"Told me what?"

"You'd best go on and tell him," said Byram. "We'll be to Scully's in a minute."

I knew Scully as a man who owned a "kitchen farm" on the road south of town. Everybody who didn't have his own garden went to Scully's for whatever vegetables were in season.

"What's going on here, Jacob?"

"Calm down, Ben. We're just going to a little meeting. Me and Byram thought it might be a good idea if you came along. I *did* speak up for you."

"What kind of a meeting?"

"Just friends and neighbors," he said. "Keep your mind open."

"Pretty much half the people in town," put in Byram.

"But they don't like to be seen by outsiders," said Jacob. "That's why you'll have to wear this."

From his knapsack he pulled a white towel.

Then I realized it wasn't a towel at all. It was a pointed white hood with two holes cut for eyes.

I stopped dead in my tracks.

"A Klan meeting?" I said.

"Keep your voice *down*, Ben," Jacob said. "We're standing right here beside you. We can hear."

"You must be insane," I said. "I'm not going to any Klan meeting. Don't you know it's illegal? The Klan's been outlawed for years."

"Tell the sheriff," said Jacob. "He's a member."

As soon as I got over my shock at finding that my old best friend was a Ku Klux Klansman, I knew Chaney was right. I *had* to go along. This was exactly the kind of information Theodore Roosevelt had sent me down here to uncover.

Chapter 77

Through the holes in my hood I saw at least fifty men in white hoods and robes, walking in loose ranks along the dirt road. Jacob, Byram, and I fell right in with their step.

No one said anything until we were all inside Scully's large old barn and the doors had been closed.

One man climbed up on a hay bale and ordered everyone to gather around. I followed Jacob toward the back wall of the barn.

"Our first order of business," he said, "is to announce that we have a special guest attending our meeting this evening."

He waved his hand—*was he waving in*

my direction? There was no way he could know who I was, not under that hood.

Without a word Jacob reached over and snatched the hood off my head.

I stood revealed. The only man in the place without a mask covering his face.

A murmur ran through the crowd.

"Benjamin Corbett," said the man on the bale. "Welcome, Ben. You are among friends here. We're not the ones tried to hurt you."

I sincerely doubted that. But then he took off his hood and I recognized Winston Conover, the pharmacist who had filled our family's prescriptions for as long as I could remember.

One by one the men around me began taking off their hoods. I knew most of them. The Methodist minister. A farm products salesman. A conductor on the Jackson & Northern railroad. A carpenter's assistant. The county surveyor. The man who did shoe repairs for Kline's store. Sheriff Reese and his deputy. The man who repaired farm implements at the back of Sanders' General Store.

So this was the dreaded Ku Klux Klan.

As ordinary a group of small-town men as you're likely to come across.

"Ben, we appreciate you showing up to let us talk to you." It was Lyman Tripp. Jovial, chubby Lyman had the readiest smile in town. He was the undertaker, so he also had the steadiest business of anyone.

"Maybe you'll see that we ain't all monsters," he said. "We're just family men. We got to look out for our women and protect what's rightfully ours."

I didn't quite know what he meant by "rightfully ours."

Byram Chaney tied a gold belt around the waist of his robe. He climbed up on the hay bale from which Doc Conover had just stepped down.

"All right, let's get it started," he said.

The men stood around in their white sheets with their hoods off, conducting the most ordinary small-town meeting. They discussed the collection of dues, a donation they'd recently made to a widowed young mother, nominations for a committee to represent the local chapter at the county meeting in McComb.

Just when it began to seem as harmless as a church picnic, Byram Chaney said, "Okay now, there must be a recognizing of new business related to the niggers."

Doc Conover spoke up. "I had two colored girls come into the drugstore last week. They said they was up from Ocean Springs visiting some kin of theirs. They wanted to buy tincture of iodine. I explained to 'em, just as nice as I could, that I don't sell to coloreds. Then one of 'em started to lecturin' me on the Constitution. When I told her to get the hell out of my store, she said she'd come back with her daddy and her brother, and they'd *make* me sell 'em iodine."

"You say they's from Ocean Springs?" said Jimmy Whitley, the athletic coach at Eudora High.

"That's sure what they said."

"Johnny Ray, ain't you got a cousin in the chapter down in Ocean Springs?"

"I do, that's Wilbur Earl," said Johnny Ray.

Byram Chaney said, "Johnny Ray, why don't you talk to your cousin, find out who those girls might have been. Then we can see about getting 'em educated."

The crowd murmured in agreement.

Another man spoke. "I only want to report that that old nigger Jackie, you know, the one that used to drive the carriage for Mr. Macy? He come into my store again, looking for work."

I recognized the speaker as Marshall Farley, owner of the five-and-dime.

Jacob leapt to his feet and spoke with passion. "There you go," he said. "Niggers looking for jobs that belong to us! That old coon's had a perfectly good job all this time, driving for one of the richest men in the county. Now he wants more. He wants a job that could go to a fella like me, a good man with a family to feed."

In place of the polite murmur, a wave of anger now rolled through the crowd. I understood something new about these men. They weren't filled just with hate; they were filled with at least as much *fear*. Fear that the black man was going to take everything away from them—their jobs, their women, their homes, all their hopes and dreams.

Then I realized Jacob was talking about me. "So if you ask me, I think it's high time we teach our guest a thing or two," he was saying. "He needs to know we aren't just a bunch of ignorant bigots. I make a motion that we give over the rest of our meeting to the proper education of Ben Corbett."

I looked around and couldn't believe what I saw. Half a dozen men, in a rough circle, were coming right at me. Then they were upon me, and they had me trapped for sure.

Chapter 78

Feeling sick to my stomach now, my brain reeling, I rode in the back of an open farm wagon with Jacob, Byram Chaney, and Doc Conover. I was the one with hands bound behind his back.

Cicadas made a furious racket in the trees, their droning rhythm rising and falling. We were driving south out of town into the swamp, an all-too-familiar journey by now.

I was almost as terrified as I was angry. When I spoke to Jacob, I could barely keep from screaming.

"How could you do this? The one man I thought I could trust!"

"Stay calm, my friend."

"I'm not your friend," I said.

"Ben, you can't help it if you got some

mistaken ideas about us," he said. "You'll find out, we're nobody to be scared of. We're fair-minded fellows, like you. I just ask you to keep an open mind."

"By going to the swamp to watch you lynch another black man?"

"I said, *stay calm*."

After a time we came into a clearing. I could have sworn this was the place where somebody hanged me. Where I almost died. But it was a different spot altogether.

Two men in white robes stood near a crude wooden platform. Between them they held a man in place, with a rope around his neck.

His face was turned away from me.

"Let's go closer," Jacob said.

"This is close enough," I said.

But it wasn't my decision to make. Byram Chaney lifted his reins and drove the wagon into the clearing for a better view of the murder.

Slowly the man on the platform turned to face the crowd. He was a small man. Frightened. Pathetic. On his nose he wore gold-rimmed spectacles.

The man was white.

Chapter 79

"His name is Eli Weinberg," Byram Chaney told me in confidential tones. "He's a crooked little Jew from New Orleans. He talked three different widow ladies out of a thousand dollars each. He was selling deeds to some nonexistent property he said was down in Metairie."

"And he would have got away with all that money," Jacob said, "but the fellows found him yesterday, hiding in the outhouse at the McComb depot."

Eli Weinberg decided to speak up for himself. "Those are valid deeds, gentlemen," he said in a quavery voice.

"What are you doing?" I said. "You can't hang him, he might be telling the truth!" I felt my whole body shaking. "Why don't you look into what he says?"

"We did look into it," said Doc Conover. "We got word from our brothers that he's been fast-talking his way into towns all over this part of the country."

"So have him arrested," I said.

"This is better," Conover said. "We get the job done, no waiting, no money wasted on lawyers and trials and such. And we let them other Jews know they better think twice before coming to Eudora to steal from the likes of us."

"The likes of you?" I said. "Hell, you're all murderers!"

Eli Weinberg heard my voice. He twisted around in the hands of his captors to see who might have spoken in his defense. "Murderers! Yes, that man's right! You are all murderers!"

Jacob said, "You're missing the point, Ben. The Klan is here to fight against *all* injustice. We're not here just to educate niggers. We're here to educate anyone who needs educating."

I narrowed my eyes and shook my head. "You're crazy, Jacob. You and your friends are just a bunch of crazy killers."

Eli Weinberg shouted out, "Listen to him! He's right! You're all crazy killers!"

Those were the last words he spoke.

Someone jerked hard on the rope, and Eli Weinberg's body flew into the air. His cheeks inflated. His eyes bugged in their sockets. His face turned an awful dark crimson, then slowly faded to gray. Vomit spilled from his mouth. His body jerked and trembled horribly.

Within seconds he was dead.

A few seconds after that, the brilliant flash of Scooter Willems's camera illuminated the dark night.

Chapter 80

The hangman's bowie knife made quick work of the rope. They let Eli Weinberg's body fall to the ground with a thud. I had seen ailing farm animals put down with more respect.

"You reckon we oughta bury him?" a man said.

"Leave him where he lies," said Chaney. "He said he had a son in Baton Rouge. We'll get word to our brothers down there. The son can come fetch him."

"Jews are supposed to be buried before sundown on the day they die," I said.

"It figures you would know all about Jews," said Doc Conover.

Chaney climbed aboard the wagon

and took the reins. As we jolted out of the clearing, Jacob reached down to untie my ankles. "Turn around and let me do your hands," he said.

I will confess it—I felt a wash of relief. They didn't intend to kill me tonight.

Without any warning a stiff breeze swept over us, along with a spatter of oversized raindrops. The breeze died for a moment, then the rain was on us, lashing us with windy sheets of water.

I noticed that Doc's wet white robe had become translucent, so I could read his name stitched on the pharmacist's jacket he wore underneath.

"What you think, Ben?" Jacob asked as the wagon wheels slogged through the mud. "Is the Klan making a little more sense to you now?"

If Jacob hadn't been a friend my whole life, I would have punched him right then. "Listen to yourself, Jacob. You just killed a man. Do you hear me? *You killed him."*

I thought he was going to snap back at me, but the fire suddenly died in his eyes. He shook his head, in sorrow or disgust. He stared down at his callused hands.

"You . . . will . . . never . . . understand," he

said. "I'm a fool to even try. You're not like us anymore. You don't understand how things have changed."

"Let me tell you what else I don't understand," I said. "How you—the one I always thought was my friend—how could you do this to me, Jacob? Jacob, *I was your friend.*"

"I did it to help you," he said. "To keep you alive." His voice was weak, pathetic.

The rain was beginning to slacken. The wagon slowed to a stop outside Scully's barn, where the evening's festivities had begun.

"Come on, Ben," Jacob said in a low voice. "Let's go home."

"I don't think so." I turned away and set off walking in the direction of Eudora.

"Where the hell you going?" he called after me.

I didn't answer or even look back.

Chapter 81

A silk banner with elegant black letters ran the length of the wall.

WELCOME HOME, BEN

This was the banner that had hung in the dining room for the big family celebration the day I returned from my service in Cuba. Half the town turned out to cheer the decorated Spanish-American War veteran who had distinguished himself under the famous Colonel Theodore Roosevelt.

Now the banner was dingy, the silk stained brown with drips from the leaky roof. I was standing not in my father's house on Holly Street but in the “long house” out back, a former slave quarters.

It was to the long house that I had come after I left Jacob. It hadn’t housed an actual slave since well before I was born. At the moment it seemed to be serving as a storage room for every piece of castoff junk my father didn’t want in the house.

It was also home to the dogs, Duke and Dutchy, the oldest, fattest, laziest bloodhounds in all of Mississippi. They didn’t even bother to bark when I opened the door and stepped inside.

I lit an old kerosene lantern and watched the mice scurry away into corners. As the shadows retreated, I realized that all the junk piled in here was *my* junk. My father had turned the long house into a repository of everything related to my childhood.

The oak desk from my bedroom was shoved against the wall under the welcome banner. Piled on top of the desk were pasteboard cartons and the little desk chair I had used before I was old enough to use a grown-up one.

I lifted the lid of the topmost carton. A

musty smell rose from the books inside. I lifted out a handful: *A Boy's History of the Old South, My First Lessons in Arithmetic,* and my favorite book when I was a boy: *Brass Knuckles, Or, The Story of a Boy Who Cheated.*

Next to the desk stood my first bed, a narrow spool one decorated by my mother with hand-painted stars. It was hard to believe I'd ever fit on that little bed.

In the far corner was another pile of Benjamin Corbett's effects: football, basketball, catcher's mitt, slide trombone, the boxer's speed bag that once hung from a rafter in the attic.

I lifted the corner of a bedsheet draping a large object, and uncovered the most wonderful possession of my entire childhood: a miniature two-seater buggy, made perfectly to scale of white-painted wicker with spoked iron wheels. I remembered the thrill it gave me when our old stable hand Mose would hitch up the old mule, Sarah, to my buggy. He would lift me onto the driver's seat and lead the mule and me on a walk around the property. I must have been all of six or seven.

Before I knew what was happening, I was crying. I stood in the middle of that dark, musty room and let the tears come. My shoulders shook violently. I sank down to a chair and buried my head in my hands. I was finally home—and it was awful.

Chapter 82

A familiar voice brought me out of a deep sleep. These days I came awake instantly, and always with an edge of fear. It was only when I blinked at the two figures smiling down on me that I was able to relax.

"Near 'bout time for breakfast," said Yvella, my father's cook. Beside her was Dabney, the houseman. Each held a silver tray.

"Way past time," said Dabney. "In another hour it'll be time for dinner."

Among the items on Dabney's tray were a silver coffeepot emitting a tendril of steam from its spout and a complete place setting of Mama's best china.

Yvella's tray offered just about every

breakfast item known to southern mankind: grits, fried eggs, spicy link sausage, homemade patty sausage, griddle cakes with sorghum syrup, a basket of baking-powder biscuits, butter, watermelon pickles, and fig preserves.

"Yvella, you don't expect me to eat all this?"

"Yes, suh, I sure do," she said. "You too damn skinny."

"I *have* lost some weight here recently," I said and rolled my eyes.

"Yeah, I heard all about it," she said.

"How'd y'all know I was here . . . *in the guest quarters?*"

"Duke come and told me," Dabney said.

I realized that I was standing in front of them shirtless, wearing only my drawers. I looked around for my clothes.

"Don't you worry about it, Mister Ben," Yvella said. "I seen plenty worse than that. I took your clothes to the wash."

Dabney brought over a filigreed iron tea table I remembered from Mama's flower garden.

"I didn't tell your daddy you's here," he said. "I figure you'd want to tell him yourself. But why don't you come on and sleep in the house, Mister Ben. That big old house just rattling around with hardly nobody in it, you out here sleepin' with the dogs."

"We'll see," I said. "Thank you for the invitation."

Along with the coffee, Dabney had brought me a straight razor, shaving soap, a tortoiseshell comb and brush, and a stack of fresh clothing—my old clothes, laundered and folded. I was probably skinny enough to fit into them now.

"God bless you both," I said.

"You the one that needs the blessin', from what I hear," Yvella said. "You best keep out of trouble."

"I will try," I said. "Listen, I have a favor to ask both of y'all."

"Your father don't need to know, and we ain't gonna tell him," said Dabney.

"The same goes for me," said Yvella. "And now I got a favor to ask of you."

"What is it?"

"Would you eat them damn biscuits before they get cold?"

Chapter 83

As soon as I poured the last of the coffee, Duke and Dutchy started barking—insistent, urgent, annoying barks. They ran up and down along the wall underneath the cobwebby window.

I went over and was astonished to see Elizabeth in the bushes and with her none other than L. J. Stringer.

I motioned for them to go around to the front door.

"Damn, Ben," L.J. said, "if we wanted to come through the front door, we would have done it in the first place."

I shut the door behind them. "How'd you even know I was here?"

They looked annoyed at my stupidity.

"Don't you think those Klan boys had

somebody follow you home last night after their meeting? The whole town knows, Ben. Everybody knows who you are and where you are. *All the time*."

I felt stupid. Of course they had followed me.

L.J. straightened. "Ben, let me put it to you as simply as I know how. *Your life is in danger*."

"He's right. Actually, it's a miracle you're still alive," said Elizabeth. She reached out and touched my shoulder, eyes wide with concern.

L.J. spoke in a no-nonsense voice. "People are really angry, Ben. I mean *angry*. You forget what a small town this is. Folks know you're up to something, and whatever it is, you ain't here to make them look good."

"I don't have to defend myself, L.J. There's murder going on in this town. Hell, I've seen six people with my own eyes who've been murdered, just in the short time since I got here! They nearly killed me, just for seeing what I saw."

Elizabeth spoke, her voice as gentle as L.J.'s was harsh.

"Ben, these are, or were, your neighbors," she said. "These are your friends. Most of them are good, decent people."

"Elizabeth, I don't see anything decent about men who murder innocent people. You put neighborliness ahead of simple humanity? Forgive me if I disagree."

I realized that I probably sounded like a defense attorney pleading a case. Another hopeless one?

L.J. seemed to read my mind. "No point in discussing it any further," he said. "We came here because we're afraid for you, Ben. We want to try to help. It's just a matter of time before they come for you again. And hang you good. I'll figure out some way to keep you safe."

"Thank you, L.J., Elizabeth. I really do appreciate your concern. More than you can possibly know."

"Until then, Ben, listen to me. *Do not trust anyone.* And that means *anyone*."

I knew that "anyone" included Jacob Gill, and even my father. It probably meant Dabney and Yvella too. But did it also mean the very people giving me this cautionary advice? Could I trust L.J. and Elizabeth?

"We'd best be on our way," L.J. said. "Isn't there a back door out of here?"

I pointed to it.

"Don't forget what I said, Ben. Keep your head down."

L.J. opened the little door that let onto the alley. He glanced around, then turned back. "Nobody around. Let's go, Elizabeth."

She turned to me with a smile that spoke of her concern.

"Ben, please let us help. We're your friends. Maybe your only friends."

Chapter 84

Almost midnight. Another knock came on the rear door of the long house.

I shot the bolt and the door swung open.

Moody Cross was standing there in a white jumper. And not a little terrified. She pushed past me and slammed the door shut.

"Papaw sent me."

"I guess my secret hiding place is the worst-kept secret in Mississippi," I said.

She was out of breath. "We need help. A lady from the Slide Inn sent her colored girl out to warn us. Said they's a group of men coming out to kill me and Papaw and Ricky."

"Who's Ricky?"

"My cousin, you met him at the funeral. He got run out of Chatawa, where he lived all his life. He been staying with us since you left—you know, like for protection."

Now I remembered him, a boy about the same age as Hiram, with a family resemblance to Hiram and Moody.

"What happened in Chatawa?" I asked.

"Two white men said they saw Ricky staring at a white woman. Said he was *thinkin'* evil thoughts. I guess some white folks can even see inside of a black boy's brain. There's this group of 'em—the White Raiders, is what they call 'em up there. They s'posed to be the ones coming to get us."

This seemed like more than coincidence. The horror raining down upon Abraham's family simply would not stop, would it?

"There's something else."

What else could there possibly be?

"Papaw is sick," she said. "He can't get out of his bed, got the fever and the shakes, and Aunt Henry's been there nursing him."

Moody started to cry, and I remembered something Mama always used to say: *When the time comes you want to start crying, that's the time to start moving.*

It was time for me to go get L.J. and Elizabeth.

Chapter 85

L. J. Stringer's six-seater spring wagon flew down the road, stirring the motionless air of a sticky-hot Mississippi night.

"You're going straight to hell, Ben Corbett, and you're taking me with you!" L.J. raised his crop to urge on his team.

As soon as I had gotten Moody to stop crying, we'd sneaked over to the Stringer place and surprised the whole household with our late-night knock on the kitchen door. I'd asked L.J. to help me protect Abraham, Moody, and Ricky. He'd listened and he hadn't hesitated. "I said I'd help you, Ben, and I will."

Yes, he'd heard of the White Raiders. Yes, he knew them to be a gang of killers. Finally he sighed heavily and sent his man Luther out to hitch up his team.

And now here we were, bumping and rolling our way out to Abraham's house in the Quarters. Crammed together on the back bench were Moody, Luther Cosgrove, and his brother Conrad.

Luther and Conrad were L.J.'s assistants—"my man Friday and his brother Saturday," he joked—on call twenty-four hours a day to do whatever the boss wanted done. They drove Allegra Stringer on her errands. They ran packages to McComb and Jackson and Shreveport. If L.J. needed anybody "brought into line," as he put it, it was the Cosgroves who did the bringing.

"What we're doing here is extremely foolish," said L.J. "You know that?"

"I know that," I said. "But if we don't help these people, nobody will. And they're all going to die."

L.J. shrugged and said, "Well, we can't have that. This has to stop somewhere. Might as well be right here and right now."

Chapter 86

Poor Abraham was in the parlor of his house, sleeping fitfully when we arrived. Half a dozen men came from the Quarters, as volunteers, even though they had only a couple of rifles. "Guarding Father Abraham," that's what they called it. Abraham was that beloved here.

As it turned out, the White Raiders didn't come that first night, but we continued guarding Father Abraham. As the sun went down the second evening, L.J. and I took our places on the porch. We'd been friends for a long time, but he'd gotten better and better with the years, the exact opposite of Jacob.

I arranged the other men as carefully as a Civil War general planning his lines of defense. I put two of the new men on the roof, despite Moody's protest that the sheets of tin were so old and rusty that they would almost certainly fall through.

Then L.J. dispatched five of the men in an enfilade line among the old willow trees at the edge of the woods.

"Stay awake. Stay alert," he told everyone. "Don't leave your post for any damn reason. If you need to pee, just do it in place."

As the second night watch began, our fears were as high as on the first.

Around eleven L.J. and I decided a finger of sour-mash whiskey was what our coffee needed to take the edge off. After midnight Moody came out with a fresh pot. She told me Abraham was awake.

Through the window I saw him propped up on his pillow. Between his hands he held a bowl of steaming liquid, which he raised to his lips.

"How's he doing?"

"He's got a little more energy tonight. But I ain't getting my hopes up. Aunt Henry says he's on his way."

I nodded and walked inside.

"How are you feeling, friend?" I asked.

He smiled. "How are *you,* is the question," he said. "I ain't doing nothing but laying on this bed, trying not to die. You the one doing somethin'."

"I'll keep doing my job, as long as you do yours," I said.

I was surprised how sharp he seemed, and I seized the opportunity.

"Still no word from the White House, Abraham," I told him. "Makes me angry."

"The Lord and the president, they both work in mysterious ways," he said.

"How did you ever come to know him, Abraham?" I asked. "The president, that is."

"Mr. Roosevelt's mama was a southern lady, you know. Miss Mittie. From over where I'm from, in Roswell, Georgia. And see, my sister Annie went to work for Miss Mittie, eventually went with her up to New York. She was still up there, nursing Mittie, the day she died. Died the same day as Mr. Roosevelt's first wife, Alice. Did you know his mama died the same day as his wife? I was there that day, helping Annie. That was a terrible day. I guess he never forgot it."

"*Ben!*" L.J. shouted. "The sons o' bitches are here! They're *everywhere!*"

From all around the cabin came a clatter of hooves, then an explosion of gunfire.

I lunged for the front door. I was almost there when one of the Raiders came crashing through the roof, landing on my back.

Chapter 87

Bullets were whizzing through the air as the confused-looking man picked himself up off the floor, still clutching a scrap of rusted tin he'd brought with him on his fall through the roof.

L.J. ran into the house and aimed a rifle at the fallen Raider. "Get the hell out of here or die. I see you again, you die!"

In the darkness outside I could see eight men wheeling about on horses. They wore no sheets, no hoods. They weren't bothering to hide themselves. I recognized the redheaded troublemaker I'd encountered at the trough in front of Jenkins' Mercantile.

One lout, on a big dappled quarter horse, must have weighed in at four hundred pounds. The horse struggled to keep from collapsing.

The fat man was agile, though, hopping down from his saddle like somebody a third his size. The other Raiders were getting down too, yoking their horses together.

One aimed his shotgun at the house. *Ka-blam!*

"Goddammit," L.J. grunted. He poked the barrel of his fine hand-carved rifle through the window, squeezed the trigger, and dropped the shooter in his tracks.

This was war, just like I remembered it from Cuba, except the enemy was from my own town.

L.J. called, "Take the back of the house, Ben!" So I ran to the tiny kitchen and onto the stoop.

Behind the trunk of a giant pecan tree stood Ricky, with his shotgun trained across the yard on an oak where a White Raider huddled with his rifle trained on him.

Neither of them had a clear shot, but they were banging away at each other, riddling each other's tree trunk with bullets and squirrel shot.

As I burst headlong onto that stoop, I presented a clear target for the White Raider.

He swung his gun toward me, and time seemed to slow down while I watched him turn. He squeezed off a shot. I saw the spark of the bullet strike a rock near the stoop.

The man ducked behind the oak, but he was big enough that the trunk didn't entirely conceal his belly. I braced my pistol hand on my other arm and fired.

I got him, and he hit the dirt with a thud, screaming, holding his abdomen.

His fellow Raiders had circled behind the house in a ragged line, and now attacked, sweeping the ground with gunfire, round after round. These men had come well armed; they were good with their guns. I remembered that Colonel Roosevelt called this kind of fighting "sweep in and sweep up," a strategy, he said, that was "generally used by butchers and fools."

These fools were shooting and yelling as they came, catcalling, "We got you now, niggers!" and "Run, boy! Look at him go!"

A shout came from the swamp: "They got Roy! Goddamn niggers done shot Roy!" This news provoked a fresh round of shooting. L.J. glanced at me; we had the same thought at the same instant.

We waited until the last shot, when all their weapons were unloaded at the same time.

Then we charged around the house, weapons leveled at the Raiders. "*Drop 'em!*" L.J. hollered.

They obliged, and I rushed to pick up the rifles, yelling, "Don't move—not one of you move!"

Soon two of the black men who'd been concealed along the fence line appeared, lugging a prone, struggling Raider they had lassoed and hog-tied.

"Where y'all want this one?"

"Put him down right here by the rest," said L.J.

When they came riding in, the Raiders hadn't realized they were outnumbered, but they were finding it out now. I saw a couple of smart ones leap on their horses and ride off.

But here came the huge fat man, lumbering around the side of the house with a shotgun in one hand, a pistol in the other.

"Drop your guns!" L.J. yelled.

The fat man did not obey. Instead, he pulled the trigger on the pistol. The bullet hit L.J. in the right cheek. I swear I heard the crack of his cheekbone breaking, then he fell to the ground.

I fired at the fat man and he went down hard. Stayed down, didn't move.

"L.J.! Are you all right?" I knew he was not.

"Oh, hell, yeah," L.J. said. "The damn thing just grazed me." I could plainly see that it had taken a sizable chunk of flesh out of his cheek; blood oozed down his chin. That side of his face was black with gunpowder.

I heard more commotion in front of the house, then hoofbeats. The remaining Raiders had taken this opportunity to get the hell out of there.

"Moody!" I called.

There was no answer.

L.J. made a kind of whistling sound as

he breathed through the new hole in his cheek.

"Moody, they're gone! Come on out now, I need you!"

Again all was silent.

"You'd better . . . go see . . . ," L.J. mumbled.

I rushed through the back door and stopped short at the threshold of the parlor. Abraham lay on his bed with the long barrel of a pistol pointed at his head. The man holding it had his other arm around Moody in a choke hold.

"You stop right there, Corbett," said the Raider. "They's nothin' would give me more pleasure than to finish off this old troublemaking nigger, and then you."

I didn't move.

I didn't have to.

I watched Moody's hand gliding into the pocket of her jumper. She pulled out a kitchen knife and in one smooth motion plunged it into the White Raider's back.

Chapter 88

"Ben Corbett here is a well-known nigger-lover, so I don't expect him to know any better—but L.J., *for the love of God*, I never in this world thought I would find *you* pulling such a stunt."

It was four in the morning, and we were standing in the dogtrot of the log cabin that belonged to Phineas Eversman and his family. Phineas was the chief of the Eudora police department, which consisted of him, Mort Crowley, and Harry Kelleher, who worked only part-time.

"Just hear us out, Phineas," L.J. said. When he lifted the bloody rag from his face, his voice had a sickening whistle in it. "Your town is out of control."

"Look, Phineas, you can call me every

name in the book," I said. "You can hate me and everything I stand for, but we still have five men in the back of our wagon who attacked and murdered innocent people in the Quarters tonight. We are witnesses, and we are here to swear out a formal complaint against these men. That means you are required by law to arrest 'em, hold 'em, and see that they're brought to trial for murder."

Eversman looked past me and out the front door. In the back of the wagon he saw five White Raiders tightly bound, hand and foot, by the very ropes they had brought with them for hanging Negroes.

Standing guard over these men were Cousin Ricky and eight of the ten surviving volunteer guards. Luther Cosgrove and a man named Jimmie Cooper had been gunned down. The captured men had laughed and hooted all the way downtown, promising us that their pal Phineas Eversman would soon set them free.

"Now, wait a minute, Corbett," said Phineas. "The first thing out of your mouth was that you and these Nigras killed some of the men."

"They attacked us!" I bellowed. *"We had to fight back or we'd all be dead! Are you listening?"*

"There's no need to get ugly," said Phineas. His voice was mild, but his eyes kept flicking outside to the tied-up men, as if he were weighing the risks on all sides.

L.J. pressed the bloody cloth against his cheek. "Phineas, you listen to me, now," he said quietly. "It's time, Phineas. It's time to put an end to it—the violence, all the hatred against coloreds in this town. These Ku Kluxer gangs are tearing Eudora apart, limb from limb. People are living in fear, black and white. You know me, Phineas. I've lived here all my life. I was there tonight. I saw what happened. I demand as a citizen of this town that you arrest these men for murder. Right now."

Eversman pulled his chenille bathrobe snug around his skinny body. He refashioned the knot in the belt, then made his way past us, outside to the wagon.

"Evenin', Phineas," said one of the Raiders with a chuckle. "I sure am sorry these bastards decided to wake you up for no good reason."

Eversman didn't laugh. He didn't even smile. I thought I heard a quiver in his voice, but he spoke loud and clear.

"You men are under arrest for...for trespassing, assault with a deadly weapon, and...and..."

He couldn't seem to get the words out, so I helped him.

"And first-degree murder."

Eversman glanced at me. He swallowed hard. "And first-degree murder," he said.

The men set up a howl. A dour, wiry man yelled, "Because that nigger-lover Corbett says so?"

Eversman's voice had lost its tremor. "And because his complaint is supported by our most upstanding citizen, Mr. Stringer," he said.

"Mr. Stringer is indeed upstanding," I said. "But Chief Eversman will also find that my complaint is fully and completely supported by a person even more esteemed than L. J. Stringer, if you can imagine that."

The wiry man in the wagon cast an ugly eye on me. "And who the hell that?"

"His name," I said, "is Theodore Roosevelt."

Part Five

THE TRIAL AT EUDORA

Chapter 89

Jackson Hensen, the harried senior personal assistant to the president, entered the Oval Office with a bloodred leather folder under his arm. He took one look at the president and dropped the folder. The morning's correspondence scattered all over the carpet—telegrams and official greetings from the king of England, the shah of Persia, and the Japanese ambassador, letters from congressmen, ordinary citizens, and all manner of federal bureaucrats.

"Har-de-har-har!" The president was laughing and singing. Also, he was dancing a jig. He was waving a golden Western Union telegram in the air as he capered in a circle behind his desk.

"Is anything the matter, sir?" Jackson Hensen asked.

"Does it look like there's anything the matter, Hensen?"

"Well, sir, I've never actually seen you dancing, except at state dinners. Never at your desk."

"This is the first time I've ever been happy enough to dance at my desk," Roosevelt said. "Read this." He thrust the telegram at Hensen and collapsed onto a sofa, out of breath, but still chuckling and congratulating himself.

Hensen scanned the telegram. It was stamped 11:50 p.m. of the previous night, signed CROSS AND CORBETT, and originated from a telegraph station in McComb, Mississippi. The report described in detail events that had occurred during the previous several days—lynchings, Klan meetings, the attack of the White Raiders, the gun battle, the arrest of three Raiders on charges of first-degree murder.

It was this last piece of information that so delighted the president.

"There it is!" Roosevelt shouted. "White men charged for killing black men, right down there in the heart of Dixie. Now let Du Bois and that Wells-Barnett woman try to tell me I have ignored the Negro problem!"

Hensen's eyes came up from the telegram. "It is excellent news, sir."

"Worth dancing about, Hensen?"

"Well, sir . . . certainly."

For a moment Jackson Hensen feared that President Roosevelt was going to make him dance.

"Do you know why I am *fortunate* enough to receive this most excellent news, Mr. Hensen?"

"Why is that, sir?"

Roosevelt peered around the sofa. "Where'd you go, Hensen?"

"I'm here, sir. Picking up the mail."

"Never mind that, Hensen. Get your pad, will you? I gave Margaret the afternoon off. I want to send my congratulations to Abraham Cross and Ben Corbett. What shall it be, then, a letter or a wire?"

Hensen took a little notebook and pencil from his vest pocket.

"Those men must have thought I'd forgotten all about them." He laughed, a big booming Roosevelt laugh. "I think

I showed great wisdom *not* to respond to their first report, but to let them draw their own conclusions as to what should be done."

"Yes, sir, it most certainly was wise of you." Hensen was often amazed at the depth and breadth of the president's self-regard. He licked the point of his pencil. Roosevelt perched on the edge of his desk, mindful of the fine figure he cut as he dictated his message of congratulations.

"What a magnificent ending to this project!" the president exclaimed.

Chapter 90

Phineas Eversman's first act was to release two of the five prisoners. He told us it was for lack of evidence, but I assumed there was some family connection. (There had to be; this was Mississippi.) I was so surprised and impressed that the chief had actually arrested the other three men that I offered no word of protest.

The three still in custody were named Chester Madden, Henry Wadsworth North, and, ironically enough, Lincoln Alexander Stephens, a man whose name evoked both the Great Emancipator and the dwarfish vice-president of the Confederacy. Henry North was the redheaded bully I'd encountered before, at Jenkins' Mercantile.

Some folks called it "the Niggertown Trial." Others called it "the White Raiders Trial." The *New Orleans Item* dubbed it "That Mess in Eudora." Whatever people called it, everyone was obsessed with it.

The citizens of Eudora were divided on the issues, but they certainly weren't *evenly* divided. A small group welcomed the prospect of punishment for the violent, night-riding Raiders. But many folks, unbelievable as it might seem, thought the Raiders were being treated unfairly.

The *Eudora Gazette,* a weekly four-sheeter usually devoted to social notes, was now publishing five days a week, churning out a breathless new front-page report on the White Raiders Trial every day. The formerly lazy and slow-moving editor, Japheth Morgan, was a whirl of energy, placing expensive telephone trunk calls nearly daily to consult with his "unimpeachable sources of information in the capital."

Japheth Morgan had never worked this hard before. He was losing weight and smoking cigarettes, one after another. He had dark circles under his eyes.

"You'd best settle down a bit, Japheth," L.J. told him. "This trial could end up being the death of you."

"But you don't understand," Japheth answered. "For me and for the *Gazette,* this isn't the opportunity of a lifetime, it's the trial of the century!"

The trial of the century.

As soon as he said it, I knew it was true. This *was* the trial of the century—not just for Eudora, not just for Mississippi, but for the entire country.

Chapter 91

"Notice how nobody complains about the heat anymore," L.J. said to me one morning over breakfast at his home. "Nobody talks about the mosquitoes, or the price of cotton, or any of the things that mattered before. None of those things means a damn now. All anybody cares about is the trial."

I had to smile. "I wouldn't know what you're talking about, L.J., since nobody in this town speaks to me."

"Maybe they're like me, they just hate talking to a damn lawyer."

I'd been given a bedroom on the second floor at L.J.'s, with a sitting room attached and a small balcony where my first cup of coffee was served every morning. There were fresh sheets, starched and ironed, every day; the best sausages for breakfast, aged beef for supper.

Most important, L.J. posted three armed guards around the house: one at the front, one in the back, and one baking on the roof. At L.J.'s I'd gotten the first really good night's sleep I'd had since coming back to Eudora.

L.J.'s wife, Allegra, bustled into the dining room.

"Japheth Morgan insists on seeing you two right now," she said.

Indeed, Morgan did mean *right now*. He had followed Allegra and was standing directly behind her. In his hand was a fresh broadsheet, the ink still shiny. At the top of the page I saw in enormous type the word EXTRA!!!

"I thought you two gentlemen would want to be the first to read this," Morgan said.

L.J. shook his head. "What the hell have you done now, Japheth?"

Morgan began to read aloud. "The Mississippi Office of Criminal Courts has announced the venue and date for the proceedings currently known far and wide as the White Raiders Trial. Following a ruling by the Mississippi Supreme Court, the prosecutor's petition for change of venue has been denied, and the trial will be held in Eudora, Mississippi, scene of the alleged offenses."

"Well, hell, that's no big surprise," L.J. said. "We all knew nobody else wanted to grab hold of this hot horseshoe."

"I agree," I said. "It's disappointing, but it does provide the prosecution with its first proper grounds for appeal."

"Appeal to whom?" said L.J. "The Supreme Court has ruled."

"There's another Supreme Court, in Washington," I said with a wink.

Japheth looked relieved. "Do y'all want to hear this or not?"

"Please," L.J. said, straightening his face into a serious expression. "Please read on."

"Jury selection will begin on September the seventeenth at nine o'clock a.m.," he read.

"Goddamn, what is that, *next Monday?* That's six days from today," L.J. said. "Ben, you're gonna have to scramble."

"Wait. Wait. Wait," Japheth said.

He read slowly, emphatically:

"Further, the Supreme Court has exercised its judicial discretion to appoint a judge to oversee this important and much-noted trial. The judge appointed is..."

Japheth glanced over to make sure we were listening. We absolutely were.

Then he read on:

"The judge appointed is a lifetime citizen of Eudora, the Honorable Everett J. Corbett."

Chapter 92

Son of a bitch!

It was not illegal for the Mississippi Supreme Court to appoint my father to preside over a trial in which I was assisting the prosecution.

Not illegal, but wildly unusual, and absolutely deliberate.

I could have fought it, but I already knew that I wouldn't. It gave us a second, decent ground for the eventual, inevitable appeal.

Most people in town, Japheth reported, were positively *delighted* with the news. Everyone knew that Judge Corbett was "fair" and "honest" and "sensible." Judge Corbett "understands the true meaning of justice."

"That is exactly what I am afraid of," I said.

Having spent the first part of my life listening to my father pontificate, I knew one thing for certain: he might cloak himself in eloquence, reason, and formality, but underneath it all he believed that although Negroes might be absolutely free, thanks to the detested Mr. Lincoln, nowhere was it written that Negroes deserved to be absolutely equal.

Judge Corbett and men of his class had gradually enshrined that inequality in law, and the highest court in the land had upheld its finding that "separate but equal" was good enough for everybody.

Now the trial was less than a week away, and one huge question was still outstanding: who would the state of Mississippi send to prosecute the case?

"My sources in the capital have heard nothing about it," Japheth told L.J. and me. "It's a big, holy secret."

Chapter 93

A while later, the three of us were sitting on the west veranda of L.J.'s house, watching the sunset and sipping bourbon over cracked ice.

"Well, you gentlemen are always acting so all-fired high and mighty," Japheth said, "but you've yet to give me a single piece of information that I can use. Why don't you start by sharing the names of the prosecution witnesses?"

"Watch out, L.J., he's using one of his journalist's tricks to get you to spill it," I said.

"Me?" L.J. scoffed. "What do I know? I don't know anything. I've been cut off by the entire town. I'm almost as much persona non grata as Mr. Nigger-Lover

Corbett. Everybody from here to Jackson knows whose side I'm on. And you know any friend of Ben Corbett's doesn't have another friend between here and Jackson."

I clapped his shoulder. "I appreciate what you've done, L.J."

It was right then that we heard a deep tenor voice, with a hint of something actorly in the round tones, accompanying a firm bootstep down the upstairs hall.

"If you need a friend from Jackson, maybe I can fill the bill."

We looked up to see a man whose appearance was as polished and natty as his voice. He wore a seersucker suit of the finest quality and a straw boater with a jaunty red band. He could not have been much more than thirty, and he carried a wicker portmanteau and a large leather satchel jammed with papers.

He introduced himself as Jonah Curtis and explained that he had been appointed by the state of Mississippi to prosecute the White Raiders.

"I had my assistant reserve a room at Miss Maybelle's establishment," he said.

"But Maybelle took one look at me and it turned out she had misplaced my reservation. She suggested I bring myself to *this* address."

"Welcome to the house of pariahs, Mr. Curtis," said L.J. "You are welcome to stay here in my home for as long as this trial takes."

"I do appreciate that, sir. And please, call me Jonah."

Jonah Curtis was almost as tall as I. He was what anyone would call a handsome man.

And Jonah Curtis was one other thing besides.

Jonah Curtis was a black man.

Chapter 94

One important piece of the puzzle was still missing.

Who would be defending the White Raiders?

The next morning that puzzle piece appeared. L.J. came rushing into the house yelling, “Those goddamn leaky slop buckets have gone and got themselves the best goddamn criminal defense attorney in the South!”

Jonah looked up from his book. “Maxwell Hayes Lewis?”

“How did you know that?” L.J. asked.

“You said the best.” Jonah turned to me. “Ben, if you needed a lawyer to defend a gang of no-good lowlifes who viciously attacked a colored man's house, who would you get?"

"Maxwell Hayes Lewis," I said.

"And why would you want him?"

"Because he got the governor of Arkansas acquitted after he shot his bastard son—his half Negro son—in full view of at least twenty-five people."

"So, our little pack of rats managed to get themselves 'Loophole Lewis,'" Jonah said.

Loophole Lewis. That's how he was known wherever lawyers got together and gossiped about others of their species. Lewis's philosophy was simple: "If you can't find a loophole for your client, go out and invent one."

Jonah carefully closed his well-thumbed copy of the *Revised Civil Code of the State of Mississippi*. "You know, I have always wanted to meet Counselor Lewis," he said.

Jonah must have made a special connection with the good Lord, because we were still sipping coffee ten minutes later when L.J.'s butler announced that a Mr. Maxwell Lewis was there to see us.

"I thought it would be the mannerly

thing to do, to come by and introduce myself to you distinguished gentlemen of the prosecution," Lewis said, coming in.

He was plainspoken and plain-looking. My mother would have said he was "plain as an old corn stick." Then she would have added, "But that's just on the outside, so you'd better watch yourself."

We all told Mr. Lewis we were pleased to meet him. He said he was pleased to meet us as well. No, thank you, he said, no tea or coffee for him. Bourbon? Certainly not at this early hour, he said, although he asked if he might revisit the question somewhat later in the day.

This display of southern charm was not the reason for his visit, I was sure. Fairly soon he sidled up to the real reason.

"I must say, Mr. Corbett, I was a mite surprised when I saw that the trial judge will be none other than your distinguished father," he said.

"As was I," I said. Clearly he wanted me to say more, so I stayed silent.

"It's an unusual choice, and highly irregular," he continued on. "My first instinct was to try to get a new judge from the powers that be in Jackson, but then I got to thinking about it. This is an open-and-shut case. Why bother causing a fuss? I'm sure Judge Corbett will preside with absolute fairness."

"If there's one thing he's known for," I said, "it's his fairness. And already we find ourselves in agreement, Mr. Lewis. We also believe that this is an open-and-shut case. I'm just afraid the door will be shutting on you."

Lewis chuckled at my sally. "Ah! We shall see about that," he said. "I've been checking on your record in murder trials up in Washington, D.C. And yours too, Mr. Curtis. We shall certainly see."

Chapter 95

Over the next days we transformed the sitting room off my sleeping quarters into the White Raiders War Room, as L.J. soon nicknamed our paper-strewn maelstrom of an office.

Conrad, the Cosgrove brother who had survived the assault at Abraham's house, went up to McComb every morning to collect every newspaper and pamphlet having to do with the upcoming trial. We hauled an old chalkboard up from L.J.'s basement and made two lists of possibilities: "Impossible" and "Possible."

Among the latter were some terrifying questions:

What if Maxwell Hayes Lewis leads with a request for dismissal?

Bang, the gavel falls! The case is over!

What if Abraham is too ill to testify? What if he dies before or during the trial?

Bang! The case is over!

What if Lewis tampers with the jury? It wouldn't be too difficult in this town.

What if . . . ?

We made our lists, erased them, improved and reworked them, and studied them as if they were the received word of God.

After spending a few days working beside him, I decided that Jonah Curtis was not only a smart man but a wise one. Jonah clearly had intelligence to spare, tempered with humor and a bit of easygoing cynicism—the result, I supposed, of growing up always seeing the other side of the coin toss we call Justice. He was the son of a sharecropper who spent most of his life as a slave, on a cotton plantation near Clarksdale, in the Mississippi Delta. When Jonah got his law degree and passed the bar examination, his father gave him a gift, the gold pocket watch for which he'd been saving since before Jonah was born.

It was a beautiful timepiece, but the chain, clumsily hammered together from old scraps of iron, didn't match its quality. Jonah told me that his father had made it himself, from a piece of the very chain that had shackled him to the auction block the last time he was offered for sale.

Sometimes Jonah got a little ahead of himself with his legal theories, at least as far as L.J. was concerned.

"A verdict depends on the culture of any given town," Jonah said. "A man held for killing a Negro in New York City will have a very different trial—and a very different outcome—than a man held for the same crime in Atlanta. Bring him to Eudora, and again the crime and the resulting trial would be different. We might say this White Raiders case is sui generis."

L.J. sighed heavily. "Talk English, for God's sake," he said. "Down here, we say 'soo-ey' when we're calling hogs."

L.J. already considered me the worst know-it-all in the room, so I left this for Jonah to explain.

"Sorry, L.J., it's Latin," said Jonah. "*Sui generis*—'of its own kind,' literally, 'of its own genus.' In other words, this case…well, there's never been another one anything like it."

Chapter 96

The chanting outside L.J.'s house grew louder. The voices came closer and closer.

All white?
Not right.
All white?
We fight.

I hurried to the balcony off the War Room, with L.J. and Jonah at my heels. An astounding sight met our eyes. There were black people, scores of them—two hundred or more—slowly marching down the middle of Willow Street in Eudora, Mississippi.

This was almost unbelievable. In the

South, black people were not supposed to assemble in these numbers.

L.J. let out a whistle. "That is one angry bunch of Negroes," he said.

"I think the word *I* would use is 'passionate,' " said Jonah.

Though I had never expected to see black people marching through the streets, I knew instantly what this was about. Tomorrow the trial would begin, and the first order of business was jury selection. No Negro had ever been permitted to serve on a jury in the state of Mississippi. Many of the liberal Yankee newspapers had declared it an outrage. They suggested that the White Raiders Trial might be just the occasion for the presiding judge to allow one or possibly even two colored men to serve as jurors.

We stood at the railing of the veranda, watching the marchers slowly pass. It was plain that they had taken a detour from Commerce Street to go past L.J.'s house. Some of them waved or lifted their hats to us.

Just when we thought we had seen the last of the marchers, another phalanx turned the corner onto Willow.

I was amazed. "Gentlemen. Are you seeing what I'm seeing?"

L.J. smiled. "Yessir, it's one hell of a crowd."

"Not just the *size* of the crowd," I said. "Take a look at who's *leading* it."

All white?
Not right.

L.J. squinted to see. "Those two old folks at the front?"

Jonah answered for me. "The lady is Ida Wells-Barnett," he said. "And the gentleman, if I am not mistaken, is Mr. W. E. B. Du Bois. This is history being made, indeed."

Chapter 97

When I was a boy, my mother would sometimes take me to watch my father conducting a trial.

"It's a *presiding* day," she'd say. "Let's go see Daddy scaring the pants off of everyone." And away we'd go to the courthouse.

To my child's eyes the old Pike County Courthouse looked exactly like a church. The second-floor gallery where the colored people got to sit was like the choir loft. The benches below were the pews. And my father stood at the high altar in the front of the room, delivering thunderous sermons and running the whole thing like a very strict minister who happened to wield a hammer instead of a Bible.

More than twenty years later, here I was, back in the church of Judge Everett Corbett.

But today, as L.J. and Jonah and I arranged our papers and books on the prosecution table, the old courthouse felt like something else entirely.

Not a church.

It was more like a theater now.

The upstairs colored section had been transformed into balcony seats. The benches on the main level were the orchestra seats, jammed to overflowing with an audience that had stood in line for hours to see the hottest entertainment in town. And that altar? Well, that was now center stage.

That was Everett J. Corbett's stage. He could be a dynamic, exciting performer, and I felt sure he would not let his audience down today.

Ringing the front steps of the courthouse were Scooter Willems and several dozen men like him, bristling with tripods and huge black accordion cameras. Accompanying the photographers were at least a hundred reporters flashing pencils and notebooks, trading tidbits with each other, rushing this way and that in pursuit of the latest rumors.

Inside, the colored spectators had dutifully filed upstairs to the cheap seats. The benches below were filled to maximum capacity by the white citizens of Eudora. Only the first two rows had been left empty, roped off for the pool of potential jurors.

Dominating the wall above the judge's bench was an enormous Fattorini & Sons regulator clock nearly as long as a grandfather clock, with a carved dark-wood case, elegant Roman numerals, and a pair of gleaming brass pendulums. Growing up, I always thought of it as the Clock of Justice.

Now every tick brought us closer to nine a.m.

Here came a pair of Chief Eversman's newly recruited deputies, leading in the defendants. Three White Raiders. No shackles, ropes, or handcuffs. The deputies chatted and laughed with the men as they led them to the defense table.

And then the great Maxwell Hayes

Lewis strode from the back of the room to greet the Raiders and shake their hands so that everyone in the courtroom could see how normal, how average and amiable, these men were. After a moment's discussion the defendants turned to look at our table. They looked back at each other and grinned. The sight of Jonah, L.J., and me seemed to amuse them greatly.

The bailiff entered with a solemn expression, carrying the heavy cast-iron imprinting seal, which he placed at the right end of my father's bench. This was the seal he would use to mark evidence as it was admitted.

"All rise," the bailiff called. "The court is now in session, the Honorable Everett J. Corbett presiding."

Daddy's big entrance was always a highlight. Here he came through the door at stage left, his hair gleaming with brilliantine, his silky black robe pressed to perfection by Dabney.

He lifted the heavy mahogany gavel. I was surprised to see him using the gavel I had sent him on his sixtieth birthday, since I had never received a thank-you note.

He brought the gavel down with a thunderous bang.

“There will be order!” he commanded. “There will be silence! There will be justice!”

Chapter 98

Now to pick a jury.

That summer had been one of the hottest on record. It seemed to me that God had saved up all the excess heat and humidity in the world and brought it down upon Eudora today. It was already so hot in the courtroom that the hand fans were flapping like a flock of restless birds.

Judge Corbett had evidently taken measures to spruce up the courtroom for the national press, who were allowed inside between sessions to gather scraps of news. He had ordered all the spectator benches and tables and chairs sanded and revarnished, and indeed they all gleamed as if brand-new. But the new varnish turned soft and sticky in the heat and gave off fumes that set heads spinning. I breathed the sweetish, medicinal smell; the seat of my trousers stuck to my chair.

This was going to be a very long day.

I saw at once that Judge Corbett still ran an efficient courtroom. It took only ten minutes for the first three candidates to be interviewed, approved, and seated in the jury box: three middle-aged white men.

Jonah made little fuss over any of them. I assumed he was saving his objections for an occasion when they might prove persuasive.

It didn't take long.

The clerk read a name from the list: "Patton William Taylor."

Chapter 99

From the front row rose a mousy little man commonly known as Patsy-Boy Taylor. I knew him as a helper of Lyman Tripp, the undertaker in whose wagon I had ridden to the Klan meeting at Scully's barn.

I scribbled a note and passed it to Jonah.

Taylor served time in La. State Prison for assault of Negro girl. Believe he broke her leg.

Jonah scanned the note, nodding. It was his turn to question the prospective juror first.

"Good morning, Mr. Taylor," he said. "Tell me, sir, have you ever been to Louisiana?"

"Once or twice," said Patsy-Boy.

"How about the town of Angola? Ever been there?"

The man frowned. "I reckon I have."

"And how long was your most recent stay in Angola, Mr. Taylor?"

"I don't remember."

"Perhaps I can help refresh your memory, sir," Jonah said. "Mr. Taylor, did you recently finish a five-month term in the Louisiana State Penitentiary at Angola?"

"I might've," said Taylor. "I can't quite remember."

"Your Honor, if it please the court, could you direct Mr. Taylor to answer my question?"

The ice in my father's water pitcher had melted away, but there was plenty of it in his voice. "He *did* answer, Mr. Curtis," he said. "He said that he couldn't quite remember."

"Your Honor, with all due respect, I don't believe—"

"Your beliefs are of no interest to me, Mr. Curtis," my father said. He turned to the defense table. "Mr. Lewis, do you have any objection to this gentleman sitting on this jury?"

"None whatsoever, Your Honor."

"Mr. Taylor will be sworn in to serve," my father said. The gavel came down.

By reflex L.J. and I came up off our chairs. I can't say I couldn't believe what had just happened, probably because I'd watched justice being meted out in Mississippi for too long. But *still*.

"I most strenuously object, Your Honor," Jonah said in a loud voice.

A young colored woman in the gallery called out, "That ain't justice!"

My father pointed his gavel at her. "Contempt of court. Ten days in jail and a dollar fine. Get her out of here!"

Two of Phineas's deputies ran to do his bidding. Everyone heard the woman's noisy protest as he dragged her down the stairs.

Meanwhile, my father's attention was seemingly riveted by the sight of a fly trapped in the soft varnish of his bench. The insect was hopelessly stuck, its wings buzzing. The judge closed his thumb and forefinger on the fly, plucked it up, and placed it in the center of his desk.

Bang! He brought his gavel down on that fly.

"Let me tell you something, Mr. Curtis," he said. "Let me explain something to you. I would advise you to listen, and listen well. *I am in charge of this courtroom.* Did you hear what I said?"

"Yes, sir," Jonah replied.

"What did I say?" My father's voice was deadly calm. "Repeat it for me, please."

"You are in charge of this courtroom, Your Honor."

"You're damn right I am. Now, you may object to Counselor Lewis's comments. He is your opponent; he represents the defense. But you may not ever—*ever*—object to something I have said. For any reason."

The only sound in the courtroom was the ticking of the clock and the hum of the ceiling fans.

"Thank you, Mr. Curtis. And tell those two clowns you brought with you to sit themselves down, or I'll have them removed from my courtroom."

The trial of the new century—the proceedings known as the *State of Mississippi v. Madden, North, and Stephens*—was officially under way.

Chapter 100

There they sat, three White Raiders facing *a jury of their peers*.

It was a true statement in every way. Once Judge Everett Corbett cut off all objections from our side, he quickly empaneled a jury of twelve middle-aged white men who looked just like the men they would be called upon to judge.

"We have a jury," the judge announced, "and so we will proceed to trial. Is the prosecution prepared to begin in the morning?"

"Yes, Your Honor," Jonah said.

"And I'm sure the defense is ready."

"Defense is certainly ready, Your Honor," said Maxwell Hayes Lewis.

"Then without further ado—" my father began.

Jonah Curtis stood up and dared to interrupt him again.

"Your Honor, begging the court's pardon, I feel compelled to state for the record that the prosecution has not seen a fair and representative jury selection here today."

My father's voice was dangerously soft. "All right. I have warned you, Mr. Curtis, and I will not warn you again. I am in charge of this trial. I am in charge of this courtroom. I have ruled that this jury is fit to serve."

"But Your Honor—"

Suddenly my father rose up and bellowed, *"And I will not warn you again!* Try me, my friend! Just try me once more! Challenge my jurisdiction again, and I will declare a mistrial here and summarily dismiss all the charges. Which, I remind you, is within my power."

My father turned on his heel and swept out of the room. I knew the drill: he would walk straight into his office and pull off his robe. His clothes would be damp with sweat. I pictured him settling into his swivel chair in that office lined with law books, oak filing cabinets, diplomas, and certificates of appreciation. On his desk he permitted himself one personal touch: the sad-beautiful honeymoon photograph of him and Mama, arm in arm on the boardwalk at Biloxi.

While the defendants stood shooting the breeze with their jailers, Lewis took a detour by our table.

"I guess they didn't teach y'all everything up in those Ivy League law schools," he said. "Down here, we believe the first responsibility of a good criminal attorney is to make friends with the judge."

"Oh, they tried to teach us that," Jonah said. "I guess I just didn't do a good job of learning it."

"Me either," I said. "And I've had decades of practice with the man."

Loophole Lewis chuckled genially and brought out a couple of cigars from an inside pocket. "May I offer you boys a Partagás? Best quality, fresh off the boat from Havana. I'm sure you enjoyed a few of these fellows when you were down in Cuba, Ben."

"No, sir," I said mildly. "We didn't have

much time for smoking cigars." I was about to say more when I saw Conrad Cosgrove pushing into the courtroom through the crowd.

"Mr. Corbett," he said. "A messenger brought this to the house. I figured you'd want to see it right away."

Conrad handed over a small envelope.

On the front, in an elegant hand, were the words BENJAMIN CORBETT, PERSONAL CORRESPONDENCE.

The words engraved on the back flap were just as simple: THE WHITE HOUSE.

"If you gentlemen will excuse me," I said. I didn't wait for an answer.

Chapter 101

As I walked down the courthouse steps, a reporter from the *New Orleans Item* took my elbow to ask how I thought the first day had gone.

"Exactly as expected," I said. "Justice will be served here." I took my arm back and kept walking.

I followed the cinder path around the side of the building. The giant oak trees in the square provided the only real shade in the center of town. I felt twenty degrees cooler the moment I stepped under their branches and took a seat on a bench.

I sliced the edge of the envelope with my fingernail. Inside was a single typewritten sheet on gold-embossed White House stationery.

Dear Capt. Corbett,
The eyes of America are upon you, and upon the proceedings in Eudora. I can assure you that with my own (four) eyes I am personally watching you and the trial at every moment.

I know you will continue to do your best, and I know that you will succeed in this endeavor, as we succeeded together during the late War.

Ben, know that your president is with you every inch of the way.

Sincerely yours, I remain
Your obt. servant,
Theodore Roosevelt, Pres't.

I smiled at the president's little joke about his "four eyes," but when I realized the meaning of his subsequent words, my stomach took a nervous dive. As if I didn't have enough tension to deal with, now the president of the United States was "personally watching" me "at every moment."

I read the letter again and put it back in the envelope.

A voice called, "Mr. Corbett, sir."

I looked to both sides and saw no one.

Again the voice: "Mr. Corbett? Over here, sir, *behind you*."

Chapter 102

I turned around quickly to find a tall, slender colored man standing on the sidewalk. He was perhaps ten years older than me and beautifully dressed, down to the club scarf in his pocket and the jeweled pin in his necktie.

"May I have a word with you for a moment, sir?" he asked.

"Well, of course," I said. "Come have a seat."

"I'm sorry, Mr. Corbett, I can't. That park is White Only."

I had forgotten—or maybe I'd never realized—that the old wooden benches, the little fountain, the shade of the big old eudoras, all were reserved for the exclusive use of white Eudora.

I walked across the grass to the man and extended my hand. "Ben Corbett."

"I'm a correspondent for the *Indianapolis Cross,*" he said.

"Ah yes," I said. "I've read your paper. Y'all have published some of the best general reports I've seen on the question of lynching."

"Why, thank you, sir," he said. "I'm honored that you've heard of us."

"Welcome to Eudora," I said.

"Oh, it's not my first time," he said. "I grew up in Eudora."

I looked at him harder. I rattled around in my memory, but I couldn't place where I had seen him before.

"I used to work for Mr. Jenkins at the mercantile store," he said.

All at once I knew him.

I said. "Is that—*Marcus?* Is that you?"

His eyes lit up. "You remember me?"

"I'll be damned if I'll ever forget you, Marcus," I said.

I reached out my arms and embraced him. He was surprised, but he let me do it, and even patted me on the back.

"You were the only one who helped my mother," I said. "You helped me get her to Dr. Frederick. If you hadn't, she might have died."

Marcus told me that his family had left Eudora for the Midwest not long after the time of Mama's stroke. They wound up in central Indiana, where his father worked for a cattle farmer. Marcus went on to study English at the Negro teachers college in Gary and had landed a job with the largest colored newspaper in the state.

And now, he said, he had convinced his editors to send him to Mississippi to cover the White Raiders Trial because he had a personal interest in one of the defendants. "Henry North," he said. "I knew him. You did, too."

"I did?"

Marcus said, "Do you remember that redheaded boy that worked with me at Jenkins' Mercantile? He helped us carry your mama out that day. That boy is Henry North."

Sure, I remembered the loutish boy. He was thin and rawboned in those days. He had said Mama was drunk, to leave her where she lay.

"I remember the day your mama took

sick," Marcus said, "like it was yesterday. You weren't more than about seven years old, but you acted like a grown man. You answered old Sanders back like he deserved. And you helped me carry her to the doc. I always knew you were going to turn into a fine man."

I was speechless. Marcus's words made me feel humble. The truth was that after years of remembering Marcus's example every day, as my mother had told me to do, I hadn't thought about him in quite a while.

"I've paid close attention to your law career, Mr. Corbett—helping people up in Washington, helping wherever you can. When I saw how you were turning out, I tell you, it gave me a little hope along the way."

Seeing Marcus again, hearing him speak like this, gave me a transfusion of energy. As if I'd just received new blood, a whole body's worth of it.

Without knowing it, I had given Marcus "a little hope along the way."

And now Marcus had given me hope for the difficult murder trial that lay ahead.

Chapter 103

After careful deliberation, Jonah Curtis had chosen to wear a navy blue suit, a crisp white shirt, and a bright red tie. He didn't look exactly like an American flag, but all the colors were there for the patriotic effect he intended for his opening statement to the jury.

"Gentlemen, I did not come to Eudora to make history," he began. "I was sent here by the Supreme Court of the state of Mississippi to seek justice. If in the name of justice you reach the verdict I truly believe you must reach, the state will ask you to assign a degree of punishment that you feel is appropriate for these crimes."

"Let us begin, though, not at the ending," he said, "but at the beginning. A hot summer night. You know what that means, surely I don't have to tell you. Talking to a Mississippi man about the heat is like talking to a fish about the water."

This little joke brought an involuntary smile to two or three faces among the jury.

"So there we are on that hot summer night. Sweltering. Down in the Quarters, inside a poor man's house.

"And here, on a bed in the parlor, an old man lies dying. His granddaughter is tending to him, his trembles and tremors, his rackety cough."

All the men on the jury were watching him now, even those whose expressions revealed their innate distaste for a Negro attorney dressed in a suit.

"On the porch of this home, there are two gentlemen standing guard. These are not fighters or thugs. One is an attorney, well known to the most powerful men in our nation's capital. The other is the inventor of the Stringer Automatic Baler, the most successful businessman in Eudora—heck, let's be honest—in all of south Mississippi."

There was a patter of quiet chuckling; everyone in the courtroom shot a look at L.J., beaming at this description of him.

"These gentlemen have come to the Quarters on this night," Jonah said, "because the dying man is their friend. They've heard rumors of trouble. They have a well-reasoned fear that some kind of tragedy is in the offing.

"Lord, it's hot. The old man struggles to breathe. The granddaughter cannot help the tears that come to her eyes. The old man is all she has on this earth.

"Then there comes a sound, the sound of hoofbeats on the road. There are men on horses, raising a cloud of dust in the darkness."

A couple of the jurors looked ostentatiously bored, and a man in the back row was already dozing. But the others seemed attentive, and a few were even transfixed, as if Jonah were telling them a scary story.

And that's exactly what he was doing.

"Suddenly, gentlemen, all is pandemonium—uproar and violence and chaos.

Men firing guns everywhere. Glass flying. Women screaming. Suddenly there are men all around the house, trying to shoot their way in. Trying to kill the old man. Trying to kill his granddaughter.

"The old man is terrified. The young woman throws herself over him, shielding his body with her own. The assault lasts only a few minutes, but it seems like hours and hours."

Jonah paused. He studied the faces of the jurors, each one in turn.

Finally he spoke again, in a hushed whisper.

"Two men lie dead on the ground. One is a man who's been a friend and neighbor to you all, all his life—Luther Cosgrove, an employee of Mr. Stringer for nearly thirty years. He lies dead in the side yard, shot in the face by the men on horseback. The other is a much younger man from out in the county, a fellow named Jimmie Cooper, who had come to that house of his own free will that night and volunteered to stand guard over that dying old man. Jimmie Cooper lies dead on the ground in front of the house."

Jonah paused and shook his head

sorrowfully, as if he couldn't believe the price Jimmie and Luther had paid.

"But then there is a miracle," he said. "Three of the killers are arrested. For once, they are not allowed to pull on their Klan hoods and go riding off into the darkness, unmolested, unpunished. For once, there are men who are interested in capturing the killers, in bringing them to justice—in bringing them here today, to face trial before a jury of their peers. And that, of course, is where you gentlemen come into the story."

He turned, pointed his finger at the defendants. "There they are. Mr. Chester Madden. Mr. Henry North. Mr. Lincoln Stephens."

The defendants put on the smirk they had evidently practiced beforehand, but they couldn't hold it. Their nerves and the silence in the room got the best of them.

It was now time for the most difficult, delicate portion of the opening statement. Jonah and I had spent hours in the War Room going back and forth over this part, trying to find the best way to say what he needed to say.

"Gentlemen, you may have noticed there

is one fact I left out of my account," Jonah said. "You may think it's the most important fact of all. And that is the fact that these defendants are white men. They attacked a colored family in a colored neighborhood. One of the men they killed was white. The other was black. I didn't mention any of this to you.

"And do you know why? I'll tell you why—because the pursuit of justice knows no color! The pursuit of justice admits only that which is fair, and honest, and true.

"This case is *not about race*. It is not about the black versus the white. This case is much easier than that. It's a simple matter of justice.

"Now, as the prosecutor representing the great state of Mississippi, it will be my job to show you how these three men attacked and pillaged, how they came to the Eudora Quarters planning to kill, intending to kill. How they planned and then executed the deliberate, premeditated murder of two men on a hot, awful night in the Quarters. On a night when these three men, and all the ones who got away, were hoping that justice had taken a holiday. *Well, justice has not taken a holiday here in Eudora!"*

I heard a sound from the jury box. Glancing over, I was astounded to see one of the jurors, old Lester Johnson, a retired teller from the First Bank of Eudora, clapping. So taken was he by Jonah's presentation that he was applauding. The sound was very loud in the room.

Then there was a louder sound: the gavel coming down *BANG!*

My father jumped to his feet. "Lester!" he shouted. *"Have you lost your goddamn mind?"*

Chapter 104

"Well, well, well," Maxwell Hayes Lewis said slowly. Then he rose from his chair to begin his opening statement.

Those three words were all it took for me to realize what he was up to.

Lewis was appropriating the style of Clarence Darrow, a Chicago labor lawyer renowned all over the nation as the "lawyer's lawyer." Darrow was the most effective courtroom presenter of the day, his style casual, colloquial, at times downright homey, with ample doses of country wisdom and sentiment tossed in.

Lewis scratched his head, then slid his hand down, cupping his face in his hand, squeezing his cheek, as if he were sitting in his study, lost in thought.

Then he appeared to notice the jury for the first time, and ambled over.

"Now, Mr. Curtis here says, and I quote, 'the pursuit of justice knows no color. The pursuit of justice admits only that which is fair, and honest, and true.' "

He turned around and stared hard at Jonah. But when he spoke, his voice was gentle. "Thank you for saying that, Mr. Curtis. All I have to say to that is, Amen."

The jurors visibly relaxed. The lawyer had brought them to a point of tension, then eased up.

"But let me tell you fellows where Mr. Curtis and I are absolutely *not* in agreement," he said.

Lewis's face was glistening with perspiration, and he hadn't been talking a minute yet. He mopped his face with a handkerchief, a gesture that afforded him a dramatic pause.

"We are not in agreement *on the story itself*. Mr. Curtis tells a tale of night riders galloping in and shooting up a house in a frenzy of violent and lawless behavior. I have another version of that story to tell you. Now, the story I have to tell you is about eight upstanding white citizens of

Pike County. Three of them were wrongly accused and arrested, the three gentlemen you see before you today.

"But on the night in question, there were eight. They climbed up on their horses, calmly, and in a neighborly way they rode over to Abraham Cross's house. Why did they go there? Were they looking for trouble? Well, no—the trouble had already come and found *them*."

He paused, turned around, and walked the other way along the jury box, meeting the eyes of each man in turn.

"Those eight men rode over that night to investigate a complaint against Mr. Cross's nephew, a Mr. Richard Cross, known as Ricky, a Negro who was suspected of molesting and raping a young white girl of the Cedar Bend community.

"Understand, my friends, that the prosecutor's story and this story fit together perfectly. The entire evening can be seen, from one perspective, as a gigantic misunderstanding. If the people in that house in the Quarters had not shot first and asked questions later—if they'd all been informed that they harbored a rapist in their midst, if they'd known about the assault on the girl, and the legitimate reasons my clients had for going to Mr. Cross's house that night—why, none of this would have happened.

"But even so, it *did* happen. And it is a tragedy.

"And yet, gentlemen, it is not murder. I am here to tell you about Abraham Cross—a dying man, according to Mr. Curtis, although just for your information he is still alive and well, and I wouldn't be surprised if you all get to meet him. I'm going to show you how Mr. Cross and his granddaughter and his hired gunmen, some of whom are in this room trying to intimidate you gentlemen here today..."

As he said this he was looking directly at L. J. Stringer and me.

"...I will show you how this armed band of Negroes and their white friends set about to deny my clients any access at all to the suspected man. How they, in fact, attacked my clients, and sought to visit great bodily harm upon them—even though my clients had *a written legal warrant* deputizing them and empowering them to question the accused, they were set upon by a pack of armed men.

"My clients fired their own weapons, gentlemen, in self-defense. The case is simple. It's what is known in our game as 'open and shut.' My clients are facing these terrible charges, they have been jailed and denied their most basic rights as Americans, as Mississippians."

You could see the jurors straightening with pride as he said this. "And all because of a story! A fable! A fiction, my friends. Mr. Jonah Curtis is a very eloquent lawyer, gentlemen, anyone can see that, but what he's telling you is nothing more than a bedtime story!"

Several jurors laughed out loud.

"That is right, gentlemen of the jury. A bedtime story. We have two versions being told here. Mr. Curtis has told you a fairy story, and I have told you the truth. *As God above knows it to be!*"

Chapter 105

"Goddamn them, Ben. Goddamn them all to hell!"

L.J. slammed his fist on the dining room table, rattling the crystal goblets. "Goddamn their lying, cheating asses!"

L.J. was doing all the shouting. Jonah and I were standing back, watching him scream in a way only rich men can. We didn't try to stop him or calm him down.

"The biggest lie of all," L.J. said, "is when he says these White Raiders had some kind of official warrant to come into that house after Ricky."

Jonah looked at me. "All right, Ben, how is Lewis going to demonstrate that in a credible fashion?"

"Easy," I said. "He'll put Phineas Eversman on the stand."

"The policeman?"

"Chief of police, and the only full-time officer on the force," I reminded him. "He'll put Phineas on and Phineas will lie through his teeth."

Jonah looked quizzical. "I thought Eversman was on our side. Or at least neutral."

"He was on our side for exactly one night," I explained. "He only arrested those men because L.J. pushed him into it. He's been looking for a way out ever since."

I speared a slice of Virginia ham before passing the platter to L.J.

"It didn't look like it would rain tonight, did it?" said Jonah.

"Not to me," L.J. replied. "Why?"

"That sure does sound like thunder outside," Jonah said.

I walked over to the window and pulled back the drapes. First I was surprised; then I was frightened.

"What is it, Ben?"

"About thirty, forty fellows with guns," I said, "and a few with pitchforks. They appear to be just standing there, watching the house."

"That's a mighty big crowd for Eudora," L.J. said.

"No," I said. "It's a mighty big *mob*."

Chapter 106

The mob caused us no trouble that night. For about an hour they watched us watching them through the windows, then they turned and went away. Every few minutes I peeked out the window, but the streets of Eudora stayed quiet and dark that night.

The next morning the trial began in earnest. I spent a long minute studying the face of Henry Wadsworth North, trying to match the man with what I remembered of the boy on the day Mama took sick. Too many years had intervened. This sallow, blotchy-faced fat man bore only a vague resemblance to the surly kid I remembered from Jenkins' Mercantile.

Jonah called his first witness: Abraham Cross.

Abraham was wearing his best church suit, of speckled brown wool, and a matching fedora. He rolled in in a rickety wheelchair Moody had borrowed from a crippled neighbor of L.J.'s, a nice woman who sympathized with us.

"Now, Mr. Cross," Jonah said, "why don't you take us back to the night of August twenty-fifth. Tell us what you remember."

Abraham nodded. "Well, sir, I was in the parlor, a-layin' in my bed, and Moody was tendin' after me—"

"Excuse me, sir," Jonah said. "Who is Moody?"

"Moody Cross. My granddaughter. She looks after me."

"Thank you, sir. Please go on."

"Like I say, I was a-layin' in my bed. Not quite sure if I'd been sleeping or not. But then sure enough I come awake. Sound like the cavalry done showed up outside the house. A bunch of horses, I don't know how many. And men shootin' off guns, and yellin.' Like to scared me half to death—and I don't need to be any closer to dead than I already am."

Laughter rolled through the courtroom, from whites and Negroes. My father slammed down the gavel to kill it.

Abraham continued telling his story in precise, unwavering detail. Without any prompting from Jonah, he pointed out and positively identified two of the defendants.

"That one there, I saw him through the front window," he said, pointing at the defense table.

Jonah asked him to be more specific.

"That one on the right," he said. "Stephens. He shot Jimmie Cooper dead."

"You're sure it was Mr. Stephens you saw?"

"No doubt about it," said Abraham. "And then that one there—Mr. Madden—he come into the parlor where I was, with another one of them Raiders. A man he called Harold."

"And what did Mr. Madden do?"

"He says to this Harold, 'You watch this old nigger real good. Keep your gun on his neck.' Then he went back outside, Madden did."

"And the one he called Harold—he stayed there with you?"

"Yes, he did."

"Did he keep a gun on you?"

"Yes, sir. Up against my skull. And he grabbed Moody too. Not in a nice way."

"And how did you respond to that, Mr. Cross?"

Abraham scratched his old head, closed his eyes for a moment. Then he spoke.

"Well, sir, to tell you the truth I didn't have to respond."

"And why is that?"

"Because a minute later, Ben Corbett come into the room, and my granddaughter Moody . . ."

He stopped.

"Please continue," Jonah said.

"She pushed a kitchen knife into Harold's back."

Chapter 107

"So, let me see if I've got this straight, Mr. Cross."

Maxwell Hayes Lewis stood up to begin his cross-examination of Abraham.

"You were *lying* in your living room, half asleep. Or maybe you were asleep and dreaming part of the time, you're not really certain. You woke up . . . or you think you woke up . . . you looked out that window and saw a man you *thought* was Mr. Stephens pulling the trigger on a pistol."

Jonah said, "Your Honor—"

"Overruled," my father said.

"This is supposed to be a cross-examination," Jonah said. "Could he get to a question sometime today?"

"I said overruled," my father repeated.

"Oh, I'm asking him a question," Lewis said. "I'm asking him if I've got his story straight. Mr. Cross, you said you saw this man shooting a pistol. But in fact you never saw him shoot anyone. You never saw anyone take a bullet from Mr. Stephens's gun, did you? You can't follow the path of a bullet with your eyes."

"Your Honor—"

"Hush." My father waved his hand as if Jonah were a fly that needed swatting. He turned to Abraham. "Answer the question. Are you sure who you saw?"

Abraham worked his jaw, as if chewing a wad of tobacco. Then he spoke.

"I know it was Mr. Stephens shooting, 'cause I saw him clear as day. I heard Jimmie when he fell and hit the roof. I knew that's who it was 'cause I'd watched him climb up on the roof. And I saw him again, when he fell."

Good for you, Abraham, I cheered silently. *Give it back to him. Stick him with the truth.*

"And that's the way you remember it?" Lewis said.

"Yes, sir. But not only that. That's how it *was.*"

"How is your memory these days, Mr. Cross?"

"Sharp as a serpent's tongue, sir," he said.

That got a chuckle from the spectators.

Lewis smiled too. "How old are you now, Mr. Cross, sir?"

"Mama always said I come into Miss'ippi the same year Miss'ippi joined up with the United States."

"And Mississippi became a state in 1817," said Lewis. "So that would make you . . ."

"Eighty-nine," Abraham said. "Same as Miss'ippi."

Another laugh. If the jury was anything like the audience, some of them had to be enjoying Abraham's company.

Lewis ambled over to his desk, picked up a piece of paper, and carried it to the bench. "Your Honor, if it please the court, I submit article number one as physical entry and evidence, a warrant from the chief of police to search the premises of one Abraham Cross in the Eudora Quarters."

"Very well," my father said. He took pleasure in sliding the document into the maw of his heavy iron stamp, bringing down the lever to imprint his seal and admit it into evidence.

He handed the warrant back to Lewis, who carried it to Abraham.

"Mr. Cross, would you please take a look at this document?"

Abraham slowly settled his spectacles onto the bridge of his nose and took the paper from Lewis.

"Mr. Cross, do you know how to read?"

Abraham straightened up and glared at him. "I've been reading the Good Book since I was five years old."

"In that case, would you please be so kind as to read that for me—the sentences printed at the top, in the heavy ink."

Abraham read: "'This warrant renders unto the bearers the unchallenged right to examine all house, home, and household goods of the residence denoted below, by order of the Chief of Police in the township of Eudora, Mississippi.'"

Abraham looked up at the attorney towering over his wheelchair.

Lewis said, "Please read the name on the line marked 'Residence.' "

"It's my name. 'Abraham Cross.' "

Lewis stuck his thumbs through his suspenders, a pose exactly like the photograph of Clarence Darrow I'd seen in the *American Legal Companion.*

"Now, Mr. Cross, when have you seen this document before?"

"Never in my life," Abraham said.

"Are you sure about that?"

Yes, sir, he said. He was sure. Lewis asked him the question five different ways. Jonah tried to object and was gaveled into silence.

"Didn't Mr. Stephens hand this document to you when he arrived at your house that night, Mr. Cross?"

Ah, here we go. Jonah jumped up. Objection overruled. He seemed to have reached a silent agreement with Judge Everett Corbett: he would be allowed to keep making objections as long as he understood he would be instantly overruled on every one.

"Mr. Cross, isn't it true that you saw this document, you read it, and you threw it on the ground?"

"No, sir."

"Didn't you tell Mr. Stephens that if he wanted to search your house, he'd have to shoot you first?"

"No, sir. I did not."

"Are you certain?"

"He didn't bring no paper. They rode up and started shooting. If Mr. Stephens said he did that, he is a liar. And if you say he did it, sir, you would be a liar too."

Chapter 108

After Abraham finished testifying and Moody took him home to put him back to bed, Jonah challenged the admissibility of Phineas Eversman's search warrant.

My father looked mildly amused. "It's a search warrant, Mr. Curtis. It looks like a thousand others that I've seen over the years," he said.

Since his profane outburst in the direction of the applauding juror, I thought, my father had been unusually patient with Jonah. He must have realized how bad that eruption would look once all these "two-bit newspaper reporters" put it into print.

Jonah decided to tack in another direction. "Your Honor, I know you are well aware that under the rules of civil procedure, all documents entered as evidence must be shared with all counsel *before* commencement of trial," he said. "The first time I saw this was a few minutes ago."

My father peered down his nose at the spectacle of a Negro lawyer daring to cite civil procedure to him. "Now, Mr. Curtis, you being from up in Jackson and all, and educated up in the North, well, I'm sure you are accustomed to practicing before the big-city courts like they have up there, with your civil procedures and all that," he said. I had seen him perform this act before: the simple country judge, working his way through the facts of the case with nothing but his good ol' horse sense. "But down here in Eudora," he went on, "we do things in a simple and logical fashion. Mr. Lewis hands me a document, I take a look at it. I ask myself if it looks authentic. In this case I thought it did, and I admitted it into evidence. I'm sorry you didn't get to see it earlier—Mr. Lewis, you should've showed it to him—but I'm not going to throw it away or declare a mistrial on account of a thing like that. Mr. Curtis, is that all right with you? Yes? Let's proceed."

He was so folksy, so mock-reasonable, that it made my stomach queasy. It was obvious that this judge was not the least bit worried about being overturned on any appeal. That could only be because he knew there would never be an appeal: Sheriff Reese and his deputy were Klansmen, and Phineas Eversman, the only other law enforcement officer in Pike County, had crossed over to their side. The defendants would be acquitted, they would go free, and no one would ever disturb them on these murder charges again.

"Now, I want both sides to listen," my father said. "I'm going to recess this proceeding until tomorrow morning. Just because every reporter in America is interested in this case, doesn't mean I don't have other matters to adjudicate. This afternoon I will devote myself to the trial of a man who's been charged with public drunkenness and urination. I'm going to have to settle a fence-line dispute between a planter and one of his colored sharecroppers. And I'm going to listen to that old German butcher, Henry Kleinhenz, tell me one more time why Sam Sanders should not be allowed to sell chicken parts at the general store."

He banged his gavel once.

"Until tomorrow, nine o'clock. *Sharp*."

Chapter 109

"All rise! This court stands adjourned!"

My father swept out of the room. Everyone in the courtroom started talking at once, the newspaper reporters pushing through the crowd, hastening to beat each other to the telegraph stations at the depot.

Through the window I saw that the sunny morning was giving way to dark-bottomed clouds. Everyone had been hoping for rain, if only to cool things off for an hour or two before the sun heated it all up again.

Maxwell Hayes Lewis stepped over to the prosecution table.

"Mr. Curtis, gentlemen—I just want to say, I am mighty sorry for forgetting to show that search warrant to you fellows before we got started this morning."

I looked him right in the eye. "Ah, Mr. Lewis, that is perfectly understandable. I'm sure you were too busy manufacturing that warrant this morning to bother showing it to us."

Lewis chuckled. "Ben, I am sorry to see you have become such a cynic."

"Let me tell you something, Mr. Lewis." I straightened all the way up so as to look down on him from the maximum height. "You got Phineas to fake a warrant for you, and you found some justice of the peace who was happy to sign it and postdate it, and you got my father to admit it into evidence with a wink and a nod. But Jonah has a whole bunch of witnesses who saw what your clients did that night. They saw the death and destruction. And they will testify."

The affable smile disappeared from Lewis's face. He was gathering his wits for a comeback when Conrad Cosgrove burst into the near-empty courtroom, shouting.

"Mr. Stringer! Mr. Corbett! Come on out here, you got to see this!"

I followed the others down the center aisle to the doorway. Outside, the trees in the square were swaying in the breeze from the oncoming storm. A soft patter of rain had just started to fall.

Right in front of the door, in the center of the lawn fronting the courthouse, was a sight I had never witnessed before.

A huge cross was planted there.

And it was burning.

Chapter 110

That evening a nervous and troubled prosecution team met for supper in the dining room of the Stringer home. Allegra, who usually took her meals with the children, decided to join us.

"Louie, isn't it just amazing how our Ella can turn one little handful of crabmeat into a she-crab soup worthy of Galatoire's in New Orleans?" Allegra said.

I was thinking, *I never knew his name was Louie. Even way back in grammar school, he was always L.J.*

L.J. had no time to answer. At that moment a rock exploded the glass of the window above the dining table and skipped across the room. A second rock smashed through the window beside it, then a third. Glass flew everywhere.

"The girls!" Allegra screamed and hurried up the stairs.

I ran after L.J. into the center hall. He opened his gun cabinet and took out three rifles: one for me, one for him, one for Jonah.

L.J. moved quietly along the walls of the front rooms, reaching up to cut off the gaslights so that we could see out and the people outside couldn't see in.

I saw at least fifty men milling about out there. They looked like the mob from the previous night, only larger. And they were chanting:

Free the Raiders!
Let 'em go!
Free the Raiders!
Let 'em go!

They carried rifles, pistols, and pitchforks, and torches to light their way. I saw some of them holding big branches they must have pulled down from the trees on their way. One man had a bullwhip he kept cracking with a pop like a pistol shot.

Free the Raiders!
Let 'em go!

L.J. stuck his head around the window frame. "Let the jury decide who goes free," he shouted.

A rock came hurtling across the veranda to shatter the porcelain urn on a pedestal behind me. Another rock crashed through a stained-glass panel beside the front door.

"L.J., get your head in!" Jonah cried. "Don't be a fool. Or a martyr."

L.J. stood in full view of the mob, waving his arms, trying to quiet them down, but soon realized that Jonah was right. He stepped back from the window.

"You've got to get Allegra and the girls out of here," I said.

He nodded. "I'll have Conrad hitch up the carriage. Allegra's got a sister up in Pricedale. This whole town has gone crazy."

As L.J. ran from the room, Jonah turned to me. "This town was crazy long before tonight," he said.

I was sorry to say that I had to agree.

Chapter 111

Jonah and I watched from the rear balcony as L.J.'s carriage clattered down the back drive and onto the Old Laurel Road. The crowd in front continued chanting for another half hour or so, but then the rain picked up and extinguished their torches, and their anger, at least for tonight.

Before long I was seated in the ground-floor parlor with a snifter of brandy and a pot of coffee. Two of L.J.'s housemen were sweeping up the broken glass and bringing in planks to nail over the windows. Quite the sight. And quite the night.

A knock came at the door. I looked up to see Nelson, one of the houseboys.

“There’s a Miz Begley here to see you, sir,” he said.

I went and met Elizabeth in the front alcove. Her bonnet was glistening from the rain, and she looked uncharacteristically disheveled.

She reached out and took my hand. “Oh, Ben, I was in the courtroom today,” she said. “It’s awful, just awful. We all see what’s happening. How can I help?”

I led her to L.J.’s study, toward a green damask sofa, where we sat. Elizabeth untied the bow of her bonnet and shucked it off. Her hair went flowing onto her shoulders.

“I want to help you Ben. Please let me in. These hangings, all of it, has got to stop. Most of us in town want it to stop.”

“I don’t know what to say, Elizabeth. L.J. just took Allegra and their kids out of town.”

“Don’t push me away again. Please. I live here. I have more to gain, and to lose, than you do. *Ben?*”

After a brief silence, I told her about a plan that had been forming in my head. It was quite a daring one, and I wasn't sure if I could pull it off.

"Elizabeth," I said. "You already *are* a help to me. Just knowing that I have your support and trust means everything to me."

Chapter 112

Since the night we had convinced Phineas to arrest the White Raiders, I'd known that if this trial ever came about, winning three guilty verdicts would be close to impossible. But this was the first time I had ever considered that it might be *completely* impossible.

I couldn't think of a way to combat all the lies, the false testimony, the faked documents, the bigoted jurors—and, of course, the overwhelming and nearly laughable prejudice of the presiding judge.

Jonah Curtis, on the other hand, seemed to be clinging to his little tiny ray of hope. He kept urging me to have the courage to stand by him; he intended to fight Loophole Lewis to the bitter end.

So it was that Jonah went after every scrap of evidence with passion, intelligence, and no little amount of cunning. He did constant battle with my increasingly impatient father. On the third day of the trial, everyone was astonished when Judge Corbett actually upheld one of Jonah's objections. "Don't let that give you any ideas," my father growled.

The next day Jonah put an emotional Conrad Cosgrove on the stand.

"That's right, Mr. Curtis," Conrad said, "they was at least eight of 'em coming from all directions. They never said a word, they just started shootin' everything and everybody in sight."

And later: "Yes, sir, Mr. Curtis, I seen my brother Luther take that man's boot to his head at least six, seven times. Hard enough and long enough to kill him. I was standing closer to him than I am right now to you."

But then Maxwell Hayes Lewis always got his chance at rebuttal.

"Now, Mr. Cosgrove, my dear Mr. Cosgrove, would you say that your opinion of what happened that night is influenced at all by your sorrow at the death of your brother?"

Conrad pondered the question, then shook his head. "No, sir. I do feel sad that Luther is dead, but that doesn't have a thing to do with my opinion about what happened that night."

It was a small trap, but Conrad had walked right into it.

Loophole Lewis pounced. "So the testimony you gave to Mr. Curtis just now was your *opinion*, not fact?"

"Well, sir," Conrad said slowly, "it is my opinion, like you said, but it's based on what I saw. And that's just a fact."

"But you're not absolutely certain of those facts, are you? How could you be?"

Jonah climbed to his feet again. "Your Honor, Mr. Lewis is purposely trying to confuse this witness."

Judge Corbett looked over his spectacles. "If the witness is so easily confused," he said, "then perhaps you made a mistake *calling* Mr. Cosgrove to testify in the first place."

And so it went. In that steamy courtroom, ripe with the smell of sweat and Rose of Sharon eau de toilette, the good people of the Eudora Quarters took the stand and swore to tell the truth and nothing but the truth. And they did. And then Maxwell Lewis ripped them apart.

One by one, Loophole Lewis plowed his way through our witness list. Whether defiant or docile when they took the stand, every one of those witnesses eventually stepped down looking foolish, stupid, or wrong.

It happened every single time.

At last Jonah stood up.

"If it please the court, the people call Miss Moody Cross to the stand."

Chapter 113

My God. She was dressed like a grown-up.

I had never seen her wearing anything but one of the three identical white jumpers she rotated through the laundry basket so that she always appeared to be wearing the same spotlessly clean dress. Today she looked like a grown woman: a formal blue skirt, a neat white blouse. On her feet were lace-up boots polished to a high shine. She wore white gloves and a straw hat.

Last night we had gone over and over the questions we would ask. "Just tell the truth," Jonah kept saying, "and everything will be fine."

"What are you talking about?" she

scoffed. "In that courtroom the truth ain't worth a bucket of piss."

"Charming," I said. "Try not to say that."

Jonah said, "The truth is the only weapon we have, Moody. So we have to use it."

"Maybe so," she said.

I should have listened more carefully to that phrase of hers.

Under Jonah's patient questioning, Moody told the same story her grandfather had told. The same story Cosgrove told. The same story every one of the witnesses from the Quarters had told.

By the time Jonah turned to Maxwell Lewis and said, "Your witness," the gentlemen of the jury looked about ready for some dinner and a nice nap.

Lewis said, "Miss Cross, are you a permanent resident of the house where your grandfather lives, over there in the Quarters?"

"Yes, sir, that's right. I live with him and take care of him."

All morning I had been noticing that Moody sounded more mature. She had managed to hide the edge of anger that so often came into her voice. She was speaking carefully, politely.

"I wouldn't really call it a house, though," she added. "It's more like a shack. But we do all right."

"Now, would you say your first notice of the alleged intruders on that night was when they rode up, supposedly shooting their weapons and yelling?"

"Oh, no, sir," she said in a very clear voice. "I would say my first notice was when Mr. North there, and Mr. Stephens, knocked on the door and showed me their search warrant."

Chapter 114

Sweet Jesus in heaven! Jonah and I had never discussed this with her. We had certainly never planned for her to say such a thing. But say it she had:

"...and showed me their search warrant."

With those words Moody changed the whole atmosphere of the courtroom and the direction of this entire murder trial.

Jonah looked at me wide-eyed. Together we stared at Moody on the witness stand.

I thought I detected a hint of amusement behind her serious expression. She watched Loophole Lewis swivel all the way around to shoot a goggle-eyed look at my father. She heard the defendants whispering frantically among themselves. She was aware that her words had set off a buzz of confusion in the gallery. Even the jurors had snapped to wakefulness.

And Moody was enjoying every minute of it. Maybe she knew our cause was lost, and she was out to confound everybody. To confuse us. To throw the whole trial up in the air and see where the pieces came down.

This was every lawyer's nightmare: the rogue witness, off on her own.

My father banged his gavel several times. "Order!" The buzz subsided. "Mr. Lewis?"

Lewis turned back to the witness stand. "Now, Miss Cross," he said, "every previous witness, including your grandfather, claimed that they never were presented with a search warrant that night."

"I know that, sir," she said. "Papaw's getting pretty old now; he doesn't always notice everything. And when those men came with the warrant, there wasn't anybody out in front of the house except me. I was the only one."

I'm sure that almost everyone else

thought Maxwell Lewis looked as confident as ever, but I saw signs that he was flustered. He was forgetting to slouch casually against the railing of the jury box. He was standing at attention and speaking a little too quickly. His countrified Clarence Darrow lilt had all but vanished. Moody had rattled him.

"This is, to say the least, a most unusual bit of testimony, Miss Cross."

"Why is that, sir? You-all said they came there with a search warrant. You said they showed it to us. All I'm saying is . . . well, that's exactly what happened."

She was lying. I knew it for sure. I was with Abraham in the parlor that night, and I knew nobody came to the door with any warrant. All had been quiet, there was a clatter of horses, then the Raiders started shooting at anything that moved.

Maxwell Lewis put on an uncomfortable smile. "All right, they showed you the warrant," he said. "And then what happened next?"

Suddenly I knew where Moody was going with this, why she was lying. What she was hoping to demonstrate with her lie.

Damn! It was brilliant! Why hadn't I thought of it?

But of course, if I *had* thought of it—if I'd even asked her to do such a thing—I could have been disbarred.

As it was, she was on her own.

"Well, sir," she said to Lewis, "I was looking over the warrant, you know, and I said, 'I still don't think y'all have the right to do this. But if that's what the paper says, I reckon we've got no choice but to let you come on in.' "

"You said that?" Lewis turned to the jury, hoping they would share his skepticism.

None of them even noticed. Their eyes were on Moody. She had them under her spell, and they were finally listening.

"Yes, sir, I did, and I no sooner got the words out of my mouth than a bunch of 'em rode up on their horses and started shootin' and yellin' and everything. Just like Papaw said."

"If we can," Lewis said, "let's return to the issue of the search warrant."

"Yes, sir," said Moody, as proper and polite as I had ever heard her.

"Now, who showed it to you?"

"Mr. North was the one holding the paper," she said. "And Mr. Stephens was with him."

"You are absolutely certain they presented that warrant to you?"

"Well, yes, sir, I mean—that's what happened. Just like y'all said. Don't you believe me?"

She looked the very picture of confounded innocence.

Maxwell Lewis turned to my father and shrugged.

My father spoke from the bench in a dangerous growl: "Moody Cross. You have sworn to tell the truth in this court. Do you understand that?"

"Oh, I certainly do, Your Honor, that's just what I'm doing," she said. "For the life of me, I can't figure out why me telling the truth has got y'all so confused. It's almost like you're *angry* at me."

She even had the nerve to smile. I thought, *Don't get carried away now, don't go too far. You've got them right where you want them*.

Before she took the stand, Moody and her grandfather had been uncooperative liars, uppity Negroes, troublemakers.

Agitators defying a legal search warrant. Now they were innocent citizens who had agreed to a search of their premises and then, without warning, were unfairly and savagely attacked. For no reason at all.

Chapter 115

The moment Moody stepped off the witness stand, my father declared a recess until Monday.

I followed Moody, L.J., and Jonah down the steps of the courthouse into a barrage of questions accompanied by that acrid gunpowdery smell of flash powder exploding. Moody moved through that crowd of newsmen like a ship slicing through a wave, holding her head up, walking straight ahead.

We brushed off the last pesky reporters and walked three blocks to the Stringer house. We waited until we had Moody in the War Room before anyone spoke.

"What did you think you were doing?" I asked. "You got up under oath and told the biggest, fattest lie in the history of Mississippi. And all the time grinning like a fool!"

She was grinning like that now. "I tried to keep the smile off my face," she said.

"Why didn't you tell us you were going to do that?"

"'Cause if I had, you'd have told me not to do it. This way I could scare the devil out of that Loophole Lewis, *and* your daddy the judge, *and* Phineas Eversman, *and* everybody else who was in on the lie."

"But *you* lied in order to counter *their* lie," I shouted. "That's perjury!"

"So what?" she said. "You fight fire with fire. Lewis can't contradict me. If he does, he'll have to admit they made up that warrant out of thin air, a long time after the raid."

"Oh, I understand what you were doing, all right," I said. "I just want to know what gives you the right to—"

"Ben," said L.J. "I don't see how this hurts us. I think it can only help."

I sank onto a chair. "I think so too, as bad as that is. What do you think, Jonah?"

Jonah was looking out the narrow second-floor window.

"It must be six-thirty. The usual mob is beginning to form," he said.

Then he turned from the window and faced the three of us.

"So, what do you think?" I repeated.

"I think what Moody did was... interesting. I must say, I did enjoy watching Loophole Lewis and Judge Corbett squirming like worms on a hook..."

I smiled. We had all enjoyed that sight.

"...but it won't make any difference," Jonah finished. "I'm afraid it won't."

"Yes, it will," Moody protested. "It'll cast doubt in their minds. It'll make it seem like we tried to cooperate, and they attacked us anyway."

Jonah shook his head. "Oh, Moody. Those jurors have lived here their whole lives. They don't *care* who's telling the truth and who's lying! The phony warrant? Some of the jurors were probably down at the town hall when Eversman was writing it up."

There was silence then. A long minute of it.

The chanting outside began again.

Free the Raiders!
Let 'em go!

Moody stood and smoothed her blue skirt. She adjusted her straw hat and slipped on her white gloves.

"I got to go. Papaw is in bad shape. Coming to the court, he didn't hardly know who he was," she said.

Without thinking about it I leaned over and kissed her on the cheek. "Tell Abraham I'm coming out tomorrow to see about him."

Jonah said, "Thank you for trying to help, Moody. From the bottom of my heart."

Chapter 116

It was time to try out the plan I had concocted. Maybe it was even past time, too late. Moody and L.J. had come with me. Jonah wanted to but knew he couldn't. After all, he was representing the great state of Mississippi, and we were about to break the law in too many ways to count.

"Stinks bad in here," Moody said.

The awful smell was everywhere, a sharp, nauseating odor, like a cross between bad patent medicine and rancid moonshine. It was the foul scent of the chemicals Scooter Willems used to develop his photographs.

I had just climbed through an unlocked window, with Moody and L.J. behind me, into Scooter's old cabin off the East Point Road. Now we were in his studio, one large room with black curtains dividing it into three. The front part was a portrait studio, with a backdrop and a stool for the subject to pose on. In the middle section two large wooden tables held trays of foul-smelling chemicals. But it was in the last section that we found what we'd come for: boxes and boxes of Willems's photographs, with dozens more pinned to the walls.

There was one box full of nothing but photographs of lynchings. Scooter Willems had been busy these past months. Beside that box sat a stack of postcards manufactured from the photos, souvenir pictures of hanged corpses, burned bodies, twisted victims, like the one I'd received in the mail.

"God Almighty," Moody said. "The man has taken pictures of everybody who ever got hanged."

"Look here," said L.J., working his way along the wall. "These are all from the Bobby Burnett lynching."

I held up the lantern to see.

"First, take a look at poor old Bobby

hanging there," L.J. said. "Now look who's standing next to him. *There*. By his feet."

There they were, plain as day in the flickering lamplight: Chester Madden and Lincoln Alexander Stephens, two of the three White Raiders on trial. They grinned up at the bloated, bloody, bursting head of Bobby Burnett.

One by one I pulled the photographs down from the wall, gathering them in a manila folder I found on Scooter's desk.

"Look at this!" Moody exclaimed, holding a photo up to the light.

I came up beside her. There was her brother Hiram, dead on the ground, with a rope around his neck. His grinning killers each had a foot on his body, as if he were a prize lion they'd slain on safari.

L.J. pointed to the man on the end. "I'll be damned if that ain't Lester Johnson."

I almost stopped breathing. "And now he sits on our jury."

Then I recognized the man beside him. It was Jacob, Jacob Gill, with his foot resting on Moody's dead brother. I felt my eyes filling.

Scooter Willems was nothing if not

thorough. Everyone who'd ever had a hand in a lynching in this part of Mississippi had been assiduously recorded, their faces plainly recognizable. Some of the lynchings were of victims I'd heard about, others were news to us.

The horror increased with just about every picture. Before we were through, we'd seen the faces of many prominent Eudora citizens enjoying a night out, a night of murder and mayhem.

What a record of guilt! What amazing evidence! I couldn't take the pictures down fast enough.

"Just put 'em all in the box," I said. "We need to get out of here."

"No, y'all can stay," I heard.

Chapter 117

The black curtain was yanked aside, and the studio flooded with light. At first I couldn't make out who they were, but there were five of them. Their torches were much brighter than our lantern, and they dazzled us.

"I don't recall inviting any of you folks here," a voice said. That high nasal whine had to be Scooter Willems's.

As he moved his torch I saw them all.

Two men with guns whom I didn't recognize.

Phineas Eversman, chief of police.

And Senator Richard Nottingham, Elizabeth's husband.

"Go ahead and finish packing up," said

Nottingham, waving his pistol. "Saves us having to do it."

Another man stepped into the cabin. "Yeah, y'all get to work, would you?" I knew that voice. And that face. It was Jacob Gill.

" 'Preciate you gathering 'em up for us, Ben," he said. "We were just gonna have ourselves a little evidence-burnin' party."

"We knew we'd find you here," Phineas said with a smirk on his face.

L.J. growled, "How did you know? Who the hell told you we were comin' here?"

There was a silence, then the others looked at Richard Nottingham. Finally he said, "My wife."

The words stabbed me in the heart. I felt my throat closing and thought I might be sick.

"Elizabeth was spying for me. She told us every word you ever said, Corbett. She's a good girl. Thanks for keeping us up to date. It was damn useful to Maxwell Lewis."

Phineas took the box of photographs from Moody. One of the pictures caught his eye. "We don't need this one," he said.

He handed it over to me. "In case you want a souvenir."

It was a picture of me—half naked, hanging from a lynching tree.

Scooter did a fine job with the picture. The detail was crisp; you could see every leaf on the tree. The dog licking my bloody foot, the flies swarming over my face.

"You always took a nice picture, Ben," said Jacob Gill.

Chapter 118

"All right now, Ben, we tried your plan, and you might say it didn't work out so well. So now we're going to try my plan."

Jonah was not in the mood to butter me up.

"You know those photographs would have worked," I said bitterly. "All right, all right, tell me *your* plan."

"Well, it's not quite as audacious as yours. Matter of fact, it's very logical, very well thought out."

"Damn it, just tell us," L.J. said.

"Tomorrow," Jonah said, "I want Ben to give the summation to the jury."

L.J. didn't hesitate a beat before answering, "That is a fine idea."

"No, it isn't," I said. "I was there on the

night of the murders. I'm a witness but you've chosen not to put me on the stand. You're the one who's been telling them the story of these crimes all along. Why change now?"

"You know why," said L.J.

"Because I'm white?" I said. "That's no reason!"

"It never hurts," Jonah said with a faint smile. "Look, you come from here," he explained. "You know these people. The judge is your father. These jurors will trust you more than they will me. And not because you're white—because you were there. You can give a summation that comes from your heart. For God's sake, you've been lynched yourself. You have to tell them a story, Ben. They need to hear it from you."

I dreaded the truth in what he was saying. The next thing he said cinched it for me:

"I tried the case. I fought the case. I pled the case. But all along, even before I got here, it was always your case, Ben."

Chapter 119

It looked as if half of America had come to tiny Eudora for the conclusion of the White Raiders Trial.

Outside the courthouse that morning, hundreds and hundreds of spectators jammed the town square. Little boys had climbed trees for a better view of the action. Photographers muscled their tripods through the crowds, jostling for the best angles. A few of the more enterprising had bought out Russell Hardware's entire stock of ladders to get an over-the-heads-of-the-crowd view.

Judge Everett Corbett had petitioned Governor Vardaman for state militiamen from Jackson to keep order. The soldiers had set up temporary wooden fences along the sidewalk in front of the courthouse to control the spectators who'd been flooding into Eudora by train, carriage, horseback, and on foot.

Inside the courtroom there was no question who was in control: Judge Everett Corbett.

During the course of the trial, he had expelled four colored women from the gallery for reacting too loudly. He had found three reporters in contempt of court for referring in unflattering terms to his dictatorial ways. And he had sent an old colored man to jail for shouting, "The Lord hates a liar!" during one defendant's testimony.

The first thing my father did on the trial's last morning reaffirmed his imperial status.

"Now we are ready to deliver this case to the jury," he said. "The testimony has been passionate on both sides. Tempers have run high. Outside interest has been remarkable by any standard. And thus, gentlemen of the jury, we have come to the crux of the matter. You have to let the facts speak for themselves. You will now hear from the prosecutor, Mr. Curtis, his last and best argument about how you'll decide. Then you'll hear the same from Mr. Lewis. And finally, it will be entirely up to you, the jury, to make your decision, as the framers of the Constitution intended. Mr. Curtis?"

Jonah rose with an impassive face. "Your Honor, the jury has heard quite a lot from me in this trial. More than enough, I think. So I'm going to let my colleague Mr. Benjamin Corbett deliver the summation for the state."

Chapter 120

I got to my feet, a little wobbly in the legs. The dumbfounded faces of my father, Loophole Lewis, and his three murdering clients gave me at least some pleasure.

It took my father only a moment to make the calculation: I had the right to speak, and there was nothing he could do about it. He smiled, crossed his arms, and sat back in his chair.

"I wondered if we were ever going to hear from Counselor Corbett," he said. "Of course, as his father, I have heard a great deal from him over the years, and I look forward to sharing that pleasure with the rest of you."

Appreciative laughter rolled through the room. I had no choice but to smile and try for a little joke of my own. "And, of course, as the proud son of my father, I can only say I have done at least as much *listening* over the years as *talking,*" I said. "I have learned a great deal that way."

"Please proceed, Mr. Corbett," my father said, "and let us decide for ourselves if that is true."

The audience laughed again. My old dad had definitely won the first round.

I wondered what he saw, peering down at me from his bench. Did he see a Harvard Law graduate, a well-known Washington defense lawyer? Did he see a man of passion, righteousness, ambition?

No. He saw a boy crying when he fell off his rocking horse, a child furiously resisting a spoonful of the hated mashed carrots. He didn't see me. He saw a powerless boy.

So I was determined that when I finished speaking, he would see a man; he might even see the real Ben Corbett.

"Thank you, Your Honor," I said. "I will try not to disappoint you."

Chapter 121

Benjamin E. Corbett's summation to the jury:

"Judge Corbett just told you that you have to let the facts speak for themselves. The only problem with that is, facts do not have voices of their own; they can't actually speak. So I'm the one who is standing here to give voice to the facts. That is my job today, and I appreciate your willingness to give me an ear.

"It's the middle of the night in the Eudora Quarters. Three men ride up to execute a search warrant. It's two o'clock in the morning—hardly the most traditional time to conduct a search of private premises—but that is what these men have decided to do.

"Ah, but wait. There's a girl in the house, granddaughter of the old dying man. She reads the warrant and accepts it. She doesn't like it, she says, but it's the word of the law, so she will not resist. Come on in, she says. Search our house. Torment us. Question us. Rifle through our belongings. We have committed no crime, there is no actual legal reason for you to want to search here. But she allows it. She opens the door. She lets them in.

"And yet even her total submission, her complete and immediate cooperation, are not enough for these men. The search warrant was simply a ruse to get in the door. They have not come here to do anything legal.

"They are here to torture and torment, and to kill, because they think it's their right to kill anyone who gets in their way. To skirt around the law and execute anyone they decide is guilty. To evade juries like the one you gentlemen are sitting on today. They are there to kill the idea of fair trial, a jury of a man's peers. They have come to get their way by using the gun, the knife, the rope. And the terrible rule of the mob."

Calmly, meticulously, I began to lead them through the events of that night—the shooting and wounding of the guards at Abraham's house, the death by kicking of Luther Cosgrove, the fatal shooting of Jimmie Cooper up on the roof, the spectacle of poor Abraham with a gun to his head.

And finally, I told them about my part in the whole thing: why I'd gone to Abraham's house that night, how I knew the Raiders were coming, what I did and thought and felt at every moment. I explained how lucky Abraham and I had been to avoid being killed and to manage to bring these three Raiders to Phineas Eversman so the law could work as it is supposed to work.

"Now, Chief Eversman did his duty that night as an officer of the law. Not only that, he stuck his neck out, gentlemen. He did the honest, moral, upright thing—and that's not always easy to do. He arrested these men and charged them, and he saw that they were brought to trial. He may have changed his mind since then about some things, but the fact remains that Chief Eversman knew instinctively that these men had to be stopped.

"He had no choice. He saw the blood. He smelled it—that's how fresh it was. The blood of their victims was on the defendants' hands when we brought them to him. It was on the toes of their boots.

"Now you gentlemen are in the same position the chief of police was in that night. You have heard the truth from the people of the Quarters who witnessed these brutal attacks, these murders. You have seen the blood.

"Let me put it to you frankly: the evidence has not been refuted, *because it cannot be refuted*.

"Gentlemen, outside this courthouse, there is a whole nation watching us. Reporters from all over the country have come to Eudora to see if our little town can rise above itself, rise above the customs and prejudices that have held sway down here.

"But that's not why I want you to deliver the verdict you know to be right: a verdict of guilty on all counts. I don't want you to do it because I think you should rise above your prejudices, whatever they may be. Or because I want you to show the world that Mississippi is not a place where murderers get away with their awful crimes.

"I don't want you to consider what the outside world thinks. Who cares about them? I want you to think about your own soul, your own self, *inside,* where you live, when there is no one else around.

"I hope that you will find these men guilty, because it has been proven beyond any reasonable doubt that they are. The only thing that might prevent your rendering such a verdict is fear—fear that some of your neighbors will think less of you if you send these guilty men, these murderers, to prison. You must conquer that fear. The people of this country are depending on you to prove yourselves worthy of the grave responsibility they have invested in you. Show them that here in Mississippi, the light of justice is still shining."

I saw Jonah and L.J. smiling at me. I glanced up to my father. For a moment I thought I saw the ghost of a smile on his face too. Or maybe I just wanted to see it.

I turned back to the jury.

"There's someone who said it better than I ever could. And he said it in the first book of Samuel."

I recited from memory. "For the Lord seeth not as man seeth; for man looketh on the outward appearance, but the Lord looketh on the heart."

Now it was Maxwell Lewis's turn.

Chapter 122

Maxwell Lewis's summation to the jury:

"Eloquence like young Mr. Corbett's has rarely been heard in any courthouse in our nation," he said.

Then he turned to face the judge. "Wouldn't you say that's right, Your Honor?"

This time my father withheld his smile. "Let's just get on with it, Counselor."

I was anxious to see what tone Lewis would take now. Would he appear as the mighty Darrow? Would he try to play humble country lawyer? Would he be a preacher hurling fire and brimstone, or a kindly old grandpa proffering wise advice?

Of course he would be all those things.

"Gentlemen, I begin with a simple question . . . *Where is the evidence?* What the prosecution calls evidence is not what *I* would call evidence. If it seems to you that Mr. Curtis and Mr. Corbett have paraded the entire population of the Eudora Quarters in front of you, one after the other accusing these citizens of Eudora of murder, rioting in the streets, and general mayhem—well, sir, that's because that is exactly what they've done.

"But now, when you consider charges of this magnitude and gravity, you must, as Mr. Corbett told you, consider the evidence. The prosecution's evidence, mainly the statements of various witnesses, is like any kind of evidence: it's only as good as the people who give it.

"And where does this so-called evidence come from? Who are the people giving this testimony? What is the quality of these people that would lead us to believe their testimony? Well, I'll tell you.

"These allegations come from people who wash your clothes, and chop your weeds, and clean out your barns. They come from the old uncle who sits in front of the store all day, shooting the breeze. From the people who pick cotton all day. This is testimony from people who resent you because you happen to have the blessing and good fortune to be white, and therefore you have more privileges than they have."

A dramatic pause. Then he whipped around.

"And you are being asked to take their word as truth.

"Why on God's green earth would anyone suppose that you would take the word of this bunch of worthless rabble-rousers over the word of three gentlemen from Eudora?"

I shot a glance at my father, who was watching Lewis with the same contemptuous expression he'd been aiming at me since the trial began.

I wanted to shout, "The people who wash your clothes and pick your crops can tell the truth. The truth is not based on how much money you have. It's based on . . . the truth."

Of course, I did not interrupt the summation.

“Gentlemen,” Maxwell Lewis continued. “Be aware. There are forces at work here that would like nothing better than to take away your freedoms, your right to live life the way you have always lived it here. I warn you to do what you must to make sure that does not happen. Gentlemen, be alert. *And acquit these three innocent men*.”

I turned to Jonah. He shrugged.

Lewis went on in a quiet, humble voice.

“Gentlemen, I am sorry for the rough times the people in the Quarters have had. But that gives them no license to come here and lie to you. And it gives you no license to ignore the plain facts in front of you.”

What facts? I thought. Moody’s dramatic lie had undercut the entire thrust of the Raiders’ argument. They had no facts on their side. Lewis wasn’t anything like a great lawyer; he hadn’t even bothered to counter that revelation. He was counting on the famous prejudices of white juries to carry the day for him.

"Mr. Corbett quoted the Good Book to you. He quoted a verse from First Samuel. Well, I too would like to leave you with a phrase from God's holy word. The book of Exodus."

He paused, and then spoke in a clear, loud voice: "Thou . . . shalt . . . not . . . *lie!*"

That was it? That was Lewis's big dramatic finish?

I wanted to laugh, and I could swear I saw my father roll his eyes.

Chapter 123

Judge Corbett's instructions to the jury:

"All right, that brings the evidentiary phase of this proceeding to a close," said the judge.

He rubbed his chin, then adjusted his spectacles. He took a sheet of paper from a folder and placed it in front of him.

"Gentlemen of the jury, I need not remind you that many people outside Eudora are watching our little town now, because of this case. You have seen the signs of it—the streets of our town are filled with strangers, including, but not limited to, the so-called gentlemen of the press. And I understand that over at the Slide Inn Café they keep running out of chocolate pie as fast as they can make it."

He paused, waiting for a laugh.

It didn't come.

The courtroom was too tense for frivolities now.

The sight of all those soldiers outside had made everyone nervous.

"You heard the testimony as it was presented," he said. "And now it is up to you to decide the truth as you see it, using the laws of our great state of Mississippi as your guide.

"Once you decide this case," he went on, "those reporters will write their stories, and then they'll leave. Once the circus is gone and the streets are quiet again, we folks in Eudora will be left with . . . each other."

I had heard my father give his charge to a jury many times. Usually his words were dry, precise, legalistic. Today, for some reason, he was being unusually lyrical.

"And what you decide in that jury room will influence . . . for a very long time . . . the way we live our lives in this town."

Suddenly he seemed to snap out

of it. When he spoke again, he was all business.

"You will adjourn to the jury room now. I'll have the bailiff standing right outside your door, if there's anything you need."

The jury members looked at one another, waiting for a signal that Judge Corbett had finished his instructions.

But he was not quite done.

"One other thing, gentlemen. . . . I know you enjoyed hearing the defense counsel just as much as I did, but I do want to give you my point of view on a matter he chose to address."

He claimed to be speaking to the jurors, but his eyes stayed on Maxwell Lewis the whole time.

"The people who wash your clothes and pick your cotton are every bit as capable of telling the truth as any other kind of people."

Lewis's face flushed so red I thought he might explode.

But I knew exactly what my father was up to. For the spectators and journalists, some of whom he had allowed into the courtroom to hear the closing arguments, Judge Corbett was showing himself to be a courageous man, boldly making a statement of racial tolerance.

I was neither a spectator nor a journalist, however. I wasn't buying his act for a minute. I had sat through fifty-four objections that were overruled fifty-three times. My father had systematically sabotaged the prosecution's chances of getting a fair trial in his court.

The judge banged the gavel I had given him. "Gentlemen, kindly repair to the jury room and do your job."

Chapter 124

I tried to hurry past the mob of reporters. I was becoming quite adept at avoiding them, but the more skilled ones—the fellows from New York and Washington—were relentless. They pulled at the sleeve of my jacket. Some actually planted themselves in the middle of my path.

Finally, I had to push them out of my way. It was the only way to get past these rude and opportunistic fellows.

"Mr. Corbett, do you think you have a chance?"

"Jonah, why'd you let a white man give your summation for you?"

"Mr. Stringer, what's your angle? What's in it for you?"

I felt someone push something into my hand and looked down to find a twenty-dollar bill.

A reporter I recognized from Washington was grinning at me. "That's for a private interview, and there's more if it's really good!" I wadded the bill and tossed it back at him.

I heard Jonah calling to me across the throng: "See you at the War Room, half an hour."

The reporters lost interest in me and turned on Jonah. *The War Room? What War Room? What war? Do you think of this trial as a war? Do you think you will lose?*

I used this opportunity to escape. I crossed Commerce Street and hurried downtown, to the platform by the nearly deserted depot. One old colored man was attaching a feedbag to a fine brown horse hitched to a flat truck.

I found a bench in the shade near the stationmaster's house from which I could survey most of Eudora.

The mob was still swirling around the courthouse, a jam of horses and wagons and honking automobiles.

Out on the edge of town, on the dirt road leading out to the Quarters, I saw columns of smoke rising into the sky, the campfires of Negroes who'd come from all over southern Mississippi to await the verdict. I had ridden through their camp yesterday, smelling the smoke of fatback, hearing the hymns they sang.

"Sing loud so He can hear you," I said to the distant columns of smoke.

This was the first time in weeks I'd been alone, without the trial looming in front of me. It was time I did something I had put off for too long.

I took out a sheet of paper, turned the satchel over my lap, and started to write.

Dear Meg,

I have waited weeks to write this letter.

I have waited because I kept hoping that you would reply to my last. I envisioned an envelope with your return address on it. I imagined myself tearing it open to discover that you had changed your mind, that the thought of us living apart was something you had come to believe was a mistake. That you once again believed in the two of us. But that letter never arrived. I am alone, as separated from you and Amelia and Alice as if I were dead—or, perhaps, as if I'd never existed.

Meg, much has happened in the time we have spent apart. I have been involved in a highly provocative trial here in Eudora. I'm sure you've read about it in the newspapers. I will not waste time in this letter describing the trial, except to say that as I write to you now, the jury is deliberating the outcome.

I know that this might anger you, but I must tell the truth. I am convinced beyond any doubt that I am doing the right thing when I try to use my skills as a lawyer to help those who can't find justice anywhere else.

Meg, I know that I alone cannot right the wrongs of this society. But I cannot and will not stop trying. I know you feel that effort takes too much energy and time away from you, our girls, and my love for the three of you.

Should you decide to continue our marriage, I promise I shall try to be a better husband and father.

But I must also warn you that I will not (and cannot) abandon my ideals. As much as you may long for it, I cannot become just another government lawyer.

Please, Meg, give it another chance. We have so much to lose if we abandon each other. We have so much to gain if we try to move forward together.

My time here in Eudora is drawing to an end. Soon I will be coming back to Washington, and to you. I know now—I have learned—that Washington is my home. You are my home, Meg. The girls are my home.

I pray that when I open that front door, I will hear your sweet voice again, and you will speak to me with love.

Till I see you again, I remain

Your loving husband,
Ben

Chapter 125

The jury had a verdict.

My father banged his gavel furiously, but it did no good. "Quiet!" he bellowed. "I will clear this courtroom!"

Spectators pushed this way and that, tripped over one another, stumbling to find seats. My father continued hammering away at his bench. The jurors began to make their way to the jury box, blinking nervously at the uproar their appearance had provoked.

"I will clear this courtroom!" my father shouted again, but this had no effect at all on the level of noise and excitement in the room.

"Very well," he said. "Bailiff, get 'em all out of here. *Get 'em all out!*"

Those were the magic words. Instantly the courtroom came to perfect attention. The crowd fell silent, and everyone sank into the nearest available seat.

"Very well. That's much better," said Judge Corbett. "Mr. Foreman, has the jury reached a verdict?"

"Yes, Your Honor, we have."

The foreman handed a white slip of paper to the bailiff, who handed it up to my father. Though this took only seconds, it seemed much longer than that. Time was slowing, and my senses were unbearably acute.

My father opened the paper and read it with no visible emotion. He raised his head and looked my way, still betraying nothing about the verdict.

Then he spoke. "Mr. Foreman, in the matter of the *State of Mississippi versus Madden, North, and Stephens,* how does the jury find?"

In that moment, it seemed to me, all life stopped on this earth. The birds quit chirping. The ceiling fans stopped spinning. The spectators froze in midbreath.

The foreman spoke in a surprisingly high-pitched whine.

"We find the defendants not guilty."

As he uttered those impossible words, I was staring at the piggish face of Henry Wadsworth North. The hardest thing of all was seeing the joy that broke out all over his hateful visage.

A smattering of cheers went up from the white audience. Reporters rose and sprinted for the doors. A collective groan, and then sobs, arose from the Negroes in the gallery.

My father banged his gavel again and again, but no one seemed to care.

Chapter 126

After the courtroom had cleared, I sneaked out a side entrance to avoid the crowd of journalists out front, and did what I had done so many times lately. I got my bike and headed for the Eudora Quarters.

The first person I saw was the old man in the blue shack who had showed me the way to Abraham's house the first time I came out here.

"You done your best, Mist' Corbett," he called. "Nobody coulda done better."

"My best wasn't good enough," I called back. "But thank you."

He shook his head. I continued down the dirt road.

A large brown woman was coming the

other way, balancing a wicker basket of damp clothes on her head and carrying another under her arm. She picked up the conversation in midstep: "Aw, now, Mistuh Corbett, that's just the way things goes," she said.

"But it's not fair," I said.

She laughed. "Welcome to my life."

There I was, trying to explain the concept of fairness to a woman carrying two huge baskets of other people's washing.

At the crossroads in front of Hemple's store, I saw the usual two old men playing checkers. I stopped in front of their cracker barrel. "I'm sorry, gentlemen," I said.

One man looked up at me sadly. The other one said, "Well, suh, ain't nobody strong enough to beat 'em. And so what they did was, they got off scot-free. Nothin' new 'bout that."

"Ben." A soft voice, a hand on my arm. I turned. It was Moody.

She was wearing her white jumper again. She even had a little smile on her face.

"You planning to go door-to-door, explain to everybody in the whole Quarters what happened in the white man's courtroom?" she asked.

"I would," I said.

"Don't you worry your purty head about it," she said. "All the explaining in the world won't change a thing." She took me by the elbow, leading me away. The men watched us go.

"Papaw is worse sick," she said. "I think the excitement of the trial done it. You want to see him? He wants to see you."

Chapter 127

Abraham lay in the narrow iron bed in the front parlor, just the way he was lying there the night the White Raiders attacked. His voice was so faint I barely heard him. His lips were cracked and dry. "I imagine you been going around beating yourself up pretty good about this verdict, eh, Ben?" he asked.

"I thought I could accomplish something," I said. "The country was watching, from the president on down. I thought we could make a little bit of progress."

"Who's to say we didn't?" he asked.

Moody gently dabbed his forehead with rubbing alcohol, then blew lightly to cool his skin. Every time she touched his face, Abraham's eyes closed in gratitude.

I thought he must be seeing clouds, getting ready to dance with the angels.

"When you get to be as old as me, Ben, you can't help but remember a lot of things. I was thinking about my mama...one time I stole a nickel from her purse. She knew it before she even looked in there, just by peering in my eyes. She said, 'Abraham, I don't know what you guilty of, but you sho' nuff guilty of *somethin'*, so you might as well go on and confess.' I cried for an hour, then I give back that nickel."

Moody kept rubbing his face, rhythmically massaging the skin with her fingers. His eyes closed, then opened. He went on.

"I was just a young man during the war," he said. "You ever heard that expression, how they say the ground ran red with blood?"

I said I had heard it.

"I saw it with my own eyes," he said. "I saw the ground run red. I was up at Vicksburg, just after the fight. I saw...oh, Lord. Hurts to remember. I saw legs, you know, and arms, and feet, big heaps of 'em outside the hospital tent. All rottin' in the sun."

I could see the horror of it all in my mind's eye.

"But bad as it was," Abraham went on, "that's when things begun to change. A big change at the first, then they took it back. But what happened in that courtroom . . . that'll change it. You just wait. You'll live to see it."

He fell into such a deep silence that I thought he might have fallen asleep. Maybe he was beginning his passage into the next world.

But he had a few more words to say.

"Moody said you told the jury a saying from the book of Samuel," he said.

I nodded.

"That's one of my favorite passages," he said. "I sure hated to miss you. Would you say it out to me now?"

"Of course, Abraham," I said.

I cleared my throat.

"For the Lord seeth not as man seeth; for man looketh on the outward appearance, but the Lord looketh on the heart."

Then Abraham spoke the last words he would ever say to me.

"You did fine, Ben. You did just fine."

Chapter 128

"He'll sleep now," Moody said. "Maybe he won't wake up this time."

I followed her out to the little front porch. We sat in the chairs where L.J. and I had spent a long hot night waiting for the Raiders to come.

The worst heat had finally broken. You couldn't call it a cool day, exactly, but the wet blanket of humidity had lifted.

"I'm glad I got to talk to him," I said. "His words mean a lot to me."

Moody said nothing.

"I feel terrible about the way the trial turned out," I said.

I was hoping, I suppose, that Moody would say something like Abraham had said: that I had done my best and it wasn't my fault.

She turned to face me. "I know you're going to think I'm nothin' but a cold, ungrateful girl. But I don't just feel bad—I'm angry. Damn angry. Oh yeah, you did your best. And Mr. Curtis did his best. And Mr. Stringer spent all that money...but those murderers walked away free."

"You're right, Moody," I said. "They did."

"Papaw keeps saying it takes a long time for things to change. Well, that's fine for him—he's almost run out of time. I don't want to be old and dying before anything ever starts to get better."

I nodded. Then I did something I didn't know I was going to do until I did it.

I reached over and took Moody's hand.

This time she did not pull away.

We said nothing, because finally there was nothing left to say. After a few minutes she leaned her head on my shoulder and began to weep softly.

Then she pulled away and sat up. "Listen, Ben, do me a favor. I'm afraid Papaw's going to get bedsores, and Hemple's is all out of wintergreen oil. You reckon you could go into town and bring some?"

"Gladly," I said. "But only if you go with me. You've been trapped in this house for days."

"You are plain crazy, Ben Corbett," she said. "You think the people of this town want to see you and me parading together downtown? You want to get yourself lynched again?"

"I don't care," I said. "Do you care about what the people of Eudora think?"

She pondered that a moment. "No. I s'pose I don't."

She wiped her eyes with a corner of the dishtowel. "Oh, hell, Ben, what goes on in that crazy brain of yours?"

I was wondering the same thing.

"Will you go with me?" I said. "I need to do something in town."

Chapter 129

I helped Moody down from the handlebars of the bicycle. She had hollered most of the way into town, threatening bodily harm if I didn't let her down off that contraption this instant! The noise we made was enough to turn heads all the way up Maple Street, onto Commerce Street, and into the center of town.

Eudora had just begun to settle down again. The last of the photographers and reporters had gone away on the one o'clock train.

I heard the rhythmic clang of iron from the blacksmith shop, and the *pop-pop* report of a motorcar doing a circuit around the courthouse square.

A few hours ago the eyes of the

nation were upon Eudora. Now it was just another sleepy little southern town, happy to go back to living in the past, looking toward the future with nothing but suspicion and fear.

"Shall we?" I asked Moody.

"You're gonna start a riot," she said. "You know that, don't you?"

I clasped her hand tightly in mine. Then we began to walk down the sidewalk of the busiest street in Eudora.

To anyone who didn't know us, we would seem like lovers out for a romantic stroll on a late-summer afternoon.

But of course there was a complication: I was white, Moody was black. My hair was blond and straight, hers was black and tightly curled.

The citizens of Eudora had never seen anything like the two of us.

They stopped in their tracks. Some got down off the sidewalk to put some distance between us. Others groaned or cried out, as if the sight of us caused them physical pain.

Corinna Cutler and Edwina Booth came out of Miss Ida's store, a couple of plump old hens cackling to each other—until they laid eyes on our joined hands.

Both their jaws dropped.

"Afternoon, Miz Cutler," I said. "Afternoon, Miz Booth."

Their faces darkened and they hurried away.

Ezra Newcomb saw us through the window of his barbershop. He abandoned his lathered-up customer in the chair and stalked to the door. "Ben Corbett," he shouted, "I oughta take this razor to your damn throat!"

I relinquished Moody's hand and wrapped a protective arm around her shoulder. "Nice to see you too, Ezra."

Word of our coming spread down the street before us. About half the town stepped out onto the sidewalk to see what was causing the commotion.

At the drugstore I held the door for Moody.

Doc Conover stared down at us from his pharmacist's bench at the rear. "What do you want, Corbett?"

"A bottle of wintergreen oil, please," I said.

"We're fresh out," he said.

"Aw now, come on, Doc," I said. "It's for Abraham Cross. He's dying, and it would bring him relief. You've known Abraham all your life."

"I told you we're out," he said. "Now clear out of here."

"There it is, up there next to the camphor." I pointed to the row of bottles on the shelf above his head.

"You callin' me a liar?" said Conover. "Take off, or I'll have the police throw you out of here."

Moody pulled at my sleeve. "Let's go," she said.

I followed her toward the front door.

There was a crowd waiting outside to point and jeer at us. We turned left and headed down the block. "Let's go to the Slide Inn and have some iced tea," I said.

"I can't go in there," she said.

"Sure you can. Who's going to stop you?"

"Get out of here, nigger-lover!" called a man in the crowd.

We came to Jenkins' Mercantile, passing the bench where Henry North and

Marcus had carried my mother after she had had her stroke.

We walked the rest of the way to the Slide Inn, trailing our little mob of catcalling spectators.

Lunch service was over. There were only three customers in the café—two young ladies sipping coffee and an old woman chewing on a cheese sandwich.

I'd hoped Miss Fanny was on duty today, but it was another waitress who approached us. "Can'tcha read?" she said, poking her thumb at a brand-new sign posted above the cash register:

WHITES ONLY

"I'm white," I said.

Without a pause the waitress said, "You got a nigger with you. Now go on, get outta here."

"Where's Miss Fanny?" I said.

"She don't work here no more," the woman said. " 'Cause of you."

We turned to the door. I felt something hit my sleeve and I glanced down. It was a gob of spit, mixed with what looked like cheese. It could only have come from the little old lady.

When we stepped out the door our

audience had swelled to a couple of dozen angry people.

They gawked at us. They yelled. They mocked.

"Kiss me," I whispered to Moody.

She looked up at me as if I were insane, but she didn't say no.

I leaned down and brought my lips to hers.

A cry of pain ran through the crowd.

A woman's voice: "Look, he got what he wanted—a nigger girl to take to his bed."

A man's voice from behind me shouted, "Y'all goin' to hell and burn for all time!"

"Niggers! You're *both* niggers!"

"You make me sick in my gut!"

"Get out of here! Just get out!"

I whispered, "You ready to run?"

Moody nodded.

And we ran, and ran, and ran.

Chapter 130

We were halfway to the Quarters before the most persistent of our pursuers gave up. We stopped to catch our breath, but I kept an eye out, in case anyone was still following.

As it dawned on me what we had done, I realized that I was—well, I was *delighted*. Who would have thought two people holding hands could make so many wrong-minded people so very unhappy? We had put the citizens of Eudora in an uproar, and that realization warmed my heart.

I had abandoned my bicycle downtown. Maybe the mob had strung it up in a noose by now.

As Moody and I walked the muddy

boards that passed for a sidewalk, folks began coming out of their houses to have a look at us. As fast as we'd run, news of our public display seemed to have preceded us.

"Y'all damn crazy," said one old lady.

"Naw, they in love," said a young man beside her.

"Well, hell, if *that* ain't crazy, I don't know what is!"

"No, ma'am," I said. "We're not crazy and we're not in love, either."

"You just tryin' to cause trouble then, white boy?" she demanded.

"All I did was kiss her," I explained. "But we did cause some trouble."

The old lady thought about it a moment, then she cracked a smile.

It was like a photographic negative of our march through Eudora. By the time we got to the crossroads by Hemple's store, we had a crowd of spectators tagging along with us.

One of the old men looked up from his checkerboard, his face grim. "*Now* see what you done," he said to me. "You done kicked over the anthill for sure. They comin' down here tonight, and they gonna lynch you up somethin' fierce. And some of us, besides."

"Then we'd better get ready for them," Moody said.

"Ready?" said the other checkers player. "What you mean ready, girl? You mean we best say our prayers. Best go make the pine box ourselves."

"You got a gun for shootin' squirrel, don't you?" said Moody. "You got a knife to skin it with, don't you?"

The old man nodded. "Well, sho', but what does that—"

"They can't beat all of us," Moody said. "Not if we're ready for them."

The people around us were murmuring to one another. Moody's words had started a brushfire among them. "Let 'em come!" cried a young man. "Let 'em come on!"

Moody looked at me with soulful eyes. And then she did something I will never forget. I will carry it with me my whole life, the way I have carried Marcus's kindness to Mama.

She took my hand in hers again. Not for show, because she wanted to. We walked hand in hand to Abraham's house.

Chapter 131

I thought I would be standing guard alone on the porch that evening, but at midnight Moody appeared—wearing a clean white jumper, of course.

"I couldn't sleep, thinking how you hadn't had nothing to eat the whole day long." She set before me a plate of butter beans, field peas, and shortening bread.

The minute I smelled it, I was starving. "Thank you kindly," I said.

"You're welcome kindly," she said, easing down to the chair beside me.

I dove in. "There was this old colored lady who raised me," I said, "and she always sang, 'Mammy's little baby loves short'nin'—' "

"Hush up, fool!" Moody said.

I held up both hands in surrender. "All right, all right," I said, laughing.

"You can't help it, I reckon," she said, shaking her head. "No matter how hard you try, you are always gonna be a white man, the whole rest of your life."

"I expect I am," I said, taking a bite of bread.

We watched the moon rising over the swamp from Abraham's front porch. We heard the *gank, gank* of the bullfrogs and the occasional soft call of a mourning dove staying up late.

We sat in silence for a while. Then Moody spoke.

"You think they coming tonight?"

I sighed. "You know they'll want to teach us a lesson."

We heard a groan from inside. Moody leaped up and I followed her into the parlor.

Cousin Ricky was there, at Abraham's bedside, reading from the open Bible on his lap. Abraham looked too peaceful to have given out that groan just a moment before.

"You are the light of the world," Ricky read. "A city set on a hill cannot be hid."

We crept back out to the porch. After a time Moody said, "You made Papaw's last summer a good one."

"He's one of the finest men I've met," I said. "Of course, you know that."

She touched the back of my hand. It crossed my mind that we might kiss each other now. Also it crossed my mind that we might not.

I'll never know what could have been.

Suddenly there was a gunshot, then another, the clatter of hoofbeats, lots of horses.

We stood up, unable to see the men yet, but we could hear their voices in the darkness. We hurried inside before they could drop us where we stood.

"There they go, Sammy," a man yelled. "Nigger-lovin' Yankee and his nigger whore."

It was unfolding just like the first White Raiders attack: gunfire everywhere, men jockeying their horses into position in the dark, the hatred in their voices.

This time though, there was a difference.

The Eudora Quarters was ready—at least I hoped so.

Chapter 132

There had never been a fight like this one in the state of Mississippi, and maybe anywhere else in this country. One way or the other, we were about to make some history.

The Raiders must have thought we were too stupid to know what was going to happen or too scared to defend ourselves. It never occurred to them that Moody and my little stroll down the sidewalk might have been deliberate, a provocation, and that they were riding into a trap.

There were nine of them this time. That's how confident they were that we wouldn't resist. What arrogance—to come into the Quarters with this pack of their friends, nine of them among hundreds of Negroes.

"Ricky, go around!" Moody yelled through the window. "We'll meet you on the other side!"

"You stay here," I told her. "Your job is to guard Abraham." She started to argue but gave up when I placed a snap-load pistol in her hand.

I stuck a loaded pistol in each of my trousers pockets, lifted the shotgun, and swung around just in time to stop three men dead in their tracks at the door.

I recognized them at once. There was Roy, who'd been shot in the arm in the first White Raiders attack, and Leander Purneau from the cotton gin. Best of all was the fat redheaded man in the middle, the surprised-looking fellow at whose nose both barrels of my shotgun now pointed. This was none other than Henry Wadsworth North, former defendant, murderer.

In my mind I squeezed the trigger and watched his limited supply of brains spatter all over the screen door behind him. I felt a jolt of pleasure at the prospect of being the one to end Henry North's life.

But I couldn't shoot the man like this. It just wasn't in me.

His mouth twisted up into a smile. "What you gonna do, Corbett, have me arrested again?"

From out of nowhere he brought up a small pistol.

My finger tightened on the trigger. "Drop it or I'll blow your head off," I said. "Do not doubt me for a second! I *want* to shoot you!"

He let the pistol drop to the floor. All at once hands seized him and dragged him over backwards—

Here they were, the people of the Quarters, bearing guns and knives, pitchforks and sharpened sticks, clublike lengths of straight iron. A dozen men swarmed in from the porch, seizing the Raiders and dragging them outside.

Gunfire echoed, and I heard more horses—a second wave of Raiders. But here came our reinforcements too, pouring out of nearly every door in the Quarters, bearing weapons or no weapons at all, swarming down the street and around Abraham's house. They dragged Raiders down off their horses and set upon them with clubs, rocks, and farm implements.

Every blow they struck was violent payback for a lynching, a hanging, a beating, a murder. I heard the thud of club against flesh, the crack of rock striking bone. Terrible cries erupted as the colored men overwhelmed the Raiders, avenging the lynchings of their brothers, the oppression and torture and murder of fathers and friends.

I saw Doc Conover swinging a long rifle like a club at a woman who was down on her knees, covering her head with both arms. Then I saw a man knock Conover senseless with a fireplace poker to his skull.

Lyman Tripp, the undertaker, was on the ground, surrounded by men kicking him in the ribs. I remembered how happy he had been to hang a Jew, so I didn't feel sorry for him. Not for any of them.

But then, over the racket of punches and shouts, I heard more horses approaching. There were many horses, bearing reinforcements for the other side.

Chapter 133

"Corbett!" a man shouted at the top of his lungs.

I stepped out onto the porch to see none other than Phineas Eversman on a fine black mare, wearing his black cowboy hat with the badge pinned to the brim. "You are under arrest," he said, "and that nigger girlfriend of yours."

The fight was swirling all around us, defenders chasing and shouting, new waves of attackers coming in from the woods. It seemed unbelievable that Eversman would be trying to make an arrest in such a setting.

I trained my shotgun on his chest. "Get your ass down off that horse, Phineas."

"You put your gun down, Ben," said a voice behind me.

I turned to find a revived Doc Conover with a nasty twelve-gauge shotgun leveled at me.

"Hey, Ben," Doc said. "I meant to bring your oil of wintergreen, but I forgot." He chuckled.

A shot rang out and the gun flew from his hands. Conover screamed and grabbed his elbow. Ricky ran up and scrambled after his gun.

I glanced around to see who had fired the shot. Good God!—It was ancient Aunt Henry in the doorway of Abraham's shack, blowing smoke from the long barrel of a Colt revolver. She nodded at me and went back inside.

I heard a loud crack and turned to find Eversman down off his horse with a big bullwhip in his hand, a whip straight out of *Uncle Tom's Cabin*. It had a black leather-wrapped stick for a handle and three little stinger-tips at the end of the whipcord. Eversman cracked it again, with a report louder than a pistol shot.

His arm swept around, and the whip shot out and wrapped around my ankles with a sting as fierce as yellowjackets. It snatched me off my feet, and I landed hard on my back in the dirt. I felt blood running down where the whip was cutting into flesh and then Eversman was on me, hitting with both fists at once. But I was stronger, and angrier too. I managed to roll over and fling him on his back. Seizing the slack end of the whip, I wrapped it around his neck so tight that with one hard tug I could break his windpipe. He gurgled and coughed like the two men I had seen lynched—like the sound I must have made when they lynched me.

Eversman's eyes bugged out horribly. The leather cord bit into his neck, making a deep red indentation.

And then...

I let go of him. He would kill me if he could, but I couldn't kill him.

He fell into the mud. Somehow I had opened a big cut on his cheek just above his mouth. Blood oozed out. I began unwinding the whipcord from my ankles.

I stood over him, breathing hard. "You've cut your face, Phineas. Ask Doc if he's got any wintergreen for that."

Chapter 134

In the backyard I found the old checker players from Hemple's store tying up Byram Chaney, the retired teacher in whose wagon I'd been taken to the Klan rally. That rally and the lynching that followed seemed to have taken place a hundred years ago.

I heard an odd *glunk*ing sound behind me and turned to see two men with kerosene cans working their way along the side of Abraham's house, splashing fuel on the foundation.

The one nearest me was the renowned legislator Senator Richard Nottingham, Elizabeth's husband. The military jacket he wore for this night's action was too small for him; the fabric gaped open around the buttons.

"Bring a match to that fuel," I called out, "and I'll shoot you dead. Be my pleasure."

The other man was bent over, facing away from me. He whirled and pulled a handgun. To my horror, it was Jacob Gill.

"Drop your gun, Ben," he said. "I would shoot you dead too."

Around us swirled a madness of yelling, fighting, and dust, screaming, cursing, and gunfire. Yet at that moment it felt as if Jacob and I were facing off all alone in the middle of a giant, empty room.

"Why, Ben?" he croaked. "Why'd you have to come back and ruin our nice little town?"

Chapter 135

Jacob just kept walking toward me.

Finally, my face hovered inches from his, so close I could smell whiskey and bacon grease on his breath. His face was covered with stubble, the skin on his nose peppered with gin blossoms.

I lashed out and grabbed his gun hand and twisted it hard until the weapon dropped. Jacob had always been smaller, but he could whip me at least half the time when we were boys. He was wiry and strong, and not afraid to fight dirty. I remembered the venom he could turn on our enemies when we got together in a schoolyard scrap.

"Goddamn you, Ben!" he yelled. Then I saw he had a knife. I took his arm and held it with all my strength. It felt as if we stayed that way for hours, grappling, neither of us gaining an advantage, the razor edge suspended between us. My arms ached.

I looked Jacob in the eye. *"Jacob!"* I yelled at him. *"It's me, goddamn it! It's Ben!"*

But his eyes were bulging with rage, one hand now gripping my throat, the other inching closer with the blade. If he killed me here, amid all this noise and insanity, no one would ever know it was Jacob who'd done the deed. I would just be Ben Corbett, another victim in another senseless attack in a small town.

And then I *knew* that was not how it was going to happen. I was not going to die here, at the hand of Jacob Gill. That knowledge gave me strength, just enough to jerk his arm sideways and break his hold on the knife.

I kicked Jacob hard and wrenched the knife away. I got on him, kneeling on his chest with the blade an inch from his neck. I could have slit his throat right then, but instead I poked the knife into his Adam's apple, hard enough to draw blood. Jacob's eyes widened. God, I knew those eyes.

"You gonna kill me, Ben?" he said.

I flung the knife away and heard it crash into the bushes beside the smokehouse. Then I got up. There were no words for this. So I turned and walked away from the man who had once been my best friend in the world.

Chapter 136

While I was fighting Jacob, the rest of the fracas had begun to die down.

I watched Sam Sanders, owner of the general store, jump off his horse and run away into the darkness. I saw two other White Raiders flee in his wake, one of them limping badly.

"We'll come back for you, niggers," one yelled as he ran.

"You ain't won. You just *think* you won," another called.

A flurry of hoofbeats, and the Raiders were gone.

Colored people were scattered all over the yard, nursing wounds. Four white men lay trussed up in the dirt in front of

Abraham's house. I remembered Abraham talking about the earth running red with blood—and I saw blood, tiny rivers of it, here on his home ground.

On the porch near the tied-up men, Aunt Henry was dressing the leg wound of Lincoln Alexander Stephens, another of the original White Raiders who'd come calling tonight. Aunt Henry would take care of anyone, I reflected, regardless of race, creed, or degree of idiocy.

There seemed to be only one fatality—Leander Purneau, who lay flat on his back in the mud across the road from Abraham's house. I wouldn't miss him for a second.

Cousin Ricky told the captured Raiders he could kill them. Or he could tar and feather them. Or he could do what he was going to do: drive them into town and leave them, tied up, for the citizens of Eudora to find in the morning. "Tell 'em what we did to you," he said. "Tell 'em there's as many of us in the Quarters as there is of you in town. Don't come out here again, not unless you're invited. Which ain't likely."

Richard Nottingham brought his flat-wagon out of the woods. Brown hands helped him lift Leander Purneau's body up into the bed. Nottingham's shoulder was bandaged.

The battle was over. Eudora Quarters had won—at least for one night. It would not help me or the people of the Quarters to shoot one more bullet. It was finished.

And if I needed more proof, from around the house came Jacob Gill, his shirtfront stained red with blood from where I'd nicked his throat. He walked between two colored men to the wagon and climbed in the back without looking at me. So be it.

"Mr. Corbett!" I looked up. It was Ricky, standing at the front door.

"Come on back in," he said. "Abraham has passed."

At the door, Ricky put his hand on my shoulder. "You all right?"

"I am."

Moody glanced up as we came in, then went back to reading from the Bible:

"And he said, 'Jesus, remember me when you come into your kingly power.' And Jesus said to him, 'Truly I say to you, this day you shall be with me in Paradise.' "

Moody closed the Bible. She looked up and our eyes met.

We had already spoken our last words to each other.

Chapter 137

"Are you staying for Abraham's funeral?" L.J. asked. "I'll go with you, Ben."

"I don't think so," I said. "Moody already knows how I feel about him. And it's definitely time for me to head back... you know..."

"North!" L.J. said. "Go ahead, say the word! You're headed back up to damn Yankeeland to become a damn Yankee again!"

We were standing near the table in the War Room, where we'd spent so many hours plotting our strategies for the White Raiders Trial. I was just finishing packing.

"I've gone around and around in my mind, L.J., and for the life of me I don't know what I would do differently," I said. "If I had the luxury of doing it over again."

"You did as much as you could, Ben. Most men wouldn't even have tried to help."

I slipped my razor and shaving brush into the little leather kit and tucked it in my valise. "Help," I said. "Is that what we did? I think some of the help I gave ended up hurting them."

"Go ask 'em. Go to the Quarters," L.J. said, "and ask 'em if they're worse or better off for what you did.

"I can have a man drive you up to McComb so you can get the earlier train to Memphis," L.J. went on.

"No need for that. I'll just take the good old two-oh-five." I snapped the catches on my valise. "I might stop over in Memphis tonight and hear a bit of that music I told you about."

"Sure you don't want to stay here a day or two more?" L.J. asked. "Rest up?"

I shook my head. "It's time to go. I've said my good-byes, and I suspect I've worn out my welcome in Eudora. In fact, I'm sure of it. My own father said as much."

Chapter 138

Three days later I stepped off the train in Washington. My soles squeaked on the station's marble floors when I walked across them, and I once again admired the acres of gold leaf and ranks of granite arches like victory gates. A man entering Washington through this portal was glorified and enlightened by the passage.

But one man, Ben Corbett, coming home after all these months, felt as lowly and insignificant as a cockroach scurrying along an outhouse floor.

My mind was a jumble, a clutter of worries. I couldn't stop thinking about everything that had passed, and all the terrible things that might yet happen.

Meg had never answered my letters. I

thought it likely that I would return to an empty house, shuttered and forlorn, my wife and children having gone off to live with her father in Rhode Island.

I could imagine the walls empty of pictures, white sheets covering the furniture, our modest lawn overgrown with foot-high grass and weeds.

These were my dark thoughts as I made my way through happy families on holiday, returning businessmen, flocks of government workers, Negro porters in red coats, and bellboys in blue caps.

"Mr. Corbett, sir," a voice rang out down the platform. "Mr. Corbett! *Mr. Corbett!*"

I stopped, searching the oncoming faces for the source of the greeting—if indeed it was a greeting.

"Mr. Corbett. Right here. I'm so glad I found you."

He was a young man, short and slight, with wire-rimmed glasses and an intensely nervous stare. I had seen him somewhere before.

"Mr. Corbett, I'm Jackson Hensen. The White House?"

"Ah, Mr. Hensen," I said. "What a surprise to see you here."

He smiled hesitantly, as if not quite sure whether I'd made a joke. "Will you come with me, sir?"

"I'm sorry?" I looked down at his hand cupped on my elbow.

"The president would like to see you immediately."

"Oh. Yes. Of course," I said. "And I would like to see him. But first I thought I would see my family."

"I'm sorry, Mr. Corbett. The president is at the White House right now. He's waiting for you."

So I followed Hensen outside to a splendid carriage drawn by the handsomest quartet of chestnuts I'd ever seen. All the way to the White House I kept thinking, *Dear God, please see to it that Teddy Roosevelt isn't the only person in Washington who wants to see me.*

Chapter 139

Theodore Roosevelt jumped up from his desk and came charging at me with such high spirits I was afraid he might bowl us both over.

"Welcome home, Captain!" he roared. When he pumped my hand I recalled that Roosevelt didn't consider a handshake successful unless it resulted in physical pain.

"And all congratulations to you, sir, on a difficult job extremely well done," he exclaimed. "The White Raiders Trial was a smashing success."

"But Mr. President, we lost the case."

"Of course you did," he said. "I knew you would—technically—lose the case.

But you won a tremendous victory all the same."

"I don't think I understand."

He sank onto the sofa to the left of his desk and patted the seat cushion next to his, as if I were a faithful dog being summoned. I sat. The president continued.

"I don't know how much of our press you've seen while you've been away, Ben, but you've become something of a hero up here. The more progressive citizens see you as a kind of abolitionist, a figure of progress in the march of civilization toward full equality. And the coloreds in the South see you as some kind of protector, a hero. *It's damn good!*"

"Mr. President, I was just in the South," I said. "Believe me, I'm nobody's hero there."

"I'm meeting the newspaper boys in a few minutes," he said. "You'll be with me. I'll announce that I masterminded your adventure in the South. I'll disclose to them how I supported your efforts against the White Raiders. I'll pick up votes in New England, and I'll have the colored vote from now until the end of time."

"But you sent me to Eudora to investigate lynchings."

"Indeed I did. And if you'd reported back to me that lynching was a way of life among the leaders of the white South, I would have had to do something about it. Something that would enrage some white people, no matter how much it endeared me to the Negroes."

"That's why you didn't answer my telegrams?"

"It wasn't convenient for me to hear from you yet," he said. "But then we had the most magnificent stroke of luck when the Raiders Trial came along!"

He was bubbling, but I couldn't keep silent any longer.

"Luck? You call it a magnificent stroke of luck? People died. A town was torn apart."

He ignored me completely, and he was still grinning at his good fortune.

"I know there was pain, Captain. That's to be expected. Progress requires a certain amount of suffering. You did well, you worked hard, and eventually you managed to bring it all under control. I certainly chose the right man for the job." He stood up from the sofa.

I stood as well. "Is that all, Mr. President?" I said.

"The reporters are waiting, Ben. I need you to help me explain what happened."

"Is that an order, sir?" I asked.

He looked surprised. "Well, no," he said. "Don't you want to come?"

"No, sir," I said. "If I may, I respectfully decline."

Chapter 140

As I left the White House that day I noticed that my legs felt more limber, my body lighter. There was an actual spring in my step. To my astonishment I felt strangely, incredibly happy.

The White House was bathed in an intensely golden light, and as I walked northwest on the wide avenue, past the tattered rooming houses and saloons, I saw the Washington Monument sparkling in the distance like a gigantic diamond hatpin.

Certainly I was angry that Theodore Roosevelt had used me as a pawn in one of his electoral chess games. And I dreaded even more the moment when I returned home to find my house empty.

But still, there was something hopeful in the light sparkling on the monument, and the delightful smell of woodsmoke on the breeze.

I found myself remembering Abraham Cross a few nights ago, just before he drifted off to sleep.

"You did fine, Ben. You did just fine."

To have a man like Abraham say that . . . well, that's all anyone could ever ask for.

"You did fine, Ben. You did just fine."

I turned off South Carolina Avenue onto our street. Everything looked so familiar that I might have left home only a day or two ago. No one had taken a paintbrush to our peeling little house. The second-floor shutters still hung tilted and broken, and the brick walkway was still perilously uneven.

As I mounted the front steps, three months' worth of anxiety was twisting my insides into a hard knot.

I unlocked the door and stepped into the vestibule. All was still.

I walked to the bottom of the stairs and stood there a few moments. And then—

I heard Alice's little voice.

"I think I heard the front door," she said.

I knelt down to remove two identical boxes wrapped in brown paper from my valise. I shucked off the paper and opened them.

"Do you think it could be Papa?" Amelia asked.

Then—I heard Meg's voice.

"I certainly hope so," she said. "Wouldn't that be wonderful?"

I ran up those stairs clutching the gifts for my girls—identical brown, fuzzy teddy bears, the most popular dolls of the day, inspired by President Roosevelt himself.

"Daddy!" screamed my girls, all three of them.

I took the little ones into my arms. "Now, which of you is Alice, and which is Amelia?" I asked as they giggled and snuggled into my chest.

Then I reached out my free arm. "And you—you must be Meg. I've missed you so much." Then Meg came into my arms too. "I'll never leave you again," I whispered.

True to my word, I never did.

Prologue

WISTY

It's overwhelming. A city's worth of angry faces staring at me like I'm a wicked criminal—which, I promise you, *I'm not.* The stadium is filled to capacity—*past* capacity. People are standing in the aisles, the stairwells, on the concrete ramparts, and a few extra thousand are camped out on the playing field. There are no football teams here today. They wouldn't be able to get out of the locker-room tunnels if they tried.

This total abomination is being broadcast on TV and on the Internet too. All the useless magazines are here, and the useless newspapers. Yep, I see cameramen in elevated roosts at intervals around the stadium.

There's even one of those remote-controlled cameras that runs around on wires above the field. There it is—hovering just in front of the stage, bobbing slightly in the breeze.

So, there are undoubtedly millions more eyes watching than I can see. But it's the ones here in the stadium that are breaking my heart. To be confronted with tens, maybe even hundreds of thousands of curious, uncaring, or at least indifferent, faces . . . talk about *frightening.*

And there are no moist eyes, never mind tears.

No words of protest.

No stomping feet.

No fists raised in solidarity.

No inkling that anybody's even thinking of surging forward, breaking through the security cordon, and carrying my family to safety.

Clearly, this is not a good day for us Allgoods.

In fact, as the countdown ticker flashes on the giant video screens at either end of the stadium, it's looking like this will be our *last* day.

It's a point driven home by the very tall, bald man up in the tower they've erected midfield—he looks like a cross between a Supreme Court chief justice and Ming the Merciless. I know who he is. I've actually met him. He's The One Who Is The One.

Directly behind his Oneness is a huge N.O. banner—*the New Order.*

And then the crowd begins to chant, almost sing, "The One Who Is The One! The One Who Is The One!"

Imperiously, The One raises his hand, and his hooded lackeys on the stage push us forward, at least as far as the ropes around our necks will allow.

I see my brother, Whit, handsome and brave, looking down at the platform mechanism. Calculating if there's any way to jam it, some way to keep it from unlatching and dropping us to our neck-snapping deaths. Wondering if there's some last-minute way out of this.

I see my mother crying quietly. Not for herself, of course, but for Whit and me.

I see my father, his tall frame stooped

with resignation, but smiling at me and my brother—trying to keep our spirits up, reminding us that there's no point in being miserable in our last moments on this planet.

But I'm getting ahead of myself. I'm supposed to be providing an *introduction* here, not the details of our public *execution.*

So let's go back a bit....

One

WHIT

Sometimes you wake up and the world is just plain different.

The noise of a circling helicopter is what made me open my eyes. A cold, blue-white light forced its way through the blinds and flooded the living room. Almost like it was day.

But it wasn't.

I peered at the clock on the DVD player through blurry eyes: 2:10 a.m.

I became aware of a steady *drub, drub, drub*—like the sound of a heavy heartbeat. Throbbing. Pressing in. Getting closer.

What's going on?

I staggered to the window, forcing my

body back to life after two hours passed out on the sofa, and peeked through the slats.

And then I stepped back and rubbed my eyes. Hard.

Because there's no way I had seen what I'd seen. And there was no way I had heard what I'd heard.

Was it really the steady, relentless footfall of hundreds of soldiers? Marching on my street in perfect unison?

My street wasn't close enough to the center of town to be on any holiday parade routes, much less to have armed men in combat fatigues coursing down it in the dead of night.

I shook my head and bounced up and down a few times kind of like I do in my warm-ups. *Wake up, Whit.* I slapped myself a couple of times for good measure. And then I looked again.

There they were. Soldiers marching down our street. Hundreds of them as clear as day, made visible by a half-dozen truck-mounted spotlights.

Just one thought was running laps inside my head: *This can't be happen-*

ing. This can't be happening. This can't be happening.

Then I remembered the elections, the new government, the ravings of my parents about the trouble the country was in, the special broadcasts on TV, the political petitions my classmates were circulating online, the heated debates between teachers at school. None of it meant anything to me until that second.

And before I could piece it all together, the vanguard of the formation stopped in front of my house.

Almost faster than I could comprehend, two armed squads detached themselves from the phalanx and sprinted across the lawn like commandos, one running around the back of the house, the other taking position in front.

I jumped back from the window. I could tell they weren't here to protect me and my family. I had to warn Mom, Dad, Wisty—

But just as I started to yell, the front door was knocked off its hinges.

Witch & Wizard.

Books by James Patterson

FEATURING ALEX CROSS

Alex Cross's Trial (with Richard DiLallo)
Cross Country
Double Cross
Cross
Mary, Mary
London Bridges
The Big Bad Wolf
Four Blind Mice
Violets Are Blue
Roses Are Red
Pop Goes the Weasel
Cat & Mouse
Jack & Jill
Kiss the Girls
Along Came a Spider

THE WOMEN'S MURDER CLUB

The 8th Confession (with Maxine Paetro)
7th Heaven (with Maxine Paetro)
The 6th Target (with Maxine Paetro)
The 5th Horseman (with Maxine Paetro)
4th of July (with Maxine Paetro)
3rd Degree (with Andrew Gross)
2nd Chance (with Andrew Gross)
1st to Die

FEATURING MICHAEL BENNETT

Run for Your Life (with Michael Ledwidge)
Step on a Crack (with Michael Ledwidge)

THE JAMES PATTERSON PAGETURNERS

Daniel X: Watch the Skies (with Ned Rust)
MAX: A Maximum Ride Novel
Maximun Ride: The Manga I (with NaRae Lee)
Daniel X: Alien Hunter (graphic novel; with Leopoldo Gout)
The Dangerous Days of Daniel X (with Michael Ledwidge)
The Final Warning: A Maximum Ride Novel
Maximum Ride: Saving the World and Other Extreme Sports
Maximum Ride: School's Out—Forever
Maximum Ride: The Angel Experiment

OTHER BOOKS

Swimsuit (with Maxine Paetro)
Against Medical Advice: One Family's Struggle with an Agonizing Medical Mystery (with Hal Friedman)
Sail (with Howard Roughan)
Sundays at Tiffany's (with Gabrielle Charbonnet)
You've Been Warned (with Howard Roughan)
The Quickie (with Michael Ledwidge)
Judge & Jury (with Andrew Gross)
Beach Road (with Peter de Jonge)
Lifeguard (with Andrew Gross)
Honeymoon (with Howard Roughan)
SantaKid

SantaKid
Sam's Letters to Jennifer
The Lake House
The Jester (with Andrew Gross)
The Beach House (with Peter de Jonge)
Suzanne's Diary for Nicholas
Cradle and All
When the Wind Blows
Miracle on the 17th Green (with Peter de Jonge)
Hide & Seek
The Midnight Club
Black Friday (originally published as *Black Market*)
See How They Run (originally published as *The Jericho Commandment*)
Season of the Machete
The Thomas Berryman Number

For previews of upcoming books by
James Patterson and more information
about the author,
visit www.JamesPatterson.com.

About the Authors

James Patterson is one of the bestselling writers of all time, with more than 170 million books sold worldwide. He is the author of the top-selling detective series of the past twenty years—the Alex Cross novels, including *Kiss the Girls* and *Along Came a Spider,* both of which were made into hit movies. Mr. Patterson also writes the bestselling Women's Murder Club novels, set in San Francisco, and the new series of *New York Times* #1 bestsellers featuring Detective Michael Bennett of the NYPD. He won an Edgar Award, the mystery world's highest honor, for his first novel. He lives in Florida.

James Patterson's lifelong passion for books and reading led him to launch a new website, ReadKiddoRead.com, which helps parents, grandparents, teachers, and librarians find the very best children's books for their kids.

Richard DiLallo is a former advertising creative director. He has had numerous articles published in major magazines. He lives in Manhattan with his wife.